Dornford Yates is the pseudonym of Cecil William Mercer. Born into a middle-class Victorian family, his parents scraped together enough money to send him to Harrow. The son of a solicitor, he qualified for the Bar but gave up legal work in favour of his great passion for writing. As a consequence of education and experience, Yates' books feature the genteel life, a nostalgic glimpse at Edwardian decadence and a number of swindling solicitors. In his heyday and as a testament to the fine writing in his novels, Dornford Yates' work was placed in the bestseller list. Indeed, 'Berry' is one of the great comic creations of twentieth-century fiction, and 'Chandos' titles were successfully adapted for television.

Finding the English climate utterly unbearable, Yates chose to live in the French Pyrénées for eighteen years before moving on to Rhodesia where he died in 1960.

ADÈLE AND CO.
AND BERRY CAME TOO
AS BERRY AND I WERE SAYING
B-BERRY AND I LOOK BACK
BERRY AND CO.
THE BERRY SCENE
BLIND CORNER
BLOOD ROYAL
THE BROTHER OF DAPHNE
COST PRICE
THE COURTS OF IDLENESS
AN EYE FOR A TOOTH
FIRE BELOW
GALE WARNING
THE HOUSE THAT BERRY BUILT
JONAH AND CO.
NE'ER DO WELL
PERISHABLE GOODS
RED IN THE MORNING
SHE FELL AMONG THIEVES

DORNFORD YATES

SHE PAINTED
HER FACE

HOUSE OF
STRATUS

This edition published in 2001 by House of Stratus, an imprint of House of Stratus Ltd, Thirsk Industrial Park, York Road, Thirsk, North Yorkshire, YO7 3BX, UK.

www.houseofstratus.com

Typeset by House of Stratus.
Printed and bound in Great Britain by
Antony Rowe Ltd., Chippenham, Wiltshire.

A catalogue record for this book is available from the British Library and the Library of Congress.

ISBN 1-84232-981-2

To my beautiful dog, 'The Knave', who, in his short life, gave me all that he had, and, by so doing, left behind him a bankrupt who can never be discharged.

Contents

1	The Unfinished Statement	1
2	We Spy Out the Land	18
3	I Open a Lady's Eyes	42
4	We Make an Enemy	59
5	Rats in a Trap	86
6	'Old Harry' Receives	105
7	Love Upon the Terrace	130
8	A Stalled Ox and Hatred Therewith	146
9	Into the Mouth of Hell	176
10	I Am Hoist with My Own Petard	193
11	The Fall of the Curtain	214
12	I Look Out of a Window	241

1

The Unfinished Statement

I became a beggar when I was twenty-two.

The blow was as heavy as swift, for till then I had always been given the best that money could buy. From the day I was born I had wanted for nothing at all, and, though my parents were dead, I had never been led to expect any other estate. And then, one fair June morning, when the sills of the windows of Oxford were gay with flowers, I learned that my sole trustee had gambled my fortune away.

By the help of the Dean of my College, I soon obtained work in London for which I was paid just thirty-five shillings a week, and though I believe that I might have done better than that, in my efforts to rise I met with so much unkindness that I presently withdrew from a battle for which I was ill-equipped.

I had another reason for staying in Red Lead Lane.

I had a companion in misfortune – a man of some fifty summers, who, too, had seen better days. His name was Matthew Gering – or so he said: for though he looked English enough, his speech sometimes betrayed an alien blood. That he was of gentle birth was unmistakable and I think that he may have been gifted – till misery dulled his wits. He seemed the better for my coming to share his lot, and after two or three months I moved to the humble lodging at which he had lived by himself for thirteen years. It was soon after this that I knew that I could not leave him, if only for pity's sake.

This was the way of it.

The manager of the warehouse at which we were used as clerks was a man upon whose vitals class hatred seemed to feed. Disappointed of bigger game, he preyed with a bitter fury on what he had. For fifteen years poor Gering had been his butt, enduring 'the slings and arrows' of what I can only describe as 'a mind diseased': but my arrival did something to take the strain, for he had to divide his attentions if I was to have my share of inhumanity.

And so I stayed where I was for nearly two years, when two things happened together, to set me free.

One gusty, April morning poor Gering could not rise, and when I had brought him a doctor, against his will, the latter told me plainly that he was a dying man.

"He has no resistance," he said. "A chill could have put him out – and this is congestion of the lungs."

Of course I did what I could, but when I came back from my work on the following day, I knew at once that Gering had seen his last dawn. And so did he.

"Not very long now," he said quietly…

It must have been near ten o'clock, and we had spoken no word for nearly an hour, when he put a hand under the blankets and drew out a sheet of foolscap, folded in four.

"I would like you to read this," he said. "I wrote it down years ago. But no one has ever read it. It – it would not have been well received. I have even considered all day whether I should show it to you – you who have done so much for a broken man. You see, I am like a dog that has been ill used for so long that he is suspicious of kindness and ready to bite the hand that makes to caress his head."

With his words he began to cough, and the paroxysm which followed frightened me out of my life. At least five minutes went by before the seizure had passed, and this left him so weak and shaken that even a child would have known that the end was at hand. Indeed, I had forgotten the paper, when his trembling fingers thrust it against my sleeve.

I sat back on my heels and read the following words:

My true name is Rudolf Elbert Virgil and I am the ninth Count of Brief – an ancient Austrian House. My mother died when I was three. Her only other child was my twin-brother, born half an hour after myself. He was, as they say, a bad hat. In 1910 I married an English girl and a daughter was born to us in 1912. We lived with my father at Brief, which stands to the east of Innsbruck, from which it is distant a hundred and twenty miles. In the spring of 1914 my father received some news from the English police. My twin-brother was under arrest on a charge of forgery. I left for England that night to see what could be done. Arrived in London, I sought a solicitor, and, on my going surety, my brother was admitted to bail.

The case was unanswerable. And from what the solicitor said it was perfectly clear that if Ferdinand stood his trial, he would be sent to prison for several years. When we were at last alone, my brother fell on his knees and begged me in the name of our mother to help him to make his escape. Like a fool, I agreed to do so.

The day was Thursday. Early on Friday, I left my brother in my rooms and went out to make arrangements for him to leave. All I did, I did surreptitiously. A ship was to sail for South America at noon on the following day. I booked his passage in an assumed name. I procured him an outfit and had the things sent on board. That evening I returned to my rooms to tell him that all was well. A telegram from Brief was awaiting me. My father and wife were both dead. They had been killed that day...in a car...on the Innsbruck road. The news stunned me. As a man in a dream, I did as my brother said, for now it was I that was helpless and he that took charge. All I knew was that I must get back…

That night he packed for me and told me what he had done. I was to leave the next day by the two-o'clock train. He had arranged everything. All that I had to do was to go to the Bank the next morning and draw for him the money which he was to have. That he dared not do, though I gave him my cheque. And when I had drawn the money – five hundred pounds – I was to bring it to the station from which his train would be leaving at half-past ten.

As he said, so I did. I had no brain to argue. The only thing I could see was the Innsbruck road.

They arrested me on the platform…

They thought I was Ferdinand. I do not blame them at all. You see, he was my twin-brother. Only my wife and my father could tell us apart. AND THEY WERE DEAD.

When they searched me, they found the money – and Ferdinand's ticket for the boat. Unknown to me, he had put this into my pocket – to gain his terrible ends. And he had left for Innsbruck whilst I was still at the Bank, by an earlier train, of course. He was across the Channel before I went to my cell.

So he and I changed places.

He took my father's title and all that was mine, and I was sent to prison for seven years.

My daughter became his daughter, my life became his life. You see, it was so easy. Only my wife and my father had known why I went to England. For the rest, I had gone away and now had come back. If my manner seemed in any way strange, the double loss I had suffered was blamed for that. And Ferdinand was careful. He even denied my cheque for five hundred pounds. He said that I had forged it.

Seven years is seven years. By the time I came out of jail, my cause, which had always been hopeless, was dead and

*buried as though it had never been. So I changed my name
and sought work – I had to have bread.*

*That is my story. I cannot prove it, of course. I can only
say it is true.*

MG

As I folded the paper, the dying man caught at my arm.

"Do you believe it?" he whispered.

"Every word, sir," said I. "I wish you had told me before. I'm
young and I might have done something – "

"Listen. I say in that statement that I have no proof. *But I
have.* I have always had it – a proof that I could not use."

Shaking with excitement, poor Gering raised himself up, and,
since it seemed best not to thwart him, I put my arm about him
to lend him strength.

"The House of Brief has a secret – which has passed from
time immemorial from father to son. Only two persons know
this: and they are the Count and his heir. Ferdinand cannot
know it: but I who was the first-born – *I know the secret of our
House.* And to you, who have been my son, I will pass it on. It
may be that you can use it, but I cannot see so far. By rights,
Elizabeth – that was my daughter's name…"

And there his voice faltered and died, and the light in his eyes
slid into a sightless stare. As I made to lay him back on his
pillows, he lifted a trembling hand, to make the fretful gesture
of a man who would brush aside something that spoils his view.

"I am losing control," he quavered. "Old visions I have not
summoned are closing in. What was it that I was saying?"

"Never mind, sir," said I. "Let it go. When you have rested a
little – "

"No, no," he cried, starting up. "I know that it was important.
What was it, Exon? What was it?"

He was breathing hard now, and the sweat was out on his
face. To bring him peace at the last, I did as he said.

"You spoke of a secret, sir. The secret of Brief."

"Yes, yes. That was it," he gasped. "Listen. The great tower of Brief – the great tower. There is a doorway there which no one would ever find. You must go up, counting your steps. And when you have…"

And that was as far as he got.

For a moment the poor jaws worked. And then the head fell sideways and the body went slack in my arms.

So died the ninth Count of Brief. And the secret of his House with him.

Two days later I learned that an uncle of whose existence I had been hardly aware had recently died in Australia, leaving me all he had. And he was a very rich man.

Though my adversity lasted no more than a short two years, it would have been strange indeed if it had not altered my outlook for good and all. My values were radically changed, and I found not worth the picking nine-tenths of the fruit which was once more within my reach. I cared for none of those things which had lately seemed to me to compose a young man's life. For the ways of the world of fashion I had no use, and all my pleasure was in the countryside. Only the company of Nature seemed to be able to banish the spectre of Red Lead Lane; and the song of a bird succeeded where costly distractions failed. Indeed, for the whole of that summer I moved in the English country from inn to inn, spending not a tenth of my income and every day more thankful for my deliverance.

With the approach of winter, I grew more self-possessed, and before November was in, I had settled down in a very pleasant manor, which had been a famous seat, but was now an hotel. The peace and dignity of my surroundings, the beauty of the old building and the gentle breath of tradition, with which every chamber was quick, did much to complete my cure by recommending to me the work of men's hands; and I think I can say that with the new year I entered the plain state of mind in which, for better or worse, I have been ever since. This was reserved and sober, but not unnatural. I did not shun, though I never sought company. Extravagance made me uneasy, whatever its guise. And if I could help it, I never spent a night in town.

It must not be thought that I had forgotten Gering or the statement of his which I held. I remembered him constantly, and more than once I wondered if it was not for me to take action upon the facts which I knew. And then it always seemed best to let sleeping dogs lie. I had looked up the House of Brief and had found two things – first, that the pseudo-Count was still a widower and, secondly, that on his death the title would pass to his daughter, the Lady Elizabeth Virgil, now twenty-four years old. The dreadful injustice, therefore, was over and done: it had in fact come to an end with Gering's death: and though the wicked flourished, the good was beyond his reach. In a word, there was no wrong to be righted. There was, of course, a scoundrel who richly deserved the fate which parricides used to meet: but, if I were to publish the truth *and be believed*, the scandal would cost the daughter extremely dear. But if I let things alone, she would in due course succeed to the dignity which was hers. In due course... That was the fly in the ointment with which I salved what sense of duty I had. In fact, she *was* the Countess. When Gering died in my arms, the Lady Elizabeth Virgil became the Countess of Brief.

And then a strange thing happened.

Summer was coming in, and I had been out in my car for the whole of the day. I entered my rooms in the evening, to bathe and change, when I saw upon my table an envelope covering something, but not addressed. Opening this, I found a passport within – and knew at once that some servant had made a mistake. A guest had arrived from abroad and the office had asked for his passport, from which to fill up the form which the police required. And now it had been returned – to me, instead of to him.

The passport was that of Percy Elbert Virgil, born in London in 1910, and domiciled at Brief. And the face was the face of a clever unscrupulous blackguard, with as close-set a pair of eyes as ever I saw.

I sent the passport back to the office, lighted a cigarette and sat down to think things out.

Unknown to Gering, before he had been arrested, his brother had had a son. That son was now twenty-six and dwelled in his father's house. And father and son were both evil. How did the Lady Elizabeth fare between two such wolves?

Her position was ugly. I mean, she stood in the way. Ferdinand's secret was safe – at the price of allowing his niece to sit in the seat of his son...*and heir*...I found it hard to believe that there were not times when he found that price very high. The wicked seldom care for the children of those they have wronged, and when they are bound to prefer them before their own flesh and blood...

I began to feel ill at ease.

It was, of course, none of my business. I happened to know the truth, but that was all. Gering had made no request: he had simply told me his tale. But then he had not been aware that his brother had a child of his own: and he had not expected that I should ever be free. For all that, it was none of my business.

I put out my cigarette and began to change.

Even if I made it my business, what could I do? It had never entered my head to doubt the truth of the statement which Gering had made. But how on earth could I prove it? By declaring the existence of some secret I did not know? By alleging the existence of a doorway 'which no one would ever find'? The thing was absurd. I had no proof. Gering himself had done nothing, because he had known very well that there was nothing to be done. And yet...

If I did not like Percy's portrait, the moment I saw him that evening I liked him less. Not at all resembling his uncle, he was a tall, dark man, over-dressed and scented, old for his age. His supercilious air denied the dignity which it was meant to boast: his elegance of gesture was vulgar: but the way in which he treated the servants was offensive beyond belief. His mouth was big and unkindly, and now and again a curious glint would enter and leave his eyes. But he looked a capable man: more than capable – shrewd. I could see him committing crime, but I could not see him arrested for what he had done. It occurred to me that his mother must have been wise. She had had no truck with Gering. After all, a rich brother-in-law is of very much better value than a penniless husband in jail.

I had been something surprised that such a man as he should choose such an hotel, but I saw that he sat at the table of one of the residents – a quiet, sad-faced old fellow, whose name I knew to be Inskip, who used to go up to London twice in the week. The two spoke hardly at all, and I had no doubt that business was to be done. I found myself hoping that Inskip knew what he was about.

That night I took Gering's statement and read it again. Then I took pen and paper and wrote down the verbal statement which he had made to me. After that, I made two fair copies and sealed the originals up to be lodged at my Bank. And then I went to my bed, proposing to sleep on a matter which seemed to call at least for inquiry, into which I was not armed to inquire. And yet nobody else could do it. There was the rub.

But, though I was weary enough, I could not rest – because I had called up spirits which now would not let me be. The life and death of Gering and the horror of Red Lead Lane demanded recognition in detail and would not be denied, and it was not till day was breaking that out of sheer, mental exhaustion I fell asleep.

When Winter called me that morning, I asked him if he could tell me what Inskip's profession was; and he said at once that he was a diamond merchant and added that he had heard say that he was 'a very big man'.

Winter was the valet who always attended to me. He was an excellent servant, quick and deft and willing and very quiet. He did for me much that could not be called his duty, and, because he was so pleasant, I had come to know him better than anyone else I had met since Gering died. He was only thirty years old, and I sometimes used to wonder that a man so strong and upstanding should have chosen a valet's life: but he told me once that, though he had been trained for a chauffeur, the only posts he could get would have held him in Town, and I think that, to be in the country, he would have broken stones for the roads.

That day I went to London myself – with a vague idea of engaging a private detective to shadow Percy Virgil and follow him out to Brief: but, instead, I purchased some Austrian ordnance maps and then, on a sudden impulse, walked into a motorcar dealer's and spent an hour discussing the virtues of various cars.

From this it will be seen that I was as good as halfway to leaving for Brief myself. Indeed, all that held me back was the thought that however shameful the state of affairs there might be, I could do nothing at all to put them right. I had a fine bow to bend, but not a single arrow to fit to its string – an agonizing position, if game got up. I knew. Impotence had his head-quarters in Red Lead Lane.

And then another thing happened.

Winter did not call me next day – for the first time for nearly six months. As the man who had taken his place made to leave the room –

"Where's Winter?" I said. "He's not ill?"

"He's gone, sir. He left last night."

"Gone?" said I.

"That's right, sir. He's – left the hotel."

After breakfast I asked the porter for Winter's address, and fifty minutes later I ran my friend to earth at his sister's home.

When I asked him why he had left, he looked distressed.

"I lost my temper, sir. That's one of the things a servant's paid not to do. In a sense it wasn't my fault, but the manager couldn't pass it. If I'd been placed like him, I wouldn't have passed it myself."

I bade him tell me the facts.

"It was that foreign gentleman, sir. Mr Virgil, I think was his name. He was to have left this morning. I expect he's gone. He's – he's not a nice way with servants. I waited upon him as well as ever I could, but – well, I don't think he fancied me and I really believe he set out to twist my tail. He rang for me seven times in the same half-hour. 'Do this,' he'd say, and stand there and watch me do it: and when I was through, 'Do that.' And at last I turned. 'Do it yourself,' I said, 'and be damned for the cad you look.' I give you my word, I was angry. I believe if he'd answered me back, I'd have knocked him down. But he jumped for the telephone…"

"I don't blame you at all," said I. "And next time, perhaps, there won't be a telephone."

"Next time?" said Winter, staring.

I laughed.

"I was thinking aloud," I said. "Never mind. Would you like to be my servant? I'm going abroad."

Looking back upon the order of our going, I cannot believe that any enterprise was ever undertaken with so hazy a plan of action or so indistinct a goal. All I knew was that I meant to put up at some village not far from Brief and from there somehow to observe the state of things prevailing within that house. But because I had set no course, I was perhaps the more ready to catch at such chances as happened to come my way; and but for these I should have accomplished nothing and so, of course, should have had no tale to tell.

I set out for Innsbruck in June, taking Winter with me and making the journey by road.

To Winter's pride and delight, I had purchased a fine Rolls-Royce, and though at first I felt very much ashamed of owning so handsome a car, I was very soon more than thankful for what I had done. I took with me the maps I had bought and two powerful binoculars; and a certain Bank in Innsbruck was ready to honour my cheques. And that, I think, was all – except that I carried two pistols, in case of accidents. And these lay in the Rolls' toolbox, wrapped in rubbers and hidden beneath the tools.

I crossed the Channel by night, and before the next day was over had come to Basle. There I lay at a well-known house on the banks of the Rhine, and, liking the look of the place, decided to spend a day there, before going on.

It was not that I was weary, and if I was to rest by the way, I would have preferred to stay in the countryside; but I had set out, not thinking my task would be easy, but proposing to let my embarrassments make themselves felt. And now the first one had done so. And since, so far from being outwitted or even reduced, it was likely to hang as a millstone about my neck, I felt I must have time to reflect before going on.

I could speak no language at all, except my own. I dare say this would not have mattered, if I had been but a tourist, with nothing to do but visit famous places and stay at the best hotels. But that was not my mission, and the helplessness I had known ever since I had landed in France had not only opened my eyes but had shaken me up. I could not even order a meal. As for 'pumping' some Austrian peasant...

Though I had said nothing to Winter, the more I considered this drawback, the more disconcerted I felt, and I strolled about Basle that pleasant sunshiny morning, cursing my education and wondering whether the German which Austrians spoke was as paralysing a language as that which the Swiss employed.

In this uneasy mood I presently repaired to the garage in which the Rolls was bestowed, to have a word with Winter – to whom, I may say, the curse of Babel seemed to be matter for mirth – and see that the car was no worse for her full day's run.

As I walked into the place, I saw a nice-looking fellow half-sitting on the wing of a Lowland, with his hat on the back of his head. The owner of the garage stood before him with outstretched hands, as though to declare his regret at being unable to please, but the other looked up to heaven and mournfully shook his head, and then said something or other which made the foreman beside him laugh outright. He was very plainly English and might have been thirty-five: his merry face was belying his injured air: and, to tell the truth, it did me good to see him, for his gaiety was infectious and his careless, easy manner was that of a man on intimate terms with Life, who can always count on his crony to see him through.

The moment he saw me he smiled and put up a hand. Then he touched the proprietor's arm and pointed to me.

"There you are," he said, using English. "The hour produces the man."

Recognizing me, the proprietor bowed and smiled, and I stood still and waited to know what was wanted of me.

The other went straight to the point.

"I desire your ruling," he said. "Will you be so very good as to say what this Lowland is worth? And put it as low as you dare. You see, I'm inclined to buy her: but Mr Schelling here is asking me rather too much." He turned to Schelling. "You can't say that isn't fair."

"But how can I say?" said I. "She looks all right, but– "

"Assume she's in perfect order, two years old and has done twenty thousand miles."

I raised my eyebrows and took a look at the car.

In fact, I was in a position to give the ruling he wished, for I had had a Lowland until I had purchased the Rolls.

The others watched me in silence.

At length –

"I think she'd be cheap," said I, "at three hundred and fifty pounds."

"I'm much obliged," said Herrick – to give him his name. "Well, Schelling, what about it?"

The garage proprietor sighed.

"What will you?" he said. "I go to make out a cheque."

As he made his way to the office –

"I beg," said Herrick, "that you will lunch with me. If you hadn't appeared when you did, I should now be the poorer by exactly one hundred pounds."

"But I thought – "

"I know. I was selling the car – not Schelling. I asked him three hundred pounds, and he wouldn't go beyond two. He swore she wasn't worth more, and I couldn't wait. Is that your Rolls over there?"

I told him 'yes', and we moved to where Winter was fussing about his beautiful charge. Whilst I was talking to him, Schelling returned with a cheque for three hundred pounds and, when he had pocketed this, Herrick repeated his invitation to lunch.

Ten minutes later we entered a good-looking café, where he was plainly known, for the host himself conducted us up some stairs and gave us a table beside an open window, commanding an agreeable prospect of lawns and trees.

"Now, isn't that nice?" said Herrick, regarding the pretty scene. "Sit down with Madam Nature, and your meal, however humble, becomes a repast. Of course you must have fine weather. A picnic in the rain can provoke more downright misery than anything I know. I envy you going to Innsbruck. I had a stomach ache there in 1912. Eating too many figs, I think. And the country round is superb. Then, again, the people are charming – the peasants, I mean. Always do anything for you. What about some trout to begin with? And while we're worrying that, they can squeeze us a duck."

Since I was accustomed to keep no company, the entertainment he offered was like some gift from the gods, and

I found myself talking and laughing as I had not done since I left Oxford – three years before. I never enjoyed myself so much in my life, and today I can remember that luncheon down to the smallest detail of what was eaten and said.

It was when they had brought the coffee that Herrick spoke of himself.

"I'm really a tout," he said: "at least, I was. Employed by a firm in England to sell their stuff over here. I sometimes think I was meant for better things, but when you come down to concrete, a double-blue at Cambridge is about as much good in the City as the art of elocution would be to a Trappist monk. As it was, my French and German got me the job. And it's not been too bad, you know. Quite a good screw, and out and about all day. And I've not been dismissed, you know. You mustn't think that. The English company's failed... I might have guessed when I didn't get my quarterly cheque. But I'm not too good at money, and when at last I wrote, they said the cashier was ill. And then, two days ago, I found they were bust... Hence the sale of the Lowland... Thanks to you, my dear Exon, I can now discharge all my debts and travel back to England in that degree of comfort which an insolent flesh demands."

"And then?" said I.

Herrick considered his brandy.

"I shall take a new job," he said. "Between you and me, it won't be for very long. My uncle, Lord Naseby, is failing, and I'm his heir. He hates the sight of me – a family quarrel or something: I don't know what. But he can't do me out of the money – he would if he could. But that's by the way. I've always reckoned my sentence would work out at fifteen years. And twelve were up in April, so I've only got three to go. And now tell me about yourself. You've had your cross to bear, or I'll bolt a bucket of bran."

"You make me ashamed," said I, and said no more than the truth.

With that I told him my tale.

When I had made an end –

"I don't blame you at all," he said. "When a man has no hope, one year of hell can easily break his heart. And you had two… I admit that I've had twelve years. But they haven't been years of hell, and, what is more to the point, ahead has shone certainty. Nothing so flimsy as hope. An absolute certainty. When Uncle Naseby goes out, I shall have the ancestral home and four or five thousand a year. Not a bad Rachel to wait for, my bonny boy. And a damned sight more attractive than I found her at twenty-four."

"I – I congratulate you," I said slowly, "on several things." I got to my feet. "And thank you very much for the last two hours. Will you dine with me tonight? I'm not going to dress."

"I will with pleasure," said Herrick. "Can you make it nine o'clock? I'd like to clear everything up before I come."

"Nine o'clock," said I. "I'll be in the hall."

But long before then I resolved to obey my impulse and made up my mind to offer John Herrick a job.

It was when we had dined that night and were sitting above the river, which hereabouts seemed to be a gigantic race, that I told him Gering's story and gave him the statements to read. Then I spoke of Percy Virgil and, finally, of the business which I had set out to do.

"And now," I concluded, "we come to the water-jump. I need a companion in this, an Englishman who can speak German, a man that I can talk to, who's willing to work with me if there's work to be done. In a word, I want you. Your expenses, of course, would be mine from beginning to end, and, if you say 'yes', I shall pay your fee in advance."

"I don't want any fee," said Herrick.

"I know," said I. "But I want you to feel independent: and if I've all the money, you can't. Please don't forget that I've been much poorer than you."

"All right," he said, and a hand went up to his brow. "I'm on, of course. I'll love it. And I'm greatly impressed by this business.

More than impressed. I'm dazed. You see, I know something of... Gering. In fact, I was a page at his wedding. His wife, the Countess Rudolph, was one of my mother's best friends. And I've stayed at Brief. I was only twelve at the time, and I've never been back. But I still remember the house and the seven staircase-turrets which led to the upper floors. But I never was in the great tower. The Count of Brief had his rooms there, and, if I remember aright, it was holy ground."

2

We Spy Out the Land

Now my idea had been to discover some village, not very far from Brief, at which we could take up our quarters for as long as we meant to stay. From there we could make such approaches as circumstances seemed to permit, and though these excursions demanded long and irregular hours, we should always have rest and shelter a few miles off. We could only begin, I considered, by keeping observation on Brief and thus getting to know the habits of those who lived and moved upon the estate. With that knowledge, we could go further, either by getting in touch with one of the staff or by going right up to the castle to learn what we could for ourselves.

Herrick approved these plans – if, indeed, they deserve the name, and, after two nights at Innsbruck, we left that city at six o'clock in the morning, travelling east. At nine o'clock we had breakfast, some twenty-five miles from Brief, and, after that, we set out to prove the country, working, of course, by the map and aiming at finding a reasonably comfortable lodging, which was neither too near nor too far.

Neither Herrick nor Winter nor I will ever forget that day. To and fro and around and about we went, stopping and starting and turning and losing our way, condemning this inn on sight and entering that – only to see some objection before we had tasted our beer. Some of the inns were too busy, and some were foul: this one was short of a coach-house, and that had a host that was sick, and one would have done very well – but it had no roof, because a fire had destroyed it the day before.

I must confess that the country through which we ran was some of the very finest I ever saw. On all sides forest-clad mountains were neighbouring streams and pastures and delicate woods. We climbed a majestic shoulder, only to drop to a drowsy, land-locked valley where elms rose out of deep meadows and a lazy water mirrored the drinking cows: we stole through a whispering beechwood, where the pretty speech of a brook was fretted now and again by the fluting of birds, and ten minutes later we crossed a fall of water the steady roar of which could be heard for a quarter of a mile. Now our world was a watch of summits lifting their casques of fir trees into a cloud-less sky: and now it was a comfortable pleasance, where the dawn was never challenged, where Husbandry and Nature had kissed each other.

It was half-past five that evening, and we were beginning to wonder where we should spend the night, when for the fifth or sixth time we lost our way.

As I brought the Rolls to rest –

"I decline to apologize," said Herrick. "I know I'm holding the map, but the map is wrong. Where did you get the swine?"

"It's an ordnance map," I protested. "It can't be wrong. If we'd turned to the left at – "

"If you say that again," said Herrick, "I shall tear the map into fragments and strew them about the road. I may even masticate them. D'you usually turn to the left when you're trying to get to the right?"

"Not as a rule," said I. "But from what I've seen of this country – "

"And there you're right," said Herrick. "The land's bewitched. Eighteen inns to date – and I'd swap the lot for a supper of bread and milk and a truss of hay."

"To be frank," said I, "I'm not very much surprised. But you said you knew the place. And you swore that the inns were out of the golden world."

"So they were," raged Herrick, "ten years ago. It isn't my fault they've changed. Ten years ago I stayed at an inn by Villach some twenty-five miles from a train. I paid five shillings a day, and they served my food on silver and gave me clean sheets every night, and wept when I left."

"Well, we've two hours yet," said I. "Let's give the map a rest and go as we please."

"Every time," said Herrick, and closed his eyes. "Don't wake me when we come to a village. Just go and look at the inn and then get back in the car. The rite must be observed – as a matter of form. But I don't want to know about it. I've had enough shocks today. Oh, and where's that roll I stepped on?"

Winter spoke from the back of the car.

"You gave it to the pig, sir, at Goschen."

"So I did," said Herrick. "So I did. You know, it's almost biblical. I picked at my omelet this morning – a succulent, mushroom omelet fit for the gullet of a king. And tonight I would fain fill my belly with the crusts that the swine did eat. Learn of me, Winter – and never let me do that again."

"Very good, sir," said Winter, obediently.

I let in the clutch...

For more than a mile to come we threaded a dark green forest of close-set firs, and then we passed over some ridge and began to go down between meadows of very fine grass. No signs of habitation were to be seen, but that meant little enough, for the country was very blind and more than once that day we had taken a bend to find before us a village which we had supposed to be yet a long way off. And then, on a sudden, there appeared a fork in the road.

As I set a foot on the brake, I threw a glance at Herrick, to see him asleep, and after a moment's reflection I switched to the left. I confess that the way to the right was the better road, but that climbed up once more, while that to the left led on down, and, to tell the truth, I was more for the comfort of country that man administered than the proud domain which was ruled by Nature alone. *Facilis descensus...* Before half a mile had gone by, I had an uneasy feeling that we were making the most of some private road, but since I could not turn round there was nothing to do but go on. Another two furlongs proved my suspicion just, and I rounded a bend to see our way swallowed up by the shade of two mighty chestnuts which were standing, like Gog and Magog, before a substantial farm.

Now I could not turn the Rolls round without driving past the chestnuts and so right up to the house, and since, if we were observed, we could scarcely withdraw without excusing ourselves, it seemed to me that we might as well ask where we were and then endeavour to find the farm on the map. But when I put this to Herrick, he only bade me proceed and let him be, and when I said that we could no longer go on, he said he was glad to hear it and settled himself for a further and better sleep.

I decided to force his hand, and drove up to the house.

The doors and windows were open, but no one was to be seen, and I saw at once that here was more than a farm, for the house was more important than any of those we had passed.

As Winter opened my door, a pleasant-looking woman appeared at the head of the steps...

I had no hat to take off, but I bowed and smiled. Then I pointed to the map in my hand, and, speaking, for some absurd reason, in what I believed to be French, announced that we were lost and requested the name of the house.

The woman smiled.

"I think you are English," she said.

I could hardly believe my ears, and I think my look of amazement made her laugh. Be that as it may, the two of us laughed together as though at some excellent jest, till a bright-eyed girl came running, to see what the matter might be.

Her mother addressed her in German, still shaking with mirth, and the two of them laughed together before returning to me.

"My mother," said the girl, "can only speak two or three words, but I am better, sir, if you will say what you want."

"She's better than I am," said I. "And you are extremely good. Have you ever been in England?"

"Oh, no. But every summer an English family stays here. They come in August to fish. And they have been good to teach me as much as I know."

"Do you mean that they stay here?" said I. "That they lodge with you?"

"Always," said Brenda, proudly – for I later learned that that was her name. "They have made us a beautiful bathroom two years ago."

Listen," said I. "From nine o'clock this morning my friend and I have been scouring time countryside to try and find an inn at which we could possibly stay. We could not even find one at which we could break our fast."

Brenda nodded sympathetically.

"The inns are no good," she said.

"Will you receive us?" I said. "We shan't be any trouble, and my servant here will do all he can to help."

The girl consulted her mother. I watched them with my heart in my mouth.

Then –

"We shall be pleased," she said simply, "until the end of July."

I could have flung my arms around her neck. Instead, I shook hands with them both and then ran round to rouse Herrick and tell him my wonderful news.

He heard me out in silence.

Then –

"Young man," he said, "from now on I shall take a back seat. I'm very much wiser than you – to turn to the left like that was the act of a fool – but you're one of Fortune's darlings, and that's worth all the wisdom in all the world. And now let's consider the flesh. I think we might prove that bathroom – as soon as we've had some beer."

As may be believed, we did no more that evening than minister to our needs and stroll in content about our heritage. The house, which had been a bailiff's, was full of fine rooms: our apartments were all that two men could ever desire: and the Rolls was lodged in a coach-house which would have accepted three cars. All this was well enough, but the honest goodwill that was shown to us was such as a man remembers as long as he lives. With it all, no questions were asked and we were left to ourselves.

After breakfast the following day, we returned to the map. We found our bearings at once, for the farm was marked. The name of it was Raven: and Brief lay eleven miles off. Such a distance was very convenient, for while we could have gone to the castle in twenty minutes or less, we were out of the range of such gossip as comes to a servants' hall.

The estate was large, but the castle stood to one side: and that, of course, was something, for if it had stood in the middle, unless we were ready to trespass, we could have seen nothing at all. About the estate stood mountains – so much was clear. But whether, by climbing one, we should have a fair view of the castle was more than we could divine. Still, we carefully pencilled the roads which, so to speak, by-passed Brief on the southern side, for that was the side upon which the castle was built. And then we set out to prove them. Unless the map was lying, if Brief could be commanded from any point, that point could only be reached from one of our pencilled roads.

At half-past ten that morning the three of us entered the Rolls, and I drove leisurely westward, while Herrick and Winter regarded the countryside. It seemed as well to get our surroundings by heart.

At every side road, I stopped, and we studied the map, so that, though our progress was slow, we all of us knew continually where we were. And then I turned north and on to our pencilled roads.

It was half-past twelve and we were among the mountains, when the way which we were using began to rise very steeply, after the way of a pass. This was so much to the good, but hereabouts the map and the country agreed together so ill that we could not determine the heights which we were beginning to climb. As though to confuse us still more, the road bent to and fro and doubled upon itself, while the woods through which we were moving were very thick and the trees upon either hand met over our heads. Though we were not lost, we were as good as blindfolded, and after five minutes had passed we knew not which way we were going nor whence we had come. For all that, our surroundings were lovely – a twisting, irregular tunnel of lively green, and since we could do nothing until this came to an end, we gave ourselves up to enjoying a bewildering passage which, if they had known of its beauty, a great many people, I think, would have travelled a long way to make. The air was most sweet and cool and, because of a thousand springs, the earth gave off a fragrance which put to shame the bouquet of any wine: the glare of the sun was tempered to a delicate brilliance which lighted the tenderest detail without besetting the eye: and the heavy curtains of foliage, hanging on either side, were quick with the pipe and the flutter of countless birds.

We must have threaded this natural gallery for nearly two miles, when we heard, at first very faint, the roar of falling water some distance ahead.

"And very nice, too," said Herrick, cocking an ear. "This means a break in the trees. Stop when we get there, my boy, and, as the dog to his vomit, so I will return to the map. I need hardly say that it shows no sign of water. In fact, I'm inclined to think that they guessed this bit. The temptation, no doubt, was great. Nobody seems to come here: so who on earth was ever to say they were wrong?"

Whilst he was speaking we had been rounding a bend, and, though we could not yet see it, the song of some great cascade was growing more impressive with every yard. Then we floated over a crest, and there was a bridge before us, some forty yards off.

I am sure that neither Winter nor I will ever forget the moment when we walked on to that bridge. We had never before encountered so tremendous a head of water falling from such a height; and what with the terrible might of the sheaves and tresses of foam, the everlasting roar and the definite quaking of the ground upon which we stood, we felt both dazed and abashed and looked the one to the other, as men in the presence of something they cannot conceive.

I do not know how long I stood staring, but I suddenly found that Herrick had hold of my arm. Because of the tumult I could not hear what he said, but I let him turn me about and bring me up to the parapet of the bridge.

I now had my back to the fall and at once I leaned over and down to see if the splendour below us compared with the grandeur above, but Herrick would not allow me to do as I wished, jerking my arm and shouting, until in some impatience I lifted my head.

And then I saw he was pointing – not at the raging water, but out of the gap in the trees.

A crow's mile away stood a castle, built on the spur of a foothill against the green of the woods. With the naked eye I could see four staircase-turrets, and towards the left of the pile was rising one great, round tower.

Ten minutes later, perhaps, I made Winter a little speech.

Herrick and I had strolled on, out of sound of the fall, and Winter had taken the Rolls and had caught us up.

"I want you to know," said I, "why we three are here and what we are out to do. In that castle you saw I believe there to live three people. One is the present owner, the Count of Brief: the second, his only child: and the third, a nephew of his – a Mr Percy Virgil, by name."

"The same, sir?" said Winter, shortly.

"The same," said I.

"Thank you, sir," said Winter, between his teeth.

"Now though Mr Virgil lives there, he is not the son of the house, and the castle is not his home. It is his cousin's home – and yet he lives there…

"I have reason to think that the Count of Brief prefers Mr Virgil, his nephew, before his only child: and since the Count is about as big a sweep as Mr Virgil himself, I think it more than likely that, between the two, his cousin has a very thin time. And his cousin is a girl – the Lady Elizabeth Virgil, just twenty-four years old.

"Well, we are here to find out if my suspicion is just. No more than that for the moment – I may be entirely wrong."

"I'll lay you're not, sir," said Winter. "He'd cut his own mother's throat, if she stood in his way. Cold iron, he is – cold iron: an' as truly wicked a blackguard as ever I met."

"I'm inclined to agree," said I. "But we've got to make sure. And that's not going to be at all easy, because we must not be seen. But I think the first thing to do is to keep some observation upon the castle itself. And what we are able to see may give us a line to work on…

"Mr Herrick knows the castle – he stayed there before the War. But that is as much as he knows, and we know nothing at all. So we've all got to use our wits. We're up against a blank wall, on the other side of which is the picture we want to see. Well, we've got to climb it somehow, and if it's not to be climbed – well, damn it, we'll have to go round."

If that was as much as I said, it was more than enough to fan to a flame the embers of Winter's zeal, and from that time on he was heart and soul in the business, as I shall show.

The astonishing chance which led us straight to the viewpoint to which we had hoped to come was the only stroke of good fortune we met that day. To be sure, it was handsome enough: but the fact remains that, so far as we could discover, the bridge from which we had sighted the Castle of Brief was the one and only point on the roads we had marked from which that remarkable pile could be fairly surveyed. And this was provoking, for, while the prospect it offered was all that we could have desired, as a post of observation the bridge was untenable. Apart from drowning the voice, after a very few minutes the uproar and the concussion the water made distracted the wits; the bruised and battered senses began to demand relief; and I think that no man that had stayed could have usefully given his mind to anything else.

However, we now had our bearings, and, the map proving faithful once more, we never lost them again. This to Herrick's credit, for I never saw country so blind. Unless we were high, we could see no distance at all, and when we began to rise, the forests clothing the mountains directly obscured our view. If clearings there were, we never came across them, and the very few 'windows' we found were made by other cascades and did not happen to face the way we wished. The estate of Brief itself seemed to resemble the country in which it stood, and foothills hid the castle from all of the lower roads.

By four o'clock that day we had compassed the property twice and had never seen so much as the top of the tower, but, for what it was worth, we knew the lie of the land and had marked the two entrance drives and three or four tracks which would have accepted a car. To a great extent we had the ways to ourselves, and, except in one village, called Gola, I do not think our passage excited remark. But we ran through that twice, which was foolish, and the second time, looking back, I saw a smith and his helper run out of the forge and stand staring after the Rolls, with their tools in their hands.

When I told Herrick, he sighed.

"Can't be helped," he said. "But a blacksmith's forge is as bad as a barber's shop. Gossip. And that's the worst of using a notable car. We'd better give Gola a miss for as long as we can."

It was after that that we climbed again to the bridge, and, berthing the Rolls beyond it, turned to the arduous business of proving the woods through which the cascade fell down. Except by entering these, we could not possibly tell whether or no they were hiding some coign which commanded Brief, for we could only survey them by looking up from below – an angle which showed us no more than a billowing quilt of leaves.

For three full hours we fought with that mountainside, and for all the good we did we might never have left the car. We could not even reach the head of the fall, for after perhaps two hundred and fifty feet I came to a hidden cornice of blue-grey rock, and though, in view of the tales which men of the mountains tell, I hardly like to say that this could not have been climbed, I should like to see the man that could have climbed it and, better still, the manner in which he went to work. As for finding a point of view, but for the roar of the water, we should not have known where we were, and, until I came back to the road, I never found so much as a rest for the sole of my foot.

Going down, I met Winter past speaking, clinging to the roots of a beech, but of Herrick I saw no sign till I came to a brake of brambles not more than sixty feet up. Here his hat was hanging, caught up on a venomous sucker that sprang from a monstrous bush, and, since he was not to be seen, I supposed that I had passed him by in my descent – for had he been coming down, he would not have left his hat. I, therefore, shouted his name with all my might, to be answered from the midst of the brambles by which I stood.

"I trust," he said gravely, "that you have enjoyed your stroll. I'm not going to ask if you've viewed the promised land – first, because I know the answer, and, secondly, because I am not interested in posts of observation to which only an anthropoid ape can conveniently repair. And now, if Winter's alive, you might procure my release. I'll direct the operation – I've had nothing to do for ten minutes but work it out."

"You're not hurt?"

"No. Merely disabled. If I don't breathe, I hardly suffer at all. But to move means laceration. You see, I'm embedded in something which simply must not be touched. Transgress this law, and you're savaged beyond belief." I heard him sigh. "I don't know what I've done to deserve it. I know I have certain failings, but I always thought this sort of thing was reserved for the mute of malice and people like that. Still, of course, the saints went through it... I think that's Winter coming. You might tell him to incline to the right. If he were to drop upon me, you wouldn't hear the fall for my screams. And I should go mad and kill him before I died."

So thick and fierce were the briers and so deeply was Herrick involved that a quarter of an hour went by before we could haul him out, and though both Winter and I were honestly sorry for him, our sense of decency failed before the directions he issued and the bellows of pain which he let. Indeed, we laughed so much that we could hardly stand up, much less extricate his dead weight from the welter in which he lay, and if, in the end, he had not withheld his complaints, I do not believe we should ever have dragged him clear.

That was enough for us all, and we made our way home, proposing upon the morrow to assault the neighbouring heights. These were hard of access, because they were not served by roads which the Rolls could use, but we were reluctant to trespass except in the last resort and so refused to be daunted by a prospect we could not enjoy.

The burden of the next three days will hardly go into print. Enough that we fought like madmen to wrest from the mountains and forests a secret which, if they had, they would not disclose. Such harsh and unprofitable labour I never did, and when Herrick at last declared that he would no longer abuse his long-suffering flesh, I must confess I was thankful to throw in my hand.

At four o'clock on a Thursday he leaned against a fir and stated his case.

"I do not like doing trespass, and I simply loathe doing trespass without first surveying the scene of the trespass I mean to do. But I'm not going on with these rambles, because I prefer to die in some less exacting way. A lingering illness, for instance… I am tired of unseating my intestines by efforts no goat would be such a fool as to make, and I'm sick of straining my eyeballs in an effort to see through cover which is just about as transparent as a cellar of coal. In a word, I have had my fill of futility. I, therefore, suggest that we should cut the rest of a prelude which I shall try to forget, scrap our attempts to rival the fowls of the air and enter time enemy's lines without further delay. I may say that this suggestion belongs to the spirit alone: if I took the advice of the flesh, I should enter a nursing-home."

With that, he began to retire by the way we had come, and Winter and I came after without a word.

As we drove back to Raven, we summed up what we had learned from going about the estate, and after an excellent supper, of which we were very glad, we studied the map we had marked and laid our plans.

These were, very shortly, to make for the mouth of the northern entrance-drive. There Winter would set us down and then go off for petrol, of which we were running short. If the map was true, the drive was some two miles long, but the end we had seen was flanked with fine, tall bracken, which would, at need, afford us most excellent cover from view. From the drive we could first survey and presently take to the foothills which neighboured the castle itself and so look down on the building we meant to watch: and though it would have been quicker to climb the foothills at once – for they stood close to the road running south of Brief – we should then have been unable to see ahead and might well have passed over some crest, clean into some garden or terrace commanded by every window that looked that way. How long our visit would last, we could not tell, but when Winter had taken in fuel, he was to return with the Rolls and berth her in one of the tracks.

With that, we went to bed early, for we were to rise at dawn, more or less content that the country had forced our hands and little dreaming of the ruffle which the morrow was to bring forth.

The sky was cloudless, the world was drenched with dew and the sun was not yet upon the mountains, when Winter set us down a hundred yards from the mouth of the entrance-drive. To this there were no lodge-gates, and only a board marked 'Private' distinguished its rough, brown surface from that of an ordinary road.

"The first track on the right, Winter. Back her down and take her well into the wood. You may have to wait some time, but don't go far from the car and keep out of sight of the road."

"Very good, sir," said Winter, and set a hand to his hat.

Five minutes later the Rolls was three miles off and Herrick and I were padding along the drive, one upon either side of the ill-kept road, ready to enter the bracken the moment we saw or heard any sign of life.

For a furlong the drive ran straight: then it bent to the left and the woods upon either hand began to close in: but the bracken held on and was growing tall and thick – we could see the green flood stretching beneath the trees. And then the drive curled to the right and ran into the woods.

We had covered more than a mile and the sun was up, when, something to our surprise, we heard the sound of a car. This was behind us, coming the way we had come, and at once we whipped into the bracken and kneeled down among time green stems, to let it go by.

After a moment or two, a closed car, travelling slowly, slipped into and out of our sight. The blinds of the car were drawn, and a chauffeur, wearing black livery, sat at the wheel. A glance at the number-plate showed that this was obscured.

"The return of Percy," said Herrick, "after a heavy night. I know just how he's feeling. And I'm glad I'm not his valet, if what you tell me is true."

With his words, the car disappeared, and we rose out of the bracken to hasten along in its wake.

We were now approaching the foothills among which the castle stood, but the drive was so serpentine and the trees by its sides were so thick that we could not see what was coming for more than some fifty paces beyond each bend. We, therefore, took the precaution of leaving the road for the bracken before we rounded a curve, to make sure the next reach was empty before we exposed ourselves. That we did so was just as well, for a quarter of a mile further on, I lifted my head from the bracken to see the closed car at rest in the midst of the way. One of its doors was open, and someone within was speaking with Percy Virgil, who seemed to be very angry and was pointing the way we had come.

Be sure I dropped like a stone, and Herrick, moving behind me, followed my lead.

After a moment he wriggled his way to my side.

"What do you see, Sister Anne?"

"Percy himself," I whispered. "Having a row with someone inside the car. It looked to me as though he was sending them back."

As I spoke, the car began to move backwards slowly enough.

Now the drive was not wide enough to allow any car to turn round, but a track ran out of the drive some six or seven paces from where we lay. By making use of this track, any chauffeur could turn any car, and I was ready to wager that here the car would be turned. Sure enough, in a moment or two, we saw the body swing backwards into the track. For all that, I should have been wrong, for the car did not stop until it was four or five paces clear of the drive, when the chauffeur applied his hand-brake and switched his engine off. The car had been parked.

As somebody opened the door, Percy Virgil strode out of the drive and into the track.

Here I will say once for all that throughout this tale I shall report in English such speech as was used. Much was, of course, said in German, but though, when I heard it, I did not know what it meant, Herrick translated it for me as soon as ever he could.

As he came to the car –

"Where's the wire?" snapped Virgil. "Or have you forgotten that?"

"It is here," said another man.

"And the change of clothes?"

"Also," said a woman's voice.

"All marked, as I said?"

"That is so."

"Then follow me," said Virgil, "and bring the wire."

Cautiously raising our heads, we saw the procession set out – first Virgil, then the man, then the woman, with a dog on a lead. The chauffeur brought up the rear. They passed behind the car and disappeared in the wood.

When Herrick explained what had passed, I put a hand to my head.

"What on earth does it mean?"

Herrick shrugged his shoulders.

"Unless," he said, "dear Percy is making a film…"

"Which is absurd," said I. "But so is everything else. And where does the dog come in?"

"Nothing comes in," said Herrick. "It's all preposterous. But I'm glad to have seen dear Percy – extremely glad. And I'll tell you this, my friend – if ever we should set out to get that gentleman down, we shall have to pull our socks right over our knees. He certainly looks a blackguard, but he's not the sort of blackguard that makes mistakes. I can see him committing murder, and never turning a hair: but he'd have his alibi ready – tied up and sealed and posted, before he went after his man."

I shall always find it strange that Herrick's first impression of Virgil should have agreed so very closely to mine, for though I had told him about him, I had only said that I thought him a clever, unscrupulous man. Yet, here was Herrick using the phrase I had harboured when first I saw the fellow a month before. And I must say it sobered me, for, for one thing, two heads, it is said, are better than one, and, for another, Herrick was very discerning and knew his world.

Having seen and heard what we had, I was for following Virgil, to see what his business might be, but when I suggested this, Herrick raised his eyebrows and glanced at his watch.

"As you please," said he, "but it's now getting on for five, and the out-door staff will be up and about by six. If we turn aside and start stalking Percy and Co. – and it means stalking, mark you: not whipping along a road – by the time we get back to our job, we may find that we've missed the tide."

This was sheer common sense, so I said no more. For all that, I had a feeling that Virgil was up to no good and I left him behind with reluctance and thinking all the time of the puzzle which we had been set.

Wire, a change of clothes and a dog on a lead...at half-past four in the morning...in the midst of a private park. And a closed and numberless car...and the clothes had been marked...

I think I may be forgiven for wondering what was toward.

Ten minutes perhaps had gone by when the drive curled between the foothills and then swung round to the left and began to climb. Almost at once the woods on its right fell away, and there was the castle before us, perhaps three hundred yards off.

It made a lovely picture, lit by the rising sun, for its tower and its seven turrets stood out most bold and brilliant against the blue of the sky and these and every projection that caught the light were throwing shadows so vivid that the castle looked heraldic and might have been a blazon of black and gold. It was built of grey stone and must once have been a fortress of considerable strength, but windows had later been set in its massive walls, and chimney-stacks had been added, to make it a residence. The work had been carefully done and was now itself so old that the blend of mansion and stronghold delighted the eye, and though an antiquary might have looked down his nose, the result was both strong and gentle and full of dignity.

No smoke rose from the chimneys, nor could we see any movement within or about the house, and since we could hardly have wished for a finer view, we left the drive for some bushes a few yards off to settle down to the business of searching the tops of the foothills which stood to the south. These were the lesser heights over which we had been looking the day before; if we could occupy them, without being seen, we should overlook the castle from end to end, and since their opposite sides ran down very close to the road, they would be more easy of access than any other position commanding the house.

Herrick, I think, was more excited than I, for, now that he saw the castle as he had seen and known it when he was twelve years old, he began at once to remember the plan of the house: since this was all to the good, I let him be, and myself began to survey the heights which we hoped to use.

Almost at once I remarked that on one of these, three firs were standing together to thrust a grey-green steeple into the sky: this, I was sure, could be seen from the farther side and so would make us a landmark for future use. The next thing I saw was a path which slanted up from the meadows into the woods, and when I had taken my glasses, I found that it led to an elegant belvedere. This looked unfrequented, and but for my glasses I could not have picked it out, for the trees which had been cut back had put forth new boughs. Because of the veil of foliage, nobody standing there could ever be seen from below, yet he could see as much as he wished by peering between the leaves. To reach this spot from above looked easy enough, for it hung a short thirty feet below the crest of the hill, and the ground between was covered with beech and fir.

This was enough for me. As a matter of form, I raked the neighbouring heights, but though they offered good cover, I saw no spot to compare with the belvedere. And this, of course, was natural, for the belvedere had been made to the end which we had in view, that is, to command the castle; and though in the old, quiet days, it might have been used, I found it hard to believe that man or woman today could be bothered to climb so high for the sake of a pretty prospect and nothing more. My one idea, in fact, was to make for the Rolls and then to go round by road and get to the belvedere as soon as ever I could. But Herrick, deep in memory, would not be moved.

"Why rush your fences?" he said. "We've plenty of time. I'm doing lovely work – I can even remember a picture that hung in the dining-room. That's the dining-room at the end. You can't see the stables from here – they're behind to the left. But what I'm on now is the tower. I think it rises from the courtyard – I'm almost sure. But I know that it had a door on the second floor. The courtyard's beyond that archway – not very big... You go on, if you like – I shan't be long. But I don't want to drop the thread, in case I can't find it again. The belvedere's gorgeous, of course: but I never saw the castle from there. It's because this view is familiar that everything's coming back."

I had a sudden idea.

"All right," I said. "I'll go on. And on the way I'll see what Percy's up to."

"What could be better?" said Herrick. "But don't get involved. We're here to find out – not give battle. Don't forget that."

"I promise," said I. "Don't be long," and with that, I was gone.

Retracing my steps, I did not use the drive, but moved by its side through the bracken beneath the trees. This, because I was sure that Virgil would make his way home as soon as his business was done. I had marked that he was unshaved and was wearing a scarf for a collar about his throat, and from what I knew of the man he meant to return before breakfast and rise in his regular way. And though I might now be too late to see what his business was, at least I saw no occasion for meeting him face to face. However, he did not appear, and, as I approached the track, I saw that the car was still there and had not been moved.

Now all I knew was that Virgil and his companions had passed up the track out of sight. How far they had gone or whether they had kept to the track, I had no idea, but since it seemed pretty clear that they would not be very far off, from now on I took greater precautions against being seen. When I moved, I did so gently and went on my hands and knees, and whenever I rose to look round, I did so against a tree-trunk, as though, indeed, I were stalking some wary prey.

First of all, I took a good look at the car. This was roomy and powerful and something the worse for wear. Its number-plates had been oiled and were coated with dust. One of its doors was ajar, and within I could see an old suitcase, no doubt containing 'the clothes'. But that was all, and after a long look round, I went on my way.

I dared not use the track, though I followed the line which it took, and, what with the care which I showed and the many halts which I made, my progress was very slow. For all that, I dared not hasten in case the four I was seeking were close at hand, for it must not be forgotten that, if they had come to rest, the cover which served me so well would stand them in just as good stead. Then, again, they had a dog with them.

I went on, picking my way…

It was nearly six o'clock, and I had been gone from Herrick a full half-hour when the track beside which I was moving came to an end. This to my dismay, for now I had nothing to go on, although, of course, the track might have led me wrong.

In vain I sought for a broken stem of bracken which might declare the trail which my friends had left: in vain I scanned the forest and strained my ears: but for the birds and the squirrels I might have had the world to myself.

Flat against the trunk of an oak-tree I wiped the sweat from my face. Five paces ahead a ride had been cut through the woods: though this was thick with bracken, it gave me a pretty clear view to right and to left, but the flood stretched smooth and unbroken and I could see no sign of its having been crossed.

Loth to admit defeat, I tried to think what to do. To proceed was easy enough, but, for all I knew, with every step that I took I might be going away from the party I sought. Yet to stay where I was was useless. If only there had been a hillock to add a few feet to my height, I could have looked down upon the bracken and that point of view might have shown me the traces the others had left. But there was no hillock: the ground hereabouts was sloping, but nothing more.

Suddenly I thought of the oak-tree and lifted my eyes…

If I could reach it, there was the coign I desired. One of the mighty branches was stretching out over the ride – a branch twice as thick as my loins, some twenty feet up. If I were there, I could see for a quarter of a mile, while the leaves of the lesser boughs would save me from being seen.

After a long look about me, I leaped for a sturdy sucker and swung myself up. My branch was not easy to come to, because what handhold there was was so far between, and I must confess that, whilst I fought my way up, I could not help wondering how I should ever get down. However, I would not turn back, and after two or three minutes I flung a leg over the perch upon which I had set my heart.

I now had a very good view of the whole of the ride, which sloped, on the left, to the meadows south-west of the house, and rose, on the right, to a circus, whence three other rides ran out, as spokes from a hub. Across the ride two definite trails had been left – or, rather, one and a half. The first, which stretched right across, was thirty paces away, to the left of the oak; and the second, which stretched but half-way, as far to the left again. At the end of this second trail, full in the midst of the ride, the woman was sitting alone, with her back towards me.

To say that I felt bewildered means nothing at all. What on earth she was doing there, I could not conceive, and at last I made up my mind that she must be hiding from Virgil with whom she had had some fuss. Of him or the other two men I could see no sign.

Now but for the sight of the woman, I should have at once descended and taken the other trail, but whilst I was still considering whether to follow this course, the woman got to her feet and stood perfectly still.

When I saw her do this, it came to me in a flash that, unless the woman was mad, she must be acting in concert with somebody else. And so she was. Before two minutes had passed, the chauffeur appeared.

He made his way straight to her side, when the woman handed him something and then hurried out of the ride and so out of my view.

I now felt bound to admit that Herrick must have been right when he made his idle suggestion that 'Percy was making a film'. The behaviour which I had just witnessed was not consistent with the manners of a workaday world, but the screen is above convention, as every schoolboy knows. The early hour and the talk of a change of clothes supported this point of view, and though I could see no apparatus, I had no doubt that this was somewhere at hand. And since I had no interest in such goings on, I began at once to consider how best to get down from my oak.

I had turned about and was standing upon the branch with my hands on the trunk, when the scream of a dog in agony rent the air. Half turning again, I saw the chauffeur standing where I had seen him last, holding the dog at arm's length by the scruff of its neck and flogging the luckless creature with all his might.

I was just about to cry out – for, film or no film, such cruelty was not to be borne – when I heard a galloping horse coming down from the right, that is to say, from the circus from which the four rides ran out.

Because of the leaves before me, I could not see it go by, but an instant later a bay flashed into my view. On his back was a girl, and the two were going full tilt down the midst of the ride, and making straight for the chauffeur still thrashing the dog.

So for a second or less. Then the bay turned head over heels and the girl went flying beyond him, as though shot out of a gun.

I never saw such a fall in all my life, but before I had time to think, much less descend, a man and a woman were rushing to where the girl lay. They were, of course, the two that came out of the car and they must have been standing directly in line with the bay when he came to the ground. And the chauffeur, too, was running as fast as he could.

The bay was up now and was moving off through the bracken with heaving flanks, but the girl lay crumpled up and perfectly still. To my surprise, instead of attending to her, the man and the woman between them lifted her up and began to stumble with her towards my oak. They passed directly beneath me, seeming to think of nothing but getting their burden along. Had this been the carcase of a dog, they could scarce have used it with less propriety. The girl was dead or senseless – I could not tell which: but, instead of supporting her head, they let this hang, and one of her legs was suffered to trail on the ground.

This was too much for me, and at once I began to go down; but, for all my indignation, I could not make haste, because, as I had feared, the descent was twice as stiff as the climb I had made.

I was, of course, wholly bewildered by what I had seen. An accident had occurred – I supposed in the course of the 'picture' then being made. But I could not understand any number of things. Where was Virgil? And what of the beaten dog? And what had become of the chauffeur? And why was the girl being hustled out of the way?

And there I looked over my shoulder, still twelve feet up, to see the man and the woman lay the girl down in the track which led to the car. They paid her no sort of attention, but after a hurried word, the man turned back to the ride and the woman ran down the track and out of my sight.

I think it was then that I thought that they meant her ill, for both of them need not have left her in any case. Be that as it may, I hung where I was for an instant, to let the fellow go by. Had he looked, he must have seen me, for I was fully exposed, but his eyes were fixed on something I could not see.

I leaped the last six feet, and before I turned to the girl, I looked after the man. In so doing I saw the chauffeur, walking across the ride…at the spot where the bay took his fall…*hastily coiling the wire which had brought him down.*

For a moment I stared, unable to credit my eyes.

Then I whipped to the girl, who was yet lying still as death, and, picking her up in my arms, ran out of the track and into the thick of the bracken until I could run no more.

3

I Open a Lady's Eyes

I afterwards found I had run a quarter of a mile, which shows, I think, that fear can lend a man strength which he does not possess. Be that as it may, I laid the girl down as gently as I knew how – and then lay down beside her to get my breath.

Of course I knew who she was and I knew I had seen an attempt to carry her off. And I knew that I had been sent to bring that attempt to naught. I prayed that I had succeeded – with all my heart.

And here, before going on, I will render unto Destiny the things that are his. When I remember the manifold changes and chances that steered me gradually into the nick of time, I never fail to worship the wonderful workings of Fate. I perceive that I was a puppet, now moved, now held, now switched and now thrust upon the stage, that it was not I but my Master that brought me from the County of Surrey into an Austrian oak-tree that morning at six o'clock. Had I not been there at that moment, though I had contrived to move mountains, my efforts must have been vain and Lady Elizabeth Virgil have gone to a doom more shocking than that which her father knew.

From the way she had lain in my arms I was sure that she was not dead, but I felt that she ought to have water, to bring her to life. And then I heard the speech of a rill...

Two minutes later, perhaps, a hand went up to her head.

"It's all right," said I, "lie still. You took the deuce of a toss."

Lady Elizabeth Virgil opened two large, grey eyes.

"The dog," she said. "Who was it beating that dog in that merciless way?"

"It's all right," said I. "He stopped when he saw you come down."

"And Caesar?" she cried, sitting up. "Where's Caesar – the horse I was riding?"

"Unhurt," said I. "He may be going spare, but he's not going short. And now will you please lie down and let me look round?"

After a steady stare, she did as I said.

I got to my knees and peered through the tops of the bracken, but all was still.

As I sat back on my heels –

"Why did you want to look round?"

"Because you are still in danger. You were brought down on purpose. A wire was across the ride."

Lady Elizabeth looked at me very hard.

"How do you know?"

"I saw it taken away. I saw the whole thing. The fellow was thrashing the dog to draw you that way."

There was a little silence.

Then –

"Who arranged this…melodrama?"

"Your cousin, Percy," said I. "I saw him at work."

After a long silence she let out a little laugh.

"That rings true," she said shortly. And then, "Who are you?"

"My name is Richard Exon," I said. "A – a friend of yours told me about you."

"I didn't know I had any friends."

"You've Herrick and me," I said quickly. "His mother was a friend of your mother's, and I was a friend of – of the friend I mentioned just now."

The girl regarded me straitly.

"I can't remember my mother."

"I know," said I. "The Countess Rudolph was killed before you were two years old."

With that, I got again to my knees, to throw a look round.

As I did so, I heard a car coming – gathering speed. Till then I had had no idea that we were so close to the drive, and for one distracting moment it seemed as though the closed car were heading directly for us. Then it switched to its right a short six paces away, and before ten seconds had passed we could hear it no more.

"Was that them?" said Lady Elizabeth.

I nodded.

"That's right. Gone empty away."

"What do you mean – empty?"

"They were to have taken you with them – I don't know where."

My lady sat up.

"Are you sure of this?"

"Quite sure. I'll tell you everything later." Cautiously I got to my feet. "D'you think you could manage to walk? My car's not very far off."

"There's nothing the matter with me, but why should I walk to your car?"

I hesitated. Then –

"Because I beg you," I said. "I'll tell you everything later – indeed, I will. But now we've not a moment to lose. Directly Caesar gets in, the alarm will be raised: and I don't want you to be found until after you've heard my tale. Please trust me till then. You really are in danger – what happened just now must show you that your cousin will stick at nothing to put you out of the way."

Finger to lip, Lady Elizabeth Virgil appeared to reflect. At length she rose to her feet.

"All right," she said. "I'll trust you. Where is this car?"

When I told her, she glanced about her. Then she pointed across the drive.

"That's our quickest way. But how do we come to be here? I came off in the Golden Ride."

"I carried you here," said I. "They left you halfway to the car, so I picked you up and cleared out before they came back."

A hand went up to her head.

"So far as I can make out, I've a great deal to thank you for. But I can't think as straight as I should. And when we get to your car, you are going to drive me to Brief?"

"I'd like to drive you to Raven."

"To Raven? Do you know Raven?"

"That's where we're staying," said I.

"All right. I don't care. I'd like to see Brenda again. I'll lie down there for a while. When you've been knocked out, you're never quite right till you've slept."

Though she seemed to have taken no hurt, she was not fit to walk as far as the Rolls: yet I was afraid to offer to fetch the car, in case, before I got back, the hunt should be up. There was, therefore, nothing for it. Fortune had laid on my anvil a red-hot iron. If I did not strike it now…

When she had stumbled twice, without a word I took her right arm and set it about my neck: then I put my left arm about her and held her up.

"Thank you," she said. And then, "You're awfully strong."

"You're not very heavy," said I, and spoke the truth.

With that, we went forward in silence as fast as we could: she, I think, was thankful to hold her peace, and I could think of nothing but of getting her clear of the park. For all that, I should not have been human, if I had not been aware of her beauty and the grace of the slim, straight figure that swayed in the crook of my arm.

Her head was bare, and she wore a soft, silk shirt, now smudged with green, and Jodhpur riding breeches, very well cut: but thus unadorned and shaken, she filled the eye.

45

I am given to understand that she had her mother's looks, but I find it hard to believe that the Countess Rudolph had all of her daughter's charm. I have said before that her eyes were large and grey, but I despair of disclosing the exquisite light which made them so very rare. This was a very soft brilliance, which could leap into a flame, but, once you had seen it, you never could forget it, because forever after all other eyes seemed dull. Her hair was soft and shining and black as night, and the face which it framed was strong and proud and fearless, but something sad. I think it was the droop of her lips that gave her this wistful air, but you could not have wished it absent, because that might have altered the shape of her faultless mouth. Her skin was very white and her colour was high, and she made you think of some mistress of mediaeval days, of whose beauty troubadours sang, whose favour was sought and fought for by famous men. I have seen such great ladies presented on stage and screen, but though these had the advantage of raiment, scene, and surroundings to set them off, I never saw one that looked the part so well as did Elizabeth Virgil, no matter where she was or how she was dressed. Times have changed, and knights and queens of beauty have long been dust, but the Count and the Countess Rudolph were both of proud descent, and I think that their daughter threw back to one of those lovely ghosts that fanned to a flame the flush of chivalry.

Twenty minutes had passed and I had had to carry her over a stream before I saw through the trees the flash of the Rolls. I never was so thankful, for though she made no complaint, I knew it was all she could do to stay up on her feet, and I had a dreadful fear that to strive with the effects of concussion might do her some serious ill.

Winter saw us coming and had a door open, for her to get into the car: this she did without speaking and at once lay back on the cushions and closed her eyes.

"D'you feel very rotten?" I asked.

"I'm done," she said. "That's all. I'll be all right as soon as I've had some sleep."

Herrick was not to be seen, but since he was sure to return by the entrance-drive and the road, I bade Winter take the wheel and make for the spot at which he had set us down. If he was not in sight when we got there, I meant to go on to Raven and then return, but, as luck would have it, we met him at the mouth of the track.

He was plainly bursting with news, but I was down in the road before he could speak –

"I've got her," I breathed. "She's coming with us to Raven. But don't say a word in the car – she's not too well."

Then we both got into the Rolls, and Winter let in his clutch.

"It's very seldom," said Herrick, "that Fortune makes up her mind to do a thing really well. She almost always leaves you with two or three little knots, and you have to try and untie them as best you can. As a rule, you can't: and so you have to cut them... But here she's excelled herself, for I came upon the scene of the outrage as you went off, and so I can complete the astonishing tale you've just told.

"But before I do that, let's go back. Between us, we saw the whole thing. We saw Percy meet his bullies and lead them off to the ride. There, of course, be told them exactly what they were to do, watched them fix the wire and placed them in the positions which they were to occupy – the chauffeur at the end of the ride to watch for my lady's approach, and the woman to show him his place as soon as he'd seen her go by. And when Percy had posted them, he went back to the house. That's not guesswork. *I saw him.* Two minutes after you'd left me, he whipped through the fields below me, up to the house and in by the door at the foot of a staircase turret. Back to bed, of course – and there's his alibi. Nobody saw him go out, and nobody saw him come in...

47

"My lady must have appeared just after I'd made up my mind to return to the Rolls. Any way, I didn't see her. But I saw the closed car, as you did: and, as you did, I crawled up to have a good look. Before I was through, I heard that unfortunate dog, and, without thinking what I was doing, I started along the track. Then the dog stopped screaming, and I re-entered the bracken, just about ten paces in rear of the car.

"I was wondering where you were and whether to follow the track or go back to the Rolls, when I saw the woman approaching between the trees. She was blowzed and out of breath and went by at a shambling run, and when she got to the car, she swung the door wide open and then stood biting her nails and staring the way she had come.

"Presently along comes the chauffeur, sweating great drops, with a coil of rebellious wire, and going as fast as he knew.

" 'Where is she?' he cries. 'Have you got her?'

"The woman lets out a gasp.

" 'Me?' she bleats. 'Max has got her. He sent me on.'

" 'Max hasn't got her,' cries the chauffeur, and the woman goes white as a sheet.

"The next moment, up comes Max, with his eyes bulging out of his head.

"When they told him she wasn't there, he threw the best part of a fit before my eyes. Then they all ran back in a bunch, like so many frantic beasts, to where she ought to have been. Less than two minutes elapsed before they came stumbling back, all three disputing hoarsely and, naturally, blaming each other for what had occurred. Bang opposite where I was lying the woman fell upon Max and scratched his face to glory before the chauffeur was able to pull her off. Then she fell down in a heap and burst into tears, and Max did his best to kick her till the chauffeur landed a good one and knocked him down. But for him, they'd have been there now, for he was the only one that wasn't beside himself.

" 'D'you want to be taken?' he hissed. 'That cursed horse is back in the stables by now, and in two minutes' time the hue and cry will be raised. And if we're to be found, we're done. That Jew will show us no mercy – he'll lead the pack: and he'll hound us into prison for twenty years.'

"That brought the others up to their feet and into the car, and thirty seconds later the latter was out of my sight.

"Well, there you are. We know the whole truth of the matter from first to last, and, thanks to your enterprise, we have in our hands the remarkably beautiful subject of their activities. As I said two days ago, you're one of Fortune's pets: but you know how to use your luck – I'll give you that. It would never have entered my head to carry the lady off."

"Of course it would," said I.

"No, it wouldn't," said Herrick. "I might have rescued her: but after that I should have taken her home." He glanced at his watch. "It's eight o'clock now, and she'll probably sleep till lunch. D'you propose to tell her the truth this afternoon?"

"About her father? Why not?"

"Very good," said Herrick. "And then?"

I got to my feet.

"I'm going to suggest that she stays here. It's clear that Brief isn't safe. If she is to come by her rights, we've got to get Percy down. And we've stolen a march on him – if she doesn't go back. *You see, he'll think that his bullies carried her off. There's nothing to show that they failed. And they're not likely to tell him* – from what you say."

Herrick stared and stared.

At length –

"Young man," he said, "if you go on like this, you'll be translated or something, before your time. Such wisdom is not of this world. Talk about taking Time by the forelock... Why, if you go on like this, the poor old chap'll be bald."

This was absurd, and I said so. One day your brain will work, and the next it will not. The astonishing luck I had had, had whetted my wits, and I saw the obvious plainly, instead of passing it by. But I could see nothing more. And I had an uneasy feeling that we were going too fast. Before we had entered the field, we had proved our utmost suspicions, had misled Percy Virgil and won the charge of the lady whom we had hoped to help – a handsome enough beginning, as anyone must have allowed. But peer as I would, I could not see how to go on. And the fairest advantage is useless unless you can follow it up.

Here Brenda came to say that our breakfast was served, and Herrick took occasion to tell her that no one must know that Lady Elizabeth Virgil was now at the farm.

"She has said so already," said Brenda. "No one will know."

"D'you think she's all right?" said I. "I mean, she was shaken up."

Brenda smiled.

"You need have no fear," she said. "Mother gave her one of her simples, and when she wakes she will be perfectly well." She hesitated. "But Mother says that she will not know how she came here and will remember nothing that happened after her fall."

"Good God," said I. And then, "But how can she tell?"

"From the look in her eyes," said Brenda. "She walked and talked, but she was not keeping a copy of what went on. That part of her brain was not working, so Mother says." She smiled again. "But that is of no account. You can show her your copy, you see – and I will tell her that she may believe what it says."

We had finished lunch, but Lady Elizabeth Virgil was still asleep, so, since we were both of us tired, Herrick withdrew to his chamber and I went down to the meadows, to take some rest.

The spot was peaceful. A gentle stream was lacing the sunlit fields, which neighbouring woods made into a private park: oak and elm and chestnut rose from the springing turf, and cows were contentedly grazing the clean-cut shadows they threw: on the hither side of the water, three well-grown limes were spreading a fragrant tent, and there I lay down, to consider the comfortable prospect and relish the agreeable music the birds and the insects made.

And after a few minutes I fell asleep.

I afterwards found I had slept for an hour and a half, but when I sat up with a start – for I had meant only to doze, so that I might be in attendance directly my lady came down – there she was sitting before me and waiting for me to wake up.

"Good Lord," said I. "Where's Brenda? I told her to let me know the moment you waked."

Lady Elizabeth smiled.

"I overruled your orders," she said.

She had changed her clothes and was wearing a full-skirted frock which fell perhaps three inches below her knees. This was of fair, white linen, embroidered in red; and I afterwards found that it was the dress of the country and came out of Brenda's drawer.

I begged her to excuse me a moment and stepped to the stream. There I laved my face and my hands, and then came back better fitted to tell my tale.

I took my seat before her and waited for her to begin.

"I'm told I can trust you," she said. "How do I come to be here, instead of at Brief?"

I took a deep breath. Though I had hoped she was wrong, it seemed painfully clear that Brenda's mother was right.

"I asked you," I said. "I asked you to let me bring you. And when I had told you why, you gave your consent."

Lady Elizabeth frowned.

"What was the reason you gave me? You see, I can remember nothing from the moment I took my toss. That's sometimes the way of concussion. Did you pick me up?"

"It's a curious story," said I. "May I tell it in my own way? And I'll answer what questions you like as soon as I've done."

"That's fair enough. Will you give me a cigarette?"

I did as she asked, and then I told her my tale, beginning from where we had sighted the closed and numberless car and ending with Herrick's account of its occupants' consternation on finding their victim gone. She never interrupted me once, but sat very still with her beautiful eyes on my face, and she showed no emotion at all, except that once or twice she knitted her brows.

When I had done, she lifted her head to the sky.

"I should like to thank you," she said, "before I say anything else. But for you…" A tremor ran through her. "That change of marked clothes sounds ugly. I was to be passed off as somebody else. Never mind. I'm very grateful. I think you've probably saved far more than my life."

"That's my good fortune," said I. "I just had the luck to be there."

"I don't admit that. However… How do you happen to know my cousin?"

"I don't," said I. "I only know him by sight. We were both in the same hotel about three weeks ago. In England, that was. And one doesn't forget his face."

"How did you know who I was?"

"I knew you existed," I said, "and I thought that you lived at Brief, and so the moment I saw you I guessed who you were."

She nodded, as though satisfied. Then she drew up her little feet and laced her delicate fingers about her knees.

"And now for the omnibus question – why were you and your friend on my father's estate…at four o'clock in the morning…taking care not to be seen?"

I put a hand to my head. Tremendous fences were coming: if I was to clear them all, they must not be rushed.

"We were there," I said, "to try and discover some place from which we could watch the castle without being seen."

"Why did you want to watch the castle?"

"Because I had reason to think that between the Count and your cousin your life was – well, not too easy…not what it ought to be."

Her eyes on the blowing meadows, Lady Elizabeth Virgil lifted her delicate chin.

"I want to be fair," she said quietly. "But don't sail too close to the wind. I'd like to hear you out, but you can't expect me to listen to – sheer impertinence."

"I know," I said, flushing: "I'm sorry. But will you please believe that I came from England on purpose to do what I've done today? I didn't know that your cousin would go so far. But I knew that he *might*. I knew that you stood in his way, and I knew that he and his father – "

"His *father*? His father's dead."

I got to my knees and put out my hands for hers.

"Take hold of them, please," I said. "I'm going to give you a shock."

Her eyes never left my eyes, but she did as I said.

"A year ago last April, your father died in my arms. He was the Count of Brief. The man you call father is your uncle, and your cousin his only son."

Eyes shut, head back, her underlip caught in her teeth, she held to my hands as though she would never let go, and her breath was whistling in her nostrils and the blood was out of her face.

"What…proof…have…you…of these things?"

"I will go and get it," I said.

"No, no. Don't leave me just yet. After all, I've had proof enough ever since I could think for myself. Why didn't my mother live?"

"My mother died young," I said. "I was two years old."

"As I was." She covered her face with her hands and bowed her head. "Will you tell me about – my father?"

"He was very gentle," I said. "I had no money then, and neither had he. We lived and worked together for nearly two years, and he never once complained of his bitter fate. I never knew his story until the night he died."

"Did he charge you to come and tell me?"

"No."

"Then why are you here?"

"Because I saw your cousin… No one could see your cousin and not be sure that he was a dangerous man. And I knew that you stood in his way – that, but for you, he would one day be Count of Brief. By then my luck had changed, and I had money to spend and nothing to do. So I came to see for myself. If I'd found you safe and happy, I should have kept my counsel and gone away."

"You say that – that this man is my uncle, and not my father at all: that he is Percy's father…"

"Yes," said I.

"I can well believe it," she said. "But then you say that this man is not Count of Brief."

"He never was," said I. "He was and is Count Ferdinand, the younger twin. He dispossessed your father twenty-two years ago."

She drew in her breath.

"Does my cousin know this?"

"I shouldn't think so," said I. "That's the kind of secret which a man not only keeps but does his best to forget."

She nodded thoughtfully.

Then –

"Will you show me the proof you spoke of? When you say that this man is my uncle, I know that's true. I mean, it explains – everything. But I cannot realize that he is not the Count of Brief. And what of my mother? Wasn't he married to her?"

I got to my feet.

"Your father's statement," I said, "will make everything plain." I hesitated. "Only please don't hope for too much. It'll prove what I've told you: but it wouldn't cut much ice in a Court of Law."

"I don't care about that. I want to be sure myself."

"So you shall be," said I, and made my way to the house.

On the stairs I met Herrick and told him what I had done.

"Good God," says he. "You could teach a bull to rush in. And how did she take the news?"

"Wonderfully well," said I. "Will you appear in about a quarter of an hour?"

"I shall wait till I'm sent for," said Herrick. "And then I shall probably hide. There's a lot of the gazelle in my nature. And I'm shy of attending an inquest with which I have nothing to do."

"I had to open it," said I.

"I know. I know. But then you're – exceptional. If you found that the Pope was a Mormon, you wouldn't rest till you'd seen him and had it out."

Three minutes later I faced my lady again.

"There are the papers," I said. "One is your father's statement, which he had written and signed. The other is mine, which sets out what he told me before he died. Both of these are copies. The originals lie at my bank."

She read them through twice over. Then she folded the sheets and lifted her head.

"I've no doubt now," she said quietly.

"I'm glad of that," said I. "I had nothing to go on, and yet I knew it was true. Your father was incapable of lying. I can't put it better than that."

With a sudden movement she clapped her hands to her temples and pushed back her excellent hair.

"My God," she cried. "My God, how he must have suffered. Sent down into hell by the man he was trying to save. Sent down for good – forever. Sentenced to death – for life... And what of the man who did it?" Her eyes were aflame. "What of that double-traitor that saved his body by losing his brother's soul?"

"I'll go all lengths," said I, "to help you to bring him down."

The flame in her eyes died down to the softest glow.

" 'What's Hecuba to him?' " she said quietly.

"I don't know," said I, and put a hand to my head. "I think history's repeating itself."

"And what does that mean?"

"That I want to serve you – that's all: and I've wanted to from the moment I saw your face. And I'm not alone. I know I can count on Herrick – he's with me here: he knew your father and mother before you were born. And then I can count on my servant – he owes your cousin a grudge."

Lady Elizabeth glanced at the watch on her wrist. "There's so much I want to say and so much I want to be told. But time's getting on, and if I'm to go back to the castle – "

"I beg that you won't," said I. "If you do, you'll throw away a very good card. Your cousin arranged your abduction, and now you have disappeared – according to plan. Why show him that his plan has miscarried?"

Finger to lip, my lady sat very still.

"That's sound," she said. "But it's awfully inconvenient. You'll have to lend me some money to buy some clothes."

"You must know I'd love to," I said. "I'm only so very thankful you're taking this line."

"What line?"

"Of letting me help. I mean, I'm an utter stranger, and you're – the Countess of Brief."

"If it comes to that, I am an utter stranger, and you're Richard Exon Esquire."

"That's absurd," said I. "Besides, it's a question of sex. A man – "

"I wish I could remember what happened after my fall. I can't think how I consented to let you carry me off."

"You did," said I. "I swear it."

"You must have been very persuasive. I'd never seen you before and I didn't know anything then."

"I think it was written," said I. "Fate sent me to Brief this morning – this day of all days, and when I had put a spoke in

56

your cousin's wheel, Fate impelled you to grant my – unusual request."

"Then Fate impelled you to make it: and Fate has directed you to take up my cause."

"Not at all," said I. "I've got a will of my own."

"And so have I. Fate brought you to Brief this morning – no doubt about that. But that is as much as she did. What you and I did thereafter, we did of our own free will. I don't know why we did it because my memory's gone. And I'm sorry for that, for I'd very much like to know why we did as we did. Of course I can't answer for you. You may make a practice of making 'unusual requests'. But it isn't my way to grant them – to men I don't know."

"I've told you I – "

"I know. I don't value your opinion. As a man of action you're splendid. You really are. But motives are rather beyond you – you wouldn't know one if you saw it, and that's the truth." I suppose I looked crestfallen, for she laughed and laid a hand on my arm. "And I like you for that. Oh, and try to forget you're a stranger. Let's say we made friends this morning...in the dream that I can't recapture: though you're not clear about it, I'm practically certain we did."

I thought of her sitting in the bracken, with her dark hair tumbled about her beautiful face, and of how she had said "I'll trust you" – with her steady eyes upon mine.

"I'd like to believe that," I said. "And so I shall, if you do."

Lady Elizabeth set her chin in the air.

"You speak as though we'd both had concussion. Or is your memory short?"

"No, it isn't," said I, and got up. "But I can't get away from the feeling that this morning oughtn't to count, because your memory's gone. It's difficult to explain. But we did make friends all right – without any ceremony, as children do."

"That's better," she said. She put up her hands and I drew her up to her feet. "You see, if you're to finance me, you've simply got to forget that I am the Countess of Brief."

I broke out at that.

"You're Elizabeth Virgil to me – and will be, as long as I live."

A glorious smile swept into her precious face.

"That's more like it," she said. "And now you shall give me some tea. And I'd like to meet Mr Herrick and hear if my mother was half as sweet as she looked."

We were, I suppose, some twenty yards from the house, when, happening to glance to the east, I saw a flash in the distance between the trees. One flash – that was all. But, as I saw it, I think that my heart stood still.

I knew what it was – that glitter, and whence it came. It was the screen of some car reflecting the afternoon sun: and it came from the road of approach that led to the farm.

4

We Make an Enemy

There is at Raven a window, twelve feet from the farm's front door. Masked by one of its curtains, I watched a car approach and sweep to the foot of the steps. On the other side of the window, Herrick was standing still, with his back to the wall.

In the car were four men. Two were strangers to me, one seemed faintly familiar, and Percy Virgil himself had the driving-wheel.

I shot a glance at Herrick and wondered what was to come.

Virgil switched off his engine and wiped his sinister face. Then he followed his fellows out of the car.

I heard the front door opened before they had reached the steps.

Then –

"Good evening, Brenda," said Virgil. "I'm afraid I've some serious news. My cousin's been taken – kidnapped."

Brenda snapped at her cue.

"The Lady Elizabeth? *Kidnapped*?"

"It's true enough, I'm afraid. Her horse came in without her – this morning, at six o'clock. At first we thought she'd been thrown, but it's worse than that. We found clear signs of a struggle in one of the rides."

I heard Brenda draw in her breath.

Then –

"But who would – "

"That," said Percy, "is what we want to find out. This is a sergeant of police, with one of his men." He turned to the strangers. "This girl is Brenda Revoke."

The sergeant stepped forward.

"We are seeking to trace two strangers lately seen near Brief in a fine, grey car." He jerked his head at the man whom I thought I knew. "This blacksmith saw them in Gola four days ago. And other people have seen them this side of Brief."

Brenda laughed.

"You mean our visitors?"

"There you are," said Virgil. "What did I say?"

"We do not lodge bandits," said Brenda, coldly enough. "These are two English gentlemen, who – "

"Since when have they been here?" said the sergeant.

"They came to us five days ago."

"And are they within?"

"I believe," said Brenda, "that they are taking their tea."

"Then tell them the police would like to speak with them here."

"No. Wait a moment," said Virgil. "First show us their car." He turned to the police. "If this fellow identifies it – "

"I think, perhaps," said the sergeant, but Virgil cut him short.

"Can't you see," he said, "how much it'll strengthen your hand?"

"Very well," said the other, reluctantly.

Brenda hesitated. Then she passed down the steps and led them away to the left and out of my sight...

In a flash we were both at the door *en route* for our sitting-room. As we entered the hall, Lady Elizabeth Virgil slipped from behind the front door.

"And now?" she said.

"We may," said Herrick, "we may have to call upon you. We shan't if we can help it, but Percy, er, knows no law."

She smiled and nodded.

"All right."

And then we were back in our room and had shut the door.

The position was delicate – and showed forth very clearly the infamous skill with which Percy had laid his plans. He had, of course, been looking for some such arrival as ours: and the moment he heard that we had been seen in Gola, he gave his waiting bullies the word to strike. By fastening suspicion on us, he was making sure their escape *with their precious goods*: for time that is lost in such matters is irretrievably lost, and by the time a scent has been found to be false, the one which is true has faded and died away. And we had played straight into his hands. Our movements of the last four days had been in all respects such movements as kidnappers make: our map of the district was marked as kidnappers would have marked it: and neither movements nor markings could be accounted for – except by the truth.

Quite apart from the fact that I could speak no German, Herrick was plainly the man to play our difficult hand. His wit was far quicker than mine, and he had, besides, an address which would have unsettled the hottest enemy.

"We've no time to discuss," he said, "the line we should take. But I think we must get dear Percy to help us out. This means giving something away, but charity sometimes comes off."

"You mean," said I.

"I'm not quite sure," said Herrick. "I have an idea, but it's still in a state of flux. Should it take shape, I have a horrid feeling that Percy is going to perspire. And now don't talk for a moment. If – "

Here Brenda flew in with her summons, fairly aglow with excitement and ready for any mischief that we might command.

"Have they found a map?" I said, rising.

"They are now inspecting it, sir – with their eyes half out of their heads."

"Good," said Herrick. "Where's Winter?"

"At tea in the kitchen, sir."

"Tell him to stay there," said Herrick. "And if he should be sent for, to tell the truth – except, of course, on one point. He's never seen my lady at any time."

Brenda nodded and fled, and we strolled out of the house and into the drive. The police and Virgil were there, but the smith was not to be seen. I afterwards found that he had been left with the Rolls – to raise the alarm in case we should try to make off.

I had wondered if Percy Virgil would know me again, for, while I had had good reason to study him and his ways, I had been to him no more than one of several guests at a country hotel. But he did – immediately. And though he would have concealed it, I saw him start…

Herrick was addressing the police.

"Good evening, gentlemen. I'm told that you wish to see us. If we can be of service in any way…"

The police seemed taken aback. I suppose that we did not resemble the men they had expected to see.

Then the sergeant took off his hat.

"The matter is serious," he said.

"Of course," said Herrick. "Otherwise you would first have asked us before inspecting our car."

The sergeant swallowed, and Virgil put in his oar.

"You may be strangers," he said, "but that doesn't put you above the law of the land."

"Nor, I trust," said Herrick, "beyond the traditional courtesy of its inhabitants. What is your rank in the police?"

Virgil flushed.

"I am not in the police," he said.

"Then why," said Herrick, "did you presume to address me?"

"My name is – "

"I have no desire," said Herrick, "to hear your name." He returned to the police. "You were saying that the matter was serious…"

Virgil looked ready to burst, but the sergeant went straight to the point.

"I will be plain," he said. "A lady has been abducted – a lady of high degree. She was kidnapped early this morning upon her father's estate…at Brief…some ten miles from here." He held up our map. "I think you will hardly deny that you know where that is."

"I have known where Brief was," said Herrick, "for twenty-three years."

The others stared.

Then –

"We are dealing with the present," said Virgil.

Herrick raised his eyebrows.

"Allow me to suggest," he said, "that you should keep to yourself such, er, discoveries as you may make." He turned again to the police. "Yes, gentlemen?"

The sergeant cleared his throat.

"In view, sir, of what has occurred, I must ask you to explain the markings upon this map."

"With pleasure," said Herrick.

"And I sincerely advise you to tell the truth."

"You will find," said Herrick, "that we have nothing to hide." He fingered his chin. "I stayed at Brief, as a child, in 1912. My mother and the Countess Rudolph were very close friends. Happening to be at Innsbruck a week ago, I felt a strong desire to visit the castle again. For various reasons I did not wish to leave cards. Much has happened, you know, in twenty-three years. My mother, the Count of Brief and the Countess Rudolph have died, the Lady Elizabeth has been born and, worst of all, I'm told that a vulgar blackguard, the son of an uncle of hers, has the run of the place."

A ghastly silence succeeded these moving words, the police regarding the gravel with goggling eyes and Virgil, dark red in the face, surveying Herrick with the glare of a baited beast.

Herrick continued agreeably.

"We, therefore, came here from Innsbruck on Sunday last. On Monday we started out to try to discover some spot from which we could view the castle, without going into the grounds. We only found one, and that was – too far away. Determined not to be beaten, we tried for the next three days – with the aid of that map. And all in vain... Last night we reviewed the position, and found it this – that we must either trespass or else go empty away.

"Now I do not like trespassing, but neither, I frankly confess, do I like going empty away, and in the end we decided to rise very early this morning, enter the park from the north and have a good look at the castle before anybody was up. And so...we did."

For a moment I thought that Virgil was going to faint. All the colour was out of his face, which looked peaked and thin, and he did not seem to be breathing, but might have been turned to stone. Then a shiver ran through him, and a hand went up to his mouth.

But the police had no eyes for him. The two were staring at Herrick as though they would read his soul.

"At what times," said the sergeant, "did you enter and leave the estate?"

"We entered at four and we left about half-past six."

There was an electric silence.

Then –

"I am bound to inform you," said the sergeant, "that what you have just admitted makes your position most grave. The outrage was committed this morning at six o'clock."

"Perhaps," said Herrick. "It was not committed by us."

The sergeant shrugged his shoulders.

"I shall have to – "

"I think it is clear," said Virgil, "that this gentleman is telling the truth." The two police stared upon him as though he were out of his mind. "I mean, if he were guilty, he would scarcely have made an admission which put the rope round his neck."

As soon as he could speak –

"But, sir," cried the sergeant, "a rope round the neck is harmless, unless it is tight. If every rogue was believed because he told such truths as could do him no harm – "

"These gentlemen," said Virgil, "have not the appearance of rogues."

The sergeant put a hand to his head.

"But they were there – in the park...at the hour that the business was done. Why, this map alone would warrant – "

"That is explained," said Virgil. "And what they say is quite true. The foothills conceal the castle except from the bridge which crosses the Vials of Wrath."

"Perhaps. But that does not mean – "

"Enough," said Virgil, swiftly. "For me they have cleared themselves. It only remains for you to beg their pardon and make a fresh cast. Good God, man, when time is so precious, do you propose to waste it in prying into two strangers' private affairs?"

With a manifest effort, the sergeant controlled his voice.

"Sir," he said, "if you do not wish to wait, you must leave us here. I have a sow by the ear, and until I know it's the wrong one, I will not let go." With that, he returned to Herrick. "You have said too much or too little. You were at Brief this morning from four until half-past six. Kindly relate what you did there – from first to last."

"With very great pleasure," said Herrick, folding his arms. "We left our car at the mouth of the northern drive – after instructing our chauffeur, first, to seek some petrol, and then to wait in a wood a little way off. You will understand that we did not wish to be seen."

"Is your chauffeur here?" said the sergeant.

"He is. If you would like to see him – "

"Proceed, if you please."

"Before we had walked very far, we heard a car coming behind us, using the drive. At once we lay down in the bracken until it had passed."

His face like a mask, Virgil took out his case and selected a cigarette: but I saw a bead of sweat fall on to the gold.

"It was not your car?" said the sergeant, plainly impressed.

Producing a notebook, his fellow made ready to write.

"It was not our car," said Herrick. "Others were abroad this morning…within the confines of Brief."

"Describe this car, if you please."

"It was closed and its blinds were drawn: its number-plate was obscured – I imagine, with oil and dust."

The sergeant turned to his fellow, pencil in hand.

"Have you got that down?"

The other nodded and Herrick resumed his tale, relating how the car had been met and had then been backed down the drive and into the track.

"There three people got out, and the man who had met them came up."

"Would you know them again, sir?"

"I should."

As the answer went down, I saw Virgil wipe his face.

"One of the three," said Herrick, "was a woman. She had a dog on a lead."

"A dog?" cried the police, together.

"A long-haired, black-and-white dog: a mongrel, about that size."

Struggling with his emotion –

"Sir," cried the sergeant, "I beg that you will forgive me if I have seemed something short. I have to do my duty, and your interest in Brief seemed strange. But now I know that you are telling the truth. The dog you describe was found at large in the park."

"My friend," said Herrick, smiling, "I've nothing on earth to forgive. You've been very fair with me – I shall tell your Chief Constable so, when you've laid these swine by the heels."

Though the moment called for some speech, Virgil said nothing at all – because, I imagine, he dared not trust his voice. Grey-faced, his eyes like slits, he stood a little apart, unconsciously wringing to fragments the cigarette he had taken, but had not lit.

But the police were too much excited to care for these things.

Respectfully thanking Herrick and handing him back our map, the sergeant begged that he would describe "the delinquents you so providentially saw" – and Herrick complied with a gusto which did my heart good.

His picture of Percy Virgil was actually taken from life. Lazily surveying his victim, he drew a merciless portrait of that unprincipled man: and I find it hard to believe that a rogue was ever so trounced.

Not daring to retire – much less, of course, to protest – he was forced to hear dictated a report of his personal appearance which would have provoked the most forbearing of men, and, what was far worse, to endure the utmost apprehension for fear that the police should be struck by the startling resemblance the portrait bore to himself. Over all, the realization that his shocking secret was ours must have been like an iron in his soul, which Herrick's careless disdain continually turned.

His tormentor then repeated the horribly damning words which Virgil had said to his creatures before they had entered the wood, and when the sergeant seemed puzzled about the use of 'the wire', suggested that it might have been used to trip a galloping horse.

Under cover of the flush of excitement which this suggestion induced, Herrick encouraged the impression that we had no more to disclose: this the police were ready enough to accept, because they were eager to broadcast without delay the very full descriptions of the persons they hoped to arrest. Protesting their gratitude, the sergeant requested our names, and while Herrick was writing these down, turned and exhorted Virgil to enter and start the car.

"If you'll take us to Gabble, sir, I can get on to Innsbruck from there, and in less than two hours from now every police station in Austria will be alive with orders to search for the people we want."

"Splendid," said Virgil, somehow. He turned to Herrick and bowed. "Please believe that I shall not forget today…and that I am a man who invariably pays his debts."

"Is that a threat?" said Herrick.

I saw the police open their eyes, and Virgil in desperation let himself go.

"It's a warning," he snarled. "I do not believe your tale of the numberless car. That you saw a dog this morning proves nothing at all – except that you were at hand when the outrage was done. And who would think of so using a coil of wire – except a man who had planned to employ it that way?"

"Come, come, sir," said the sergeant. "You said yourself just now that these gentlemen – "

"I have changed my mind," spat Virgil, "as you have changed yours."

"I have just remembered," said Herrick, "that one of the men was called Max. Not the leader – the burly man, who got out of the car. The leader was sharp with him, as, indeed, with them all. I think that, if you could find them, they might give the leader away."

"And the name of the leader?" sneered Virgil. "Quite sure you didn't hear that?"

Herrick raised his eyebrows, before he returned to the police.

"You would not believe me," he said, "if told you the leader's name. And so I prefer that you should apply to Max. But I'll tell you what I will do. I'll write it down for you, and I'll seal it up. And when Max has opened his mouth, you may break the seal. Thus I shall corroborate him, and he will corroborate me."

"Sir," cried the sergeant, "I beseech you to tell it us now."

"I will write it down," said Herrick. "Or, better still, Mr Exon shall write it down. You will observe that I have not mentioned the name: yet he will go off and write it – which goes to show that he knows it as well as I."

With that, he turned to me and asked me to do as he said.

When I returned to the drive Virgil was back in his car, beside himself with passion and shouting down the sergeant who seemed very much surprised.

"And if you choose," he concluded, "to take your cue from a couple of lying hounds who, if you had done your duty, would now be under arrest – by God, you can take it alone."

With that he started his engine, let in his clutch, and swung the car violently round. With storming gears, it squirted between the chestnuts and on to the road of approach. Then he changed brutally up, and it scudded out of earshot, just as an angry wasp sails out of a breakfast-room.

The police stared after the fellow with open mouths: then they turned to see Herrick with a hand to his chin.

"I gather," he said, "that you find his behaviour strange."

"I can't understand it," said the sergeant. "Ten minutes ago – "

"Quite so," said Herrick. "In fact, ten minutes ago he did his very best to get you away – because, when he heard the hour at which we had entered the park, he did not wish you to hear what I might have to tell." He took the envelope from me and held it out. "You may open that now, if you please, and read the name of the leader whom Max will betray. After that you shall have some tea, and then, we'll drive you to Gabble to take what action you please."

The sergeant ripped the envelope open and he and his fellow together peered at the sheet.

Percy Elbert Virgil

I thought they would never look up.

When at last they did, they seemed dazed; and Herrick called for Brenda and told her to give them some tea.

Her back to our sitting-room door, Lady Elizabeth Virgil looked very grave.

"Mr Herrick," she said, "you put up a wonderful show. I wouldn't have missed it for worlds: I never knew that a hand could be played so well. But you've 'scotch'd the snake, not kill'd it.' And the sooner the police find Max – well, the better for your bodily health. Have you any arms, you two?"

"We have two pistols," I said.

"Then carry them, please – from now on. I mean what I say. It may have occurred to you that this countryside favours outrage – of any kind."

With that, we sat down to tea, and, half an hour later, I drove the Rolls to Gabble, with Winter sitting beside me and the police in the back of the car.

So, for the second time, meat came out of the eater that wonderful day. A scoundrel had arranged an abduction, and we had carried off the very prize we desired: and a Judas had come upon us, to fall into the pit he had digged and to turn to esteem the suspicion under which he had meant us to lie. But when Winter heard what had happened whilst he was safe in the kitchen, discussing his tea, he put his head in his hands and would not be comforted.

It was strange to sit down to supper with Lady Elizabeth taking the head of the board, but she seemed so glad to be with us and fell so naturally into the ways we kept that, for my part, I soon forgot how she came to be there and began to accept a relation which seemed too fair to be true. I had scarcely had to do with a woman for more than three years, and now I was sitting down with one who, Herrick declared, had stepped out of the picture-books. "I warn you," he said, "she's not real. Whilst you were getting down from that tree, the fauns picked up the Countess and left a nymph in her stead. Look at those orbs... She's heard that exquisite flourish that we have no ears to hear, the fanfare with which the firmament honours the rising sun; and the echo is there in her eyes, a shred of eternity held in a peerless fee. And Percy laid hands upon her. Well, well... What's bred in the bone. Only Percy seems to begin where his father leaves off. And if I were either of them, I give you my word I should be afraid to die. Why, they'll get a civic reception when they go down to Hell."

Enough is as good as a feast, and after supper that evening we spoke of the past and present, but left the future alone. My lady told us her story – a grim corroboration of the statement her father had made. She could not remember the time when her cousin had not been at Brief. It was his home as much as hers, and though she was given precedence, he was used as the son of the house. The Count had done much for him, but little or nothing for her, and again and again she had had to fight for her rights. But for these, she would have been gone, to make her own life, for the House of Brief was divided against itself. She hated the Count and her cousin: they hated her back: and the Count was afraid of Percy, and Percy despised the Count.

By the terms of her mother's Will, she received one thousand a year. This income the Count had received until she was twenty-one, and when she had come of age he had done his best to retain the half for himself: but she had gone to the lawyers and forced his hand. Since then he had continually complained that he could not meet the expenses to which he was put, while Percy and he were always at variance – the former demanding money or money's worth, and the latter declaring with oaths that he had not the wherewithal to maintain the estate.

Her mother's Will also directed that when she was twenty-one she was to be given possession of all of her mother's jewels, and these, she told us frankly, were very valuable.

"And where are they?" said Herrick.

"In England. They were being cleaned and reset when my mother was killed, and ever since then they've lain in the jeweller's safe. I could have had them out three years ago: but what was the good? Besides, I was afraid to have them: they might have been stolen – by someone within the house. Times without number they've urged me to have them out: Percy offered to get them at last and actually wrote out a letter for me to sign, authorizing the jewellers to hand them over to him. 'Thanks very much,' I said, 'but I'd rather they stayed where they were. But I'll lend you five pounds to go on with, if that's any good.' For once he had no answer – he couldn't get round the truth. That was six weeks ago…"

A sudden apprehension stabbed at my mind.

"Oh, my God," I cried, "I'll lay a monkey they're gone."

Lady Elizabeth started, and Herrick frowned.

"Why d'you say that?" said the former.

Shamefacedly, I told her of Inskip – the 'very big' diamond-merchant, whose company Virgil was keeping when first I had seen his face.

"But he'd never dare," she cried, flushing. "I mean, if he'd forged my hand – "

" – *he would have*," said Herrick, rising, "*a very pressing reason for putting you out of the way.*"

There was a deathly silence – which I employed in cursing my reckless tongue.

Lady Elizabeth sighed.

"That's right," she said, slowly: "that's right. You know, it's painfully clear that he is his father's son."

The next day I drove her to Salzburg – a very long way: but shop any nearer she dared not, because she was too well known. Brenda came with us to help her, because she had so much to buy, and in view of the miles before us, Herrick was more than content to be left behind.

For most, of the way I drove, and she sat by my side, and before we got back that night I think I had told her all that ever I did. It was a dull enough record, but have it she would, "because," said she, "for two years you played the part which I should have played – you cared for my poor father, and I cannot know enough of the man who did that."

"Honours were even," said I. "We were both of us down on our luck, and if I befriended him, he befriended me."

"Who paid for his – his funeral?"

"Damn it," I said, "he'd have done the same for me."

"Did you put a memorial up?"

"Yes" said I. "But I'd inherited then."

"What did you have cut upon the stone?"

"*Rudolph Elbert Virgil.*"

She caught her breath.

"I'm so thankful. Anything else?"

"A line from St Luke: *But now he is comforted.*"

There was a long silence. Four or five miles went by before she turned from the landscape to speak very low.

"May I call you Richard?" she said. "And will you please drop my style?"

We held the first of our councils the following day – by the side of the stream in the meadows, before eleven o'clock.

Nature was blithe about us: the sun, a merry monarch, delighted a radiant sky, and mountain, forest and pasture lifted up grateful heads: a dulcet madrigal rode on the willing air – the sweet bird's note, the murmur of passing bees, the low of a cow and the ring of a whetted scythe: and the flowers of the field did jubilant sacrifice, dispensing the simple fragrance they keep for midsummer days.

I said what I had to say first – by Elizabeth's wish.

"To my way of thinking we've only one object in view, and that is to expose the man who for twenty-two years has passed as the Count of Brief. If we can bring this about, we shall kill two birds with one stone – we shall not only bring him down but put Elizabeth up in her proper place.

"I know nothing of the law of the land, but if I did, I'd advise that we left it alone. We should never get home by that road. And it's no good writing round, proclaiming the truth, for no one would ever believe us and he might take action against us – for libel or something like that. The only way to expose him is to make him expose himself – admit officially that what we allege is true. And that he will never do, unless we can force his hand. If we can hold above him some threat sufficiently grim, the man will do as we wish. But it's got to be a hell of a threat, to make a man cut his own throat.

"What we need is some information from which we can forge a weapon which we can use. And that will be hard to come by. It might not have been so hard twenty years ago: but the sources we might have turned to have almost certainly failed. Still, we're not in the hopeless position of not knowing where to begin, because we have one clue, which, if we can follow it up, may lead us straight to a source which is still alive.

"It is, I think, a promising clue, because it concerns a secret of whose existence the Head of the House should know. And Elizabeth knows of its existence: but her uncle does not… She knows of its existence, I say: she does not yet know what it is: but she knows *where* it is – roughly.

"*The great tower of Brief – the great tower. There is a doorway there which no one would ever find. You must go up, counting your steps. And when you have…*

"I am not disheartened by the words 'which no one would ever find', because I believe them to mean 'which no one would ever *notice*, unless he was told where to look' – and we have been told where to look.

"Now how we are to look for a doorway within the great tower of Brief, I have honestly no idea: Elizabeth can only say whether that can be done: but, if it can be done, I suggest that we should do it, before we do anything else – because, to be still more honest, I don't know what else we can do.

"One thing more. Elizabeth may not like the line I suggest. The secret, whatever it is, has been most jealously guarded for hundreds of years. It may be something that no outsider should know. And if she's the slightest feeling against our doing our utmost to find it out – well, she knows that she's only to say so for me to drop this line and never touch it again."

"My dear," said Elizabeth, quietly, "my father tried to give it to you. *It may be that you can use it* – those were his words. Do you think I would revoke his bequest? Why, he never even charged you to tell me... Never mind. Of course you're right. That doorway's our only chance. I've no idea what is behind it – no more than you. But I think it may lead to something which, as you put it, will give us the weapon we need. As for looking for the doorway – we'll have to be careful, of course, but that shouldn't be very hard. As a rule Brief sleeps very sound, and if I like to return when Brief is asleep ..." She held up a Yale key. "That's my key. It will let us into the turret which leads to my rooms. My rooms give to a landing, and the landing will lead to the tower. And nobody lives there now. The rooms are just as they were when my grandfather died: but they are not occupied. It's rather a pity, really: except for the stairs between, they make a delightful suite."

"What does it consist of?" said Herrick. "I never saw it, you know."

"Two sitting-rooms, bedroom and bathroom. Why do you ask?"

"I was wondering if they'd suit us," said Herrick. "Just for forty-eight hours, you know. I mean, this search will take time. And it would be so very convenient to be on the spot."

I stared at him open-mouthed, but Elizabeth threw up her head and began to laugh.

"You're true to type," she said. "The jester's counsel was nearly always the best. And why shouldn't Brenda come, too? She can look after us all and wait upon me."

Though the tower was unoccupied, its apartments were aired and dusted twice in the week. Every Monday and Thursday these things were done, and since the day was Sunday, we determined to take possession the following night. In this way for fifty-two hours we should have the tower to ourselves. We could easily take enough food to last us this time, and since there was water laid on, there seemed to be no reason why Brenda should not make tea whenever we pleased. We could rest in comparative comfort and, thanks to the bathroom, could make our ordinary toilet without any fuss, and, indeed, we should do very well, so far as the flesh was concerned. As for the work to be done, out of fifty-two hours Herrick and I could labour for forty or more – or nearly ten times as long as we could have laboured each night, if we had not made up our minds to stay in the tower. Add to this that to enter and leave would be the most delicate business we had to do, and this we should do once only, instead of ten several times.

Of course the plan had its drawbacks: by spending the day at Brief, we were bound to be discovered if anyone entered the tower: then again from dawn to dusk we should be cut off, for we could not leave the castle except by dark: but if we were to find our doorway without being found ourselves, I think we might have tried for a year without picking a better way.

That Sunday afternoon Brenda and Winter were told the most of the truth, for, though I am sure that both would have trusted us blindly and would have done without question whatever we asked, it would have been unfair as unwise to make such demands upon such fidelity.

Poor Winter would have given his eyes to go with us into the castle in Brenda's place – if only, I think, on the chance of encountering Percy and laying the fellow out – but I bade him remember that much would depend upon him, for that if we should be surprised or anything else should go wrong, it was he that we should look to, to bring us out of our plight.

"You see," I said, "we couldn't attempt such a show, unless there was someone outside not only who knew where we were but with whom we could keep in touch. All Tuesday and Wednesday I want you to watch the castle – especially, of course, the great tower. I shall signal to you, if I want you, and what I want you to do. We'll arrange a code later on."

Then I told him about the three firs and how, if he steered by them, he would come to the belvedere, and he seemed very much relieved to think he would be within call, instead of, as he had expected, eleven miles off.

Our slight preparations were made the following day. We bought some torches and knapsacks, and food for two days was put up. Madame Revoke was told that we were going to stay at some hunting lodge, to which her guests of the summer had two or three times repaired, and though she was something surprised that we should travel by night, instead of by day, Lady Elizabeth Virgil could do no wrong in her eyes.

For the search itself, I could not think what to take. I could hardly believe that we should have to use force: yet things which have lain undisturbed for a number of years are apt to get stiff or clogged as the case may be. In the end, after much reflection, I decided on a mallet and a chisel, some oil and two measuring-rules: if what we found were to show that this rather meagre equipment was not enough, we should have to withdraw – and return with the stuff we required.

That afternoon we rested, to save our energy for the work to come. And at half-past eleven that night Winter set us down at the mouth of the entrance drive. He was not to return to Raven, but to berth the Rolls where he could in the country beyond the foothills which rose to the south of Brief: and then at dawn he would make his way over those foothills and down to the belvedere. Half an hour later we saw the castle before us, a shadowy mass without form, charged on the sable field of the woods behind.

So dark was the night that had there been sentries posted about the house they could not have seen us moving five paces away, and since Elizabeth said that no watch was kept, we followed her boldly up to the foot of the pile. Because we were shod with rubber, we made but the slightest sound, and as we came to the walls, I heard the lisp of water which might have been set playing to cover our steps.

I afterwards learned that a fountain rose on the foothill against which the castle stood: its issue was trapped in a basin beside the source and led from there by pipes all over the house: but the overflow of the basin ran down the side of the hill to feed a considerable conduit which stood in the stable-yard. And this flowed day and night, a heavy stream of water falling into a pool and making the steady rustle which we could hear.

Elizabeth skirted the walls, and we passed three staircase-turrets, to come to a fourth. And there she stopped, before a door or postern set in its base.

I, who was next behind her, moved to her side.

"I want you to pass me," she breathed, "as soon as I've opened the door. Turn to your right up the steps, and wait till I come. I'll shut the door when you're in."

I passed the word to Brenda, who gave it to Herrick in turn.

Then Elizabeth used her key – but the door stayed shut.

In desperation she set her weight to the oak.

Then she took her key from the latch.

"My God," she said. "It's bolted. What shall we do?"

"Somewhere close by," I whispered. "Where we can talk."

She put her hand to her head. Then she nodded and made me a sign to come on.

She led us away from the turret and presently down some steps. These brought us into a garden, sunk in the slope of the ground, so that while its foot was level with the pastures to which it ran down, its head, where we stood, was twelve feet below the terrace on which the castle was built. We could here converse in safety, provided we spoke pretty low, for the sound of the water, which we could no longer hear, would absorb the hearing of anyone standing above.

"Listen," I said. "There must be windows left open a night like this. Isn't there one I can climb to?"

Elizabeth shook her head.

"You'd break your neck," she said. "And if you could get in somewhere, you'd never find your way down to open to us."

"Then, what of the tower itself? Isn't there any way I can get into that? Once inside the tower, I couldn't go wrong, and its door's in the courtyard, isn't it?"

Elizabeth shrugged her shoulders.

"There is a window," she said, "but it's heavily barred. It's on the northern side – not very high up. It's a chance in a million, but one of those bars might be loose. But why should my door be bolted? They've all spring-locks, those doors, which no one could ever force."

"Your cousin's done that," said Herrick, "because he has reason to think that Max has your key. And I don't suppose he trusts Max…"

"Come," said I. "Let's go and have a look at this window. Somehow or other we've simply got to get in."

Elizabeth led us back to the castle wall. There she turned to the left, and we followed her as we had come. Then she turned to the right, and we passed the mouth of the archway which led to the small courtyard: and after a little she turned to the right again…

Some thirteen feet up I made out what looked like a cage, sticking out of the wall. Straining my eyes, I counted four vertical bars, not flush with the wall, but projecting, which meant, of course, that the casement which they were guarding was made to open outwards into the air. This was so much to the good, for while a cage offers a foothold which an ordinary grating denies, its bars are more open to violence than such as pass directly from lintel to sill.

"Hopeless," said Elizabeth, quietly. "I thought it was lower than that."

"I think I can make it," I said. "From Herrick's shoulders, of course. And if there's nothing doing, I've only to drop." I took off my knapsack and jacket, and rolled up my sleeves. "Can I use a torch with safety, to look at the bars?"

Elizabeth nodded.

"But do be careful," she said.

Herrick spoke out of the darkness.

"I'm prepared to contribute," he said. "Be sure of that. But I'm not an acrobat. I'm willing to try and carry your fifteen stone, but as soon as you feel me going, you'd better jump. And how d'you propose to begin? Are you going to run up me, or something?"

I made him take off his knapsack and stand to the wall, and I begged him to hold his peace, because if he made me laugh, we might both come down. Then I turned again to my lady.

"Once I'm up there," I said, "we shan't be able to talk: yet there may be something I find that I want to say: in that case I'll drop my handkerchief. If I do that, will you climb on to Herrick's shoulders? And I'll lean down and tell you whatever it is."

"Yes, indeed. But, Richard, you will be careful? Supposing those bars aren't sound."

"I promise to test them," I said, "before I go up."

She was wearing the clothes in which I had seen her first, and she looked very slight and fragile against the bulk of the stronghold by which we stood. I suddenly found it outrageous that she who was the Countess should be standing without her gates, hoping to force an entry, like a thief in the night. And this, I think, made me determined that, somehow or other, I would break into that tower.

A moment later I was standing on Herrick's shoulders, with my chisel and a torch in my pockets and both of my hands on the bars.

These were in good condition, and when I had tried them once, I drew myself up by inches until I had a foot in the cage...

Within this the window was open. If I could displace but one bar, the trick would be done.

As I have said, the cage was made of four bars. All four were sunk in the stone above and below the window they were to protect: but the outer two were also tied by crossbars to the window's jambs. It was, of course, hopeless to try to move either of these, for each was held at six points: but the two middle bars were held at two points only, where top and bottom were bedded into the stone.

Holding my torch in my teeth, I inspected the four beddings carefully, one by one. There was nothing to choose between them: all were apparently sound. I put my torch away, and tested the bars themselves. The first was not rock-steady: the second, however, might have been a part of the tower.

Clinging to the cage like some ape, I fought to loosen the first, and when I stopped to take breath, I could move it an eighth of an inch.

But for the cage, I could never have done what I did. As it was, I could work with freedom, and when I was tired, I could rest: and this without the dragging, deadly oppression of what I will call self-support. Never at any time was I holding my own weight up.

Without the mallet, the chisel was of no use, and I could not have used them together, because I had to hold on: but by working the bar to and fro, I gradually crushed the cement which was lying within the sockets between the bar and the stone.

After nearly half an hour this bedding was gone, and I could move the bar sideways a full two inches each way: but wrench it out, I could not, and after a little I knew that its ends had been purposely bent – to defeat the very object I had in view. I could loosen, but I could not displace it, unless I had the strength to pull a stone from the tower.

Now the bars had been set in the wall four inches apart. By holding my bar to one side I now had a space of six inches between that bar and the next. But that was not wide enough… After a moment or two I began to try to loosen the second bar.

As well try to shake a statue – or so it seemed. As I have said, the thing was a part of the tower. But after ten frantic minutes I felt it stir.

I stopped for a moment to rip off my tie and collar and let them drop. Then I fell upon the bar, like a man possessed.

Herrick told me later that the sweat of my body kept falling as rain-water falls from a tree. If it did, I never knew it. I only knew that the tower was loosing its grip on the second bar. It did so sullenly. Twenty-five minutes went by before I had the sockets clear of cement.

If I moved the two bars I had loosened as far apart as I could, I now had a space of eight inches through which to pass: but, short of displacing a bar, I could have no more, for the iron of which they were wrought was not to be bent.

I have sometimes heard said that where a man's head will enter, there his body can pass. On that exacting night I proved that saying untrue. I could put my head into the cage, but, do what I would, I could not pass my body between the bars.

God knows I did my best to fight my way in. My shirt was in ribbons about me, my chest and my shoulders were bleeding before I rested for breath – for, now that their chance was come, the bars showed me no mercy, as I had shown them none in the hour that was past.

Breathing hard and desperate, I shook the sweat from my eyes. To be beaten by a quarter of an inch, after all I had done! Such a thing was unfair and monstrous, not to be borne. And the open window mocked me – my torch had shown me the lavatory basin within, all ready for me to bathe in: the thought of the cool, running water had helped me to launch my frantic attack on the bars. And then Elizabeth Virgil...

Since I had gained the cage, I had never looked down. She was there below, in the darkness, waiting for me to bring her into her home. I had sworn to myself to do it. I had sworn that I would not look down – until I looked out of the window I could not reach.

As I turned again to the battle, I heard her voice.

"Richard, Richard, I beg of you..."

Three feet below me, I saw her upturned face. She was standing on Herrick's shoulders, leaning against the wall.

"What is it?" I whispered. "What is it?"

"Leave it, Richard. You must. No man could do any more, but it can't be done."

It was the phrase she used that opened my eyes.

'No man could do any more.' Perhaps. *But a woman could.*

"Listen," I said, "you've come in the nick of time. Can you see these bars? The two middle ones are splayed: but I can't move them farther apart, and I'm too big to get through. But you can pass easily – and the window is open beyond... Very well. In a minute I'm going to lean down and pick you up, but not by your hands – by your belt. Put your hands above your head, as though you were going to dive, and when you come up to the bars just wriggle your way between them and get a knee on the sill."

Without a word, she put up her hands, as I said, and I disposed myself as well as I could.

Had I stayed to reflect, I might not have taken the risk, for if anything had gone wrong, she might have been badly hurt. But I think I was past reflection: to see any way was to take it without a thought.

Holding fast with my left to a cross-bar, I reached my right hand down until I touched the small of her back. Then I took her by the belt of her breeches and lifted her up.

She could not have played her part better, if we had rehearsed the manoeuvre a score of times. As she came to the bars, she turned sideways, her back to me: and before I knew where I was, she had taken her weight.

And then it was all over, and she was within the tower – standing, looking out of the window, with her delicate hands on the sill.

For a moment we regarded one another, she as unearthly fair as I was foul.

Then –

"What can't you do?" she said quietly.

I shall never forget that moment.

The iron bars were between us, the bars which I could not pass. Like some beast, I was peering between them at a beauty which was not of my world. Corruption surveyed incorruption – *and found it his heart's desire.*

I think it was the bars between us that showed me the startling truth. Any way, in that instant I knew that the service I had offered was worship and that I had been in love with the Countess from the moment, four days before, when she had lain still in the bracken, with her wonderful eyes upon mine. And in that same instant I knew that she was not for me. I had no illusions at all. The gulf between us was so great that it could not be bridged. Tradition, lineage, standing rose up about their mistress, to look me down. And decency tapped my shoulder…

I knew as well as did she that she could never repay me for all I had done. I had succoured her father and I had saved her life. I wanted no repayment: but that was beside the point – which was that *whatever I asked, she was bound to give.* I use the word 'bound' deliberately. Elizabeth Virgil threw back. To discharge a debt of honour, she would have sold her soul.

"What can't you do?" she repeated.

"When you talk like that," I said hoarsely, "you make me feel rich."

Elizabeth smiled.

"That was the idea," she said gently. "Be careful how you get down."

5

Rats in a Trap

I shall not set down in detail the search we made for the 'doorway which no one would ever find', for, for one thing, we went about it as any one else would have done, and, for another, almost the whole of our labour was thrown away. But that, I suppose, was inevitable.

There was the winding stairway, scaling the wall of the tower, and within its coils were the chambers which made the suite. From top to bottom its walls and its steps were of stone, and the flight rose without interruption, except for four landings so slight as scarce to deserve that name. It was very simply built and served or was served by five doorways, not one of which was hidden in any way; and since its form was that of the ordinary winding stair, it was hard to see how any other doorway could really be there, and harder still to divine where such another doorway could possibly lead – for on one hand you had the chambers and, on the other, the wall of the tower itself.

The door from the courtyard gave to a miniature hall which just accepted the oak when Elizabeth swung it back. This hall was but four feet square and might, in days gone by, have been held by one man against fifty who strove to pass. As you entered the hall, the stairway rose on your right, and, before you, another doorway led to the first of the chambers within the tower. These were three in number, and all would have had the same shape, but for the demands which lavatories and a bathroom had made.

Hall and apartments were panelled with old black oak, which might have belonged to the chancel of some cathedral church. I never saw woodwork so rich laid up against stone, for it was by no means a skin, as panelling usually is, but was wealthy and massive enough to have made a wall of itself. What with this and the hangings and carpets, which were of crimson throughout, the tower was like the king's daughter, 'all glorious within', and as I passed through the bedroom, to make myself clean, I felt as pretenders must feel when first they assume the purple in which they have not been born.

Before we did anything else, we bolted the door between the tower and the castle, as well, of course, as the door by which we came in: if the former were found to be fast, whoever tried it would know that somebody was or had been within the tower; but we felt we must take that risk, for otherwise we must keep continual watch and, even though watch were kept, whoever came in might very well come upon us before we were able to profit by the alarm.

After that, I made for the window whose bars I had forced aside, and roughly replaced the sockets from which the cement was gone; and since before we came in, we had gathered the scraps which had fallen whilst I was at work, there now was nothing to show that the cage had been tampered with.

Then I joined my lady and Herrick, who were surveying the stair.

If this was dark by night, it was dim by day, and we could do nothing useful without the help of a torch: so, though we had not brought Brenda with that idea; she had very soon come to Elizabeth's aid: together they shed the light, whilst Herrick and I conducted the actual search.

That the work would require great patience was presently clear, for the walls seemed to be as blank as an untouched page, yet we could not believe that a doorway could be concealed in the steps. The panelling could have been hiding a host of openings, and we were naturally tempted to turn our attention to that: but the staircase was not panelled, and we were concerned with the staircase, and not with the rooms.

You must go up, counting your steps…

Not until that time did I at all understand the portion confronting the prisoner of ancient days, who set himself to discover a way to break out of this hold: but now I know some of the trials those men endured, for though our case was different, we did as they must have done. The constant chill and the rudeness of naked stone, the furtive light, the anxious fingering of masonry, the whispered consultation, the sudden shock of unfamiliar sounds – of such was our two-day tenure of the great tower of Brief. And indeed I cannot believe that four persons, good or evil, were ever so queerly placed, living and moving in the midst of a country house whose lawful tenants were going about their business, never dreaming of the presence of strangers within their gates.

(Here perhaps I should say that we had by no means forgotten 'the son of the house': but, if Percy Virgil meant mischief, we could scarcely have been in a better or safer place, for, though he should seek us 'until the cows came home', it never would enter his head that we were about our business under his father's roof.)

It was five o'clock on the Wednesday afternoon when Elizabeth straightened her back and led the way to the bedroom where Brenda had set out some tea.

We had now been within the tower for thirty-nine hours, for more than thirty of which we had striven to find the doorway with all our might. And we were no nearer our goal than when we had bolted the doors and begun our search. At most, ten hours were left us, for by three on the following morning we must be gone.

As I stumbled into the bedroom, Herrick opened his mouth.

"I think we should face the fact that we're up against Time. We've eight hours net before us, and then we must go – *for good*. I mean, to return would be futile. What we can't find in fifty hours, we shan't find in fifty years; and to go on smearing these walls would be wasting valuable time. Besides, there's the spiritual side. If we did come back, we should come back without our hearts. We should know that our efforts were doomed before we set out. And so we have now eight hours in which to discover a secret we know is there. Myself, I think we should do it: in fact, if we don't, I shall think the less of myself. When all's said and done, it's a question of using one's brain. And that's where I think we've gone wrong. When our eyes and our hands had failed us, we ought to have let them be: to go on using them was only distracting our brains...Well, I'm going to give mine a show now – before it's too late."

With that he walked into the bathroom, to lave his head and his hands, and I sank down on the bed and did my best to marshal my weary wits.

"He's right," said Elizabeth, slowly. "One always begins the wrong way. Once we'd been over the ground, we ought to have sat down quietly and let our minds play upon the puzzle. You know. Like doing a crossword."

"That's all very well," said I, accepting some tea from Brenda, who showed no signs of fatigue. "But who could do a crossword without any clues?"

"We've got two clues. We know that a doorway exists: and we know that, to reach that doorway, we've got to go up the stair. If – "

"My God," said I, starting up.

There was a moment's silence.

Then –

"Go on," said Elizabeth, quietly. "What do you know?"

"Your father said that there was in the tower a doorway which no one would ever find. And then he used the words 'You must go up, counting your steps.' *But he never said that the doorway was on the staircase.* He said it was in the tower."

"You mean – "

"I mean that we have been looking for a doorway which we can reach from the stair: *but we ought to have been looking for something upon the stair which, when we have found it, will disclose where the doorway is.*"

"That's right," said Herrick's voice. "And the stairway bears him out. There *is* no doorway there – I think we can swear to that. *But there is a spring or something which, when we can touch it off, will open some hidden door in another part of the tower.*"

The case was now greatly altered, for though we had sought high and low, when you are looking for a doorway, you naturally do not probe places which could not be hiding a hole more than two inches square. Then again we were now released from the heart-breaking duty of striving with Reason herself, for Reason had continually insisted that, because of its shape and construction, such a stair could not be concealing the kind of opening we sought. Indeed, to say our hopes rose conveys nothing at all. All our weariness left us, and all our anxiety fled. We simply *knew* that the path we were on was the right one and very soon would bring us up to our goal.

And so it did.

Not more than an hour had gone by when I found on the thirty-sixth step a nick which might have belonged to the lid of a pencil box. It was cut in the tread of the step, close to the edge and close to the outer wall. It was choked with a cake of dirt which I had to cut out with my knife, and an obstinate film of dirt was encrusting that side of the tread; but when I had used a wet cloth to rub the stone clean, there were the parallel cracks which I had expected to see. In a word, I had found a panel – a tiny, sliding panel which, if I could draw it towards me, would discover a slot in the tread, three inches by two.

(Here, perhaps, I should say that I have now no doubt that the film of dirt on the tread was more than the natural deposit which Time will lay, and that, after replacing the panel, the late Count of Brief had washed the stone with some liquid which, when it was dry, would form an invisible skin.)

Half an hour went by before the little panel allowed me to have my way. Then at last, with a crack, it yielded, and two minutes later I drew it out of the tread.

Its withdrawal disclosed no slot, but a miniature well, rather more than an inch across: and sunk in this well was a bolt of very old iron.

At once we saw that the bolt was thus holding in place the rise of the step upon which we were now at work, and that if we could pull the bolt up, the rise would be free to be moved.

As might have been expected, the bolt was tight in its well but it was not cemented in, and after another ten minutes I managed to wheedle it out.

I then took the mallet from Herrick and tapped the rise. At once the side I had tapped retreated before the blow, but the other side started forward out of its place.

"Pivoted," breathed Herrick. "It's hung on a spindle, just like a revolving door."

One hand on my shoulder, Elizabeth lowered her torch.

There was now before us a gap, where the rise had been. This gap was split into two by the rise itself, for this had simply been turned and was now presenting its edge, instead of its face. The torch immediately showed that the gap on the right was void – that is to say, on the side on which the rise had retired: but the gap on the left was framing a block of stone, And sunk in the face of this stone was a handle, or rude, iron dog…

I can never forget how the sight of this primitive holdfast remembered the fairy stories which I had loved as a child – the magic rings which, when pulled, disclosed a secret entry into some robbers' cave, and the carving which, when depressed, caused panels to spring ajar at the head of some secret stair. And now I can only suppose that all these pretty legends are faithfully founded on fact, for there was the handle before me, and when I laid hold upon it, I was, though we did not know it, about to disclose a doorway we could not find.

Now the block of stone before us appeared to be unattached. It was very slightly smaller than the gap through which it appeared and it seemed to be resting on something which was not part of the stair. It fitted its recess as closely as does a brick loose in the wall: it was by no means loose: but the moment I touched it – I cannot say that it moved, but I knew that it was not fixed.

This very peculiar condition astonished us all, for the block must have measured at least nine inches by five, and though, for all we knew, it was only three inches deep, the weight of a stone of that size should have held it fast.

"Go on," said Herrick. "Pull it. If a genie appears, so much the better. I've quite a lot of orders to give."

I laid hold of the dog and pulled...

At once the block slid forward, after the way of a drawer that you pull from a chest. And, as you may pull a drawer clear, so I drew the block out of its housing, over the tread of the step which lay, like an apron to take it, in front of the gap.

The block was immensely heavy, for it must have been twelve inches deep, and, when I had drawn it clear, it was all I could do to lift it out of the way and on to the tread above.

To do this, I had to stand up and lift it between my legs; but the others stayed where they were.

As I laid it down –

"Do you see it too?" said Herrick.

"I – I don't understand," breathed Elizabeth. "I mean, how *can* that be there?"

"What is it?" said I, and stepped back to go down on my knees.

"It's time we went home," said Herrick. "That's what it is. When I run into black magic, that's where I get off."

Never had idle words so specious a warranty.

The block which I had withdrawn had left behind it no room.

Though I make a fool of myself, at least I will make this clear.

When you pull a drawer from a chest and lay it aside, you leave in the chest a space which is very slightly larger than the drawer which you have removed. But, though I had drawn out the block, there was no such space left, In fact, the gap was now framing another block of stone which resembled exactly the one I had taken away, except that it had no handle by which it could be withdrawn. And when I presently touched it, the same indefinable tremor told me it was not fixed.

"Can you beat it?" said Herrick, shortly.

"On the face of it, no," said I. "But there must be some simple reason for such a thing. I mean, these doings are ancient: there's no machinery here."

"There can't be a reason," said Herrick, "unless you're a conjurer. If you pick a brick out of a wall, you've a right to expect a recess. Well, there's the brick you picked out: but where's the recess?"

"There *was* a recess," said my lady. "There must have been. But now it's been filled."

"That's right," said I. "That's right. And I'll tell you another thing. It's got to be emptied again before we can put that block back."

"Do you mean to suggest," said Herrick, "that a slab of stone of that size, fixed or unfixed, can shift to and fro on its own?"

"I have it," said Brenda's voice. "The thing is a counterpoise. My uncle has one at his farm. It is very old, but its movement is silent and sure as the flight of an owl."

There was an electric silence.

Then –

"By God, the girl's right," said Herrick. "And there's the conjuring trick. Beneath these steps there's a balance; and when you drew out that block you lightened one of its scales – with two results. One was that the scale you had lightened rose in the air and thus revealed to our eyes the second weight on the scale. That is it, there – in the gap." He got to his feet. "And the other result was this – that the opposite scale sank down – *thus revealing somewhere or other the doorway we're trying to find."*

That this interpretation was good, there could be no doubt, and we all began to go down the winding stair, surveying the walls, as we went, for some gap in their masonry. We were too much excited, I fear, to use our wits. Had we done so, we should have perceived that there was but one direction in which the balance could hang and that this would bring the scale which we wished to locate very nearly above the doorway by which we had entered the tower. However, as luck would have it, we now had no need of wits, but only of eyes; and as we emerged from the staircase into the small, square hall, we saw directly before us the interspace which we sought.

I have said that the hall was panelled. On the wall which faced us one of the panels had sunk – not very much, but five inches…exactly the height of the block which I had pulled out of the stair. The gap thus shown was breast-high and fifteen inches in width. Beyond was an open space, and when I put in my hand, I could feel a faint current of air.

The panel hung on a chain, which was, of course, attached to the balance above. And so long as it hung on that chain, the panel could get no further, because the counter-weight had no room to rise. So I took the weight of the panel, while Herrick undid the chain.

(Here let me say that those that installed the contrivance so long before had left undone no convenience, however nice, however hard to devise. But for their provision, the panel's weight being gone, the counter-weight must have sunk and the chain have run up out of reach. But this was provided against, for the chain ran up through a hole which served as a guide, which was half an inch too small for the last of the links.)

Then I let the panel sink slowly into some slot in the stone…

At last it came to rest, some six inches still protruding and making a sill to the doorway which we had discovered at last.

This gave to a winding stair, precisely resembling that upon which we had passed so many wearisome hours. In a word, with the hall for landing, the stair of the tower went on down, curling slowly right-handed, into the bowels of the earth.

For the others I cannot answer, but until the way was open and we were about to go down, I had never considered to what 'the doorway' might lead: but now that we were about to discover the truth, I remembered the late Count's words and, with those for straw, began to make fabulous bricks.

It may be that you can use it…

I will not set down the pictures my fancy drew. Enough that they were all false. But I have this consolation – that not one man in a million would have predicted the scene which presently met our eyes.

Herrick declined to go down, but stayed in the hall with Brenda, "unless and until," said he, "my lady decides that she wants me on in this act." So I preceded Elizabeth, torch in hand.

For thirty-six steps we went down. And then we came to a chamber that had no door.

On the threshold I stopped and lighted a second torch, and my lady looked over my shoulder, to see what I saw.

The chamber was small – some fifteen feet by eight, and some nine feet high. Its walls and floor and ceiling were all of stone, and though there was no window, the air was by no means foul. (This, I afterwards found, was due to two vents – one low down in the wall, and the other high up at the opposite end of the room: but though I sought for their mouths, I never was able to find them, because they were too well hid.) Towards one end of the cell was a great oak stall, plainly very ancient and finely carved, and against one wall was a coffer, also of oak. There was no other furniture.

In the stall was seated a man – or what was left of one. His pose was natural. His head was up and was leaning against the back of the stall, his arms lay along its arms, and his trunk and his feet were well and truly planted on oak and stone. His clothes were those of the fifteenth century. His tunic was of diapered velvet which the passage of many years had brought to shreds and tatters, if not to dust, but a jewelled belt was still girding the crumbling loins and a chain was sunk in the ruin about the neck. Hose still hung upon the legs, which were skin and bone, and a patch, that had been a cap, was still crowning the thick fair hair. This was inviolate. The face and hands were withered, but otherwise well preserved and might have been those of a man incredibly old, but a few hours dead. The eyes, which were wide, had a curious sightless look and might have belonged to a man who was living, but blind; and the whole was in no way offensive, because, I suppose, there was no sign of corruption, but only of age. Indeed, had the hair been white, the figure would have been full of dignity: but the colour of the hair was fatal, suggesting an old man's efforts to seem to be young – one of Time's shabbier jests, for the man had not seen old age.

On the coffer were lying three things. One was a skin of parchment – or part of a skin. Upon this had been written Latin, still to be read. By its side lay the translation, clearly inscribed upon vellum and made at some later date. And between the two lay a massive signet ring.

As might have been expected, the documents told us the truth.

Here sits Elbert, Duke of Austria and Carinthia, King of Hungary, slain by his host and liegeman, Rudolf of Brief, because he came upon him defiling his wife.

With the fear of death upon her, Helen of Brief declared the following facts:

That the King and she were secretly married, before he wedded the Queen and before she deceitfully wedded Rudolf of Brief. In proof whereof she offered her marriage lines signed by the Cardinal Gaddi, lately dead of the plague, whom God reward.

That the first and third of her children, whom Rudolf believed to be his, were both the sons of the King.

Rudolf made haste to apprise the Queen of the truth.

For the sake of that injured lady, he undertook, on conditions, to hold his peace. Between them it was agreed:

That he should hold to his witness the corpse of the King, himself providing another to take its place and be interred and entombed as though it were that of the King.

That since Otto, whom he thought his first-born, was now IN TRUTH Duke of Austria and Carinthia, King of Hungary, he and his heirs should FOR EVER hold the right to call upon the heirs of her body in any stress, whose help they shall have WITHOUT FAIL by showing the King's great ring.

That her heirs shall be so instructed in perpetuity.

By Rudolf's order, Gollanx, a chemist of Innsbruck, preserved the corpse of the King. This he did according to a certain prescription which he had of a learned Venetian whose son he had saved. His raiment also he dipped against the corruption of Time.

Dated the ninth day of March in the year of Our Lord one thousand four hundred and thirty-nine (the King being dead on the seventh, having lain in state till now and to be replaced this night) and written down word for word as my lord Rudolf hath commanded by his unworthy servant and clerk

GABRIEL OF LITTAI.

Whom I slue whiles his ink was wett for he hath a long tongue and I have need of a boddy as he hath sayed.
RUDOLF OF BRIEF.

The original postscript was laboriously written in German and poorly spelt. The translation was done in German from first to last, and to this had been added two lists – one of the Lords of Brief and one of the several Heads of the other House.

Elizabeth was trembling.

"Oh, Richard, d'you know what this means?"

"It means you're a queen," said I. "But then I knew that before."

"No, no." She dabbed at the parchment. "That last name there. Not my grandfather's – the other. *Harriet Vincentia Saying, Duchess of Whelp.* She's still alive – and she's bigger than any queen. She's always known as 'Old Harry.' Her mother was English – as mine was, and if she'll take up my cause..."

"She must," said I. "It's a case of deep calling to deep."

"She's a law to herself," said Elizabeth, thoughtfully. "But if she does – well, next time you come to Brief you won't have to force any bars."

"That's right," said I, feebly enough. With a sudden movement, I set a torch in her hand. "And now I'll go for a pen. You must write your name here at once. Shall Herrick come down?"

"If you please."

I left her there and mounted the unworn stair.

The thing was absurd and childish, but now that I saw what was coming, my heart sank down. The 'rough stuff' was over, and so – my service was done. From now on, steps would be taken by a lady of high degree. Pressure would be put on the impostor: ways and means would be used which were out of my ken. And when the game had been won, I should be invited to Brief...where a servant would hold the door wide and another would take my hat. I should be ushered – *I*...that had broken into the place, to set a queen on her throne... And then I should be presented to Her Grace the Duchess of Whelp, and the Countess of Brief would tell her how good I had been – I that had held a king's daughter against my hammering heart...

I suppose that my face was betraying my state of mind, for, as I stepped into the hall, I saw Herrick throw up his head and clap his hands to his eyes.

"Oh, I can't bear it," he groaned. "Don't say that after all this – "

"On the contrary," said I, "we're practically home. I'm going to get pen and ink – for you to take down."

Leaving him staring, I entered the room on my left, passed to a table and dipped a pen in some ink. Then I came back and gave it to Herrick and watched him begin to descend.

Brenda, of course, was wide-eyed: but it was not for me to tell her what we had found.

"It's her ladyship's secret," I said: "but at least I may tell you this – that, thanks to what we've discovered, she's going to come by her rights."

"Is it very ancient?" said Brenda.

"It's nearly five hundred years old."

Brenda drew in her breath.

"And has been handed down all that time from father to son?"

"Certainly," said I. "And each of them signed his name. The signatures are down there. I think there are thirty-two."

(Here I should say that, in fact, there were thirty-three, the first twenty-five of which were those of the 'lords' of Brief. The twenty-sixth was that of the first of the 'counts'.)

"Few houses," said Brenda, "could show such a title as that."

"Very few," said I, sitting down.

"Is your family ancient, too?"

"I really don't know," said I. "I believe we go back some way, but I've nothing to show."

"The Revokes have held Raven for more than a hundred years."

"But I have no home," said I. "In fact, I'm nothing at all. It's true that I have some money – much more than I need. But that is all. I haven't even got an address."

Brenda frowned.

"You have always Raven," she said. "And when my lady is up, I think you will be welcome at Brief for as long as you live."

I smiled, and we spoke no more, but waited together in silence till Herrick came back – alone.

"Elizabeth wants you again," was as much as he said.

In some surprise, I took the torch from him and again descended the stair.

As I entered the little chamber –

"Look," said Elizabeth, pointing. "Is that all right?"

I stooped to regard the vellum.

She had written a line beneath her grandfather's name.

Elizabeth Virgil, Countess of Brief, only child of the foregoing's first-born son.

"Yes," I said. "There's no mistake about that."

She gave me the pen, and picked up the great gold ring. Then she turned to look again at the body, sunk in its stall.

"Seeing's believing," she said. "But no chemist could do today what Gollanx has done."

That, of course, was most true. By every right, the body should have been dust. Instead, it had the air of a waxwork. And that, I suppose, was why it was in no way offensive, but only remarkable.

After a long look –

"We'd better be going," she said, and turned to the stair.

I began to follow her up, throwing a beam beyond her, to light her steps, but after a little she stopped, to ask for a torch. I gave her one of my two, and by its light she examined the

100

arms on the ring. Then with a sudden movement she put this into my hand.

"Put it on my finger," she said. "You have the right."

I slid my torch into a pocket and took her left hand in mine. Then I slid the ring on to her beautiful second finger, for which it was far too big. For a moment we regarded it together.

Then –

"I'm out of my depth," I said. "There's a king down there – that I've been using as if he were a giant at a fair: and here I am standing up to a girl who's really a queen."

"I'm Elizabeth Virgil to you – and shall be, as long as you live."

"I know I said that," said I. "But now this has happened, to – to put me where I belong."

"Where do you belong, Richard?"

"To the crowd," said I, "that watches the great go by."

"Where my father stood. Where, but for you, I should be standing this very day."

"What of that?" said I. "You don't belong to the crowd, and neither did he."

Her left hand tightened on mine.

I'm afraid," she said gravely, "that he, like me, must have had a very low taste. You see, we both – took to you. And, unless I'm much mistaken, from what I've heard of 'Old Harry', she'll do the same." A smile swept into her face. "Don't look so surprised, my dear. I mean what I say. And I'll tell you another thing. As I've said, if she likes, 'Old Harry' can pull this off: but if I had to choose between your assistance and hers, I'd choose you every time – and let her go hang."

My heart burned at her words – which I could not allow.

"But that – that's fantastic, Elizabeth."

"It isn't really," she said. "And in any event it's true. You see... No, you wouldn't see – so that's no good. Let me put it like this. Till you came, I had no one to lean on. Then you came out of the blue and took the whole of my weight. Well, that has demoralized me: and now I know that I *must* have someone to lean on – that I cannot go back and stand by myself again. Now so long as you are willing, you are the person on whom I wish to lean: but you seem to have an idea that that would not be correct, because the blood in my veins is rather better than yours. Well, I'm not going to argue the point, but tell me this. Was your father a stable-boy?"

"Oh, no," said I. "He – "

"Well, that man's was," said Elizabeth, and pointed over my shoulder, down the stair. "If you don't believe me, I'll show it you in the books. Perhaps that'll make you feel better. Or must I do something to lower myself in your eyes?" I cried out at that. "Very well. Who am I to you?"

"Elizabeth Virgil," said I.

"No more?"

"No more – and no less."

"And are you content that I should lean upon you?"

Unwilling to trust my voice, I bent my head and put her hand to my lips.

I looked up to find her smiling.

"The man of action," she said.

And then she was two steps above me, climbing the stair.

There was now no cause for haste, for leave before midnight we dared not, in case Brief was not asleep: and that was the hour at which Winter was to be by the mouth of the drive. (He, of course, knew no more than that we were within the tower and that all was well, for I had twice sent him that signal a short half-hour before dawn. This, from the leads of the tower, which were easily reached.) Indeed; we were faced with the prospect of being confined for three hours with nothing to do, for though we were all worn out, excitement and impatience, between them, would not allow us to rest. But first, of course, we had to cover our tracks.

(Here let me say that I make no excuse for the outlook which I have this moment set down. It was ours, at that time: and if I am to be honest, it must be declared.)

Now that we knew the secret, it took us a very short while to return to their ancient order the elements we had displaced, but dust that the years have laid cannot be reproduced in ten minutes of time, and half an hour went by before I was satisfied with the look of the thirty-sixth step, within whose stone the key to the chamber lay. Whilst I was attending to this, with Brenda to give me light, my lady and Herrick together composed a full note of what we had found in the chamber and what the statement set forth. They were at work in the bedroom, that is to say, the uppermost room of the tower. We had used that room, and no other, because that alone was above the rest of the house, so that there we could move and converse, yet could be heard by no one who was not within the tower. To reach this room, we had to pass by the great door which gave to the second floor of the castle itself. For us this spot was always the danger-point, and, while we had laid down a carpet to swallow the sound of our footfalls as we went by, we always put out our torches before we approached the landing which served the door. It follows that, whenever we passed, we did so in darkness and silence, feeling our way.

I had finished my work on the step and, with Brenda behind me, was going upstairs to the bedroom quietly enough. We had passed by the door and I was about, being by, to relight my torch, when a sound there was no mistaking rapped out of the dark. *It was the clack of a latch.*

The two of us stood still as death.

Again the iron was raised – by somebody standing on the other side of the door...and pressure was put on the oak – which could not open because we had made it fast... Then whoever was there gave in, and the latch fell back into place.

We had been so much occupied and had become so familiar with our peculiar estate that the fears which at first had plagued us had lost their sting and we had come to ignore, if not to forget, that someone of Brief might purpose to enter the tower. This sudden catastrophe, therefore, hit me between the eyes, and I make no shame to confess that, to use the words of the Psalmist, my heart in the midst of my body was even like melting wax. Then I had myself in hand and was up the stairs in a flash, to give the alarm.

Elizabeth paled, and Herrick stifled an oath.

"If we can, we must bolt," said I. "By way of the courtyard, of course: and so to the belvedere."

"Is that step all right?" said Herrick.

"Thank God, yes," said I. "I was on my way up."

As luck would have it, our stuff was ready to hand, and before two minutes had passed, we had packed it anyhow and were ready to leave. We had intended, of course, to restore to the rooms we had used the order we had found when we came, but this was not now worth doing, and so we let them be.

As the four of us stole past the door, the latch was raised and let fall and the oak was urged, as though someone refused to allow that the bolts had been shot; but we heard no conversation, which gave us hope that no hue and cry had been raised.

As fast as I dared, I led the way down the stair…

We were, I suppose, some fifty seconds too late. As I gained the hall, I heard the sound that I dreaded some eighteen inches away – a key being tried in the door at the foot of the stair.

It was, of course, tried to no purpose. The door was heavily barred. But it meant that both exits were held, and that we were caught in the tower as rats in a trap.

6

'Old Harry' Receives

I often think that we fully deserved our plight, for, once we possessed the secret we set out to find, we should not have lost a moment in leaving the tower. To cover our tracks was essential, but that we could have done in a quarter of an hour. Then again we needed the darkness, but dusk would have served our turn. And that we had. We preferred to ignore a grave peril because for forty-three hours it had never lifted its head, losing sight of the staring fact that if it should lift its head, we were bound to be caught.

Be these things as they may, when I heard that key move in the lock, I was ready to do myself violence for throwing away the chance of escape we had had: for, had we behaved – not with prudence, but common sense, we should at that time have been nearing the mouth of the drive.

After a moment's hesitation, I led the way through the hall and into the room beyond. Then I shut the door behind Herrick, lighted a torch and threw the beam on the floor.

I touched Elizabeth's arm.

"First, tell me this," I said. "Is the roof any good?"

"I've no idea," she said, and pushed back her sable hair. "There might be a way – I don't know."

I shook my head.

To seek such a path by night would have been a desperate venture for Herrick and me: the presence of our companions ruled such an enterprise out.

"Then I can think of nothing," said I, "except to draw them away from the upper door. If we can only do that, we may still get clear. Out of the upper door, where we heard them first – across the landing you spoke of into your suite – down your staircase turret – out of the castle and up to the belvedere. Winter will still be there, if we can be quick, to lead us over the ridge and down to the Rolls."

"A feint?" said Herrick, frowning.

"That's my idea," said I. "A demonstration down here – at the lower door. I admit it's a damned thin chance, but what else can we do?"

"What sort of demonstration?" said Elizabeth.

I looked at Herrick.

"D'you think you could do it?" I said. "Disguise your voice and – and parley with them in German? I mean…"

Herrick's face was a study.

"I see," he said slowly. " 'Parley'. And how, when the parley's over, do I get out? Up a hundred steps and then through a house I don't know. Or don't I get out?"

"I shall come back." I said, "as soon as they're safe in the suite."

With my words we heard somebody pound on the lower door.

"Who is within?" they demanded. "Open at once."

Herrick looked at Elizabeth.

"Is that his lordship?" he said. "I'd like to, er, parley with him."

My lady smiled.

"That was Bertram," she said. "The steward. I'm afraid that he may get rather fussed."

"A little bit pompous?" said Herrick.

"A shade, perhaps. But a most respectable man."

"Leave him to me," said Herrick, and settled his coat. "And when I take up the running, stand by to move. If you should get clear…"

"I'll give you a flash," said I, "from the bend of the stair."

Herrick nodded and took out a cigarette.

By this time those in the courtyard were fairly assaulting the oak, and since, when the latch was drawn, the door could be moved to and fro for an eighth of an inch, a not inconsiderable uproar invaded the room.

"Put out that light," said Herrick.

As I did his bidding, he stepped to the door of the chamber and flung it back with a crash.

The uproar beyond stopped dead. Then –

"Who the devil is there?" roared the steward. "Open at once."

A thick voice replied in German.

"What does this mean – disturbing respectable people at this time of night? Go and wipe your snout, you old toss-pot, and burn the towel."

A savage hiccough subscribed this most offensive command, and Brenda, standing beside me, began to shake with mirth.

Then a wave of scandalized consequence burst on the lower door. The oak was pounded and shaken, and choking cries of protest stood out of a motley clamour of orders and threats.

I touched Elizabeth's arm and made for the stair. As we went up –

"Understand this, Bertie," said Herrick, drunkenly. "If you don't take your verminous carcase away, I'll come out and wipe your snout for you." He hiccoughed again. "Just because you're too drunk to stand up, that gives you no right to come here with your women…"

A composite yell of indignation drowned what was left of the slander and drowned it well. The demonstration was developing. Bertram and his supporters were certainly 'getting fussed.'

Two steps at a time, I leaped up that sullen stair…

Now few could have done as well as Herrick was doing below, but I was by no means sure that the outcry which he was raising within the courtyard could be heard by one who was standing by the side of the upper door – that is to say on the second floor of the house: and even if it was heard, it might not persuade such a sentry to leave his post. On the other hand, it seemed likely that the pother was yet too young for orders to have been issued or any precautions taken against the trespasser's flight: and since any moment now precautions *would* be taken – for Bertram, thirsty for vengeance, was certain to think of preventing his detractor's escape – I decided to waste no time boggling, but draw the bolts.

As the girls stumbled on to my heels, I opened the upper door...

Beyond this, curtains were hanging, heavy and thick. I cautiously lifted one, to see the broadest landing I ever knew. In its midst was an oval well, some forty feet wide, with a bronze balustrade about it and the heads of twin flights of stairs upon either side. (To give some idea of their size, each step was but two inches high and some twelve feet long.) The landing itself was dim, but a brilliance rose out of the well and the sumptuous flights of stairs ran down into light. So far as I could see, there was nobody hereabouts, but the sound of voices and movements came from a lower floor.

Elizabeth, peering beside me, caught my wrist.

"Quick," she breathed, and urged me across the carpet, past the luminous pool of the well, to a door which was close to the head of the farther stair.

An instant later, the three of us entered her suite.

"Too easy," I said, with an eye on the way we had come. "And if I'm not back in three minutes, please give me your word you'll go on. I cannot tell what may happen. If there's a hitch, it may be better for us to leave by the lower door. But we couldn't do that unless we were sure you'd escaped."

Elizabeth shook her head.

"If you don't come, I shall use my judgment," she said.

I shrugged my shoulders and went. There was no time to argue. Any moment someone might visit the upper door.

I have so far said nothing of what we were most afraid of that summer night – the entrance of Percy Virgil upon the scene. Not only was the fellow efficient – he would have secured both doors before he did anything else – but he had good cause to remember both Herrick and me; and though we made good our escape, if he set eyes upon us the police would be at Raven very nearly as soon as the Rolls. But now I disclose this dread, for as I whipped over the landing, *I heard his sinister voice.*

I think he was giving some order. Be that as it may, his unmistakable accents rang out of the well.

In a flash I was past the curtains and back in the tower and was cursing its stairway anew, because to go down it too fast was to break your neck.

As I came within earshot –

"Only let me get out," belched Herrick, fumbling the bolts of his door. "I'll teach you to talk to your betters. I warn you, Bertie, I'll tie your snout round your neck."

And there I flashed my torch – and saw him leap for the stair.

I turned and climbed before him for all I was worth...

Eighty-eight merciless steps, wedge-shaped, steep and naked, curling between walls that were hostile and, when you sought for a handhold, bruised your nails... After a little, you seemed to make no progress, to be no more than the pitiful, captive squirrel climbing his endless wheel... Up, up, up... For less than a minute, I know: but such is the power of apprehension, it seemed an age.

I was six steps short of the landing which gave to the upper door, when Percy spoke again – to bring my heart into my mouth.

"Oh, and bring my pistol, damn you. It's next to the torch."

The man was beyond the curtains masking the upper door.

Herrick and I stopped dead.

An instant later the curtains were dashed apart and a transient glimmer of light revealed our enemy.

Then –

"Who said it was shut?" he screeched. "It's open wide. By God, they've done it on you, you poisonous fools. Where's Elgar? Get hold of Elgar and tell him to watch the drive."

With that, he thrust into the tower.

He could, of course, see nothing, but his foot at once encountered the heavy length of carpet which we had laid on the steps.

"Hullo! What's this?" he muttered.

I heard him pass on to the carpet, but what further movement he made I could not tell, for the pile was tremendously thick and deadened all sound..

With Herrick one step below me, I crouched there, straining my ears. We were just clear of the carpet, standing upon the stone.

Then Virgil spoke again – and made me jump like a. foal.

"God in heaven," he yelled. "Why don't you bring that torch?"

The man was three steps above me – and coming down.

I dared not try to hit him – I could not see: but, quick as a flash, I seized the end of the carpet and jerked it downstairs towards me with all my might.

His feet whipped from beneath him, with a foul but forgivable oath, Percy Virgil fell violently on to his back. As he did so, still holding the carpet, I flung myself full upon him, enveloping him in its toils. Moved by some brilliant instinct, Herrick fought his way past us and, seizing the head of the carpet, flung this over and down.

Now since the carpet was immensely heavy and thick and more than twice the width of the winding stair, it follows that Percy Virgil was very deeply involved. To this I can swear, for when the top half of the carpet fell down upon me, I felt as though I were buried beneath some invincible bulk. I was, of course, clear in an instant, by wriggling back, but Percy could not emerge, though my weight was gone. His bellows for assistance were stifled, his convulsions, because they were frantic, did little, if any, good. Moreover, I could not go by without treading upon the welter – if not, indeed, upon him, and, since I am no featherweight, I fancy this made matters worse.

Remembering his orders to Elgar, I hurled myself up to the doorway and on to the landing beyond.

"Well done," breathed Herrick. "Which way?" The mighty landing was empty, but, as we bolted across, a man came full tilt up the staircase, the head of which was six feet from Elizabeth's door.

So dim was the light and he was making such haste that though we must almost have met, I think he would have let us go by, but I dared not take the risk and hit him, very reluctantly, full on the jaw.

As he crumpled and fell downstairs, Elizabeth's door was opened, and Herrick and I passed in.

Thirty seconds later, the four of us left the castle by way of the staircase-turret by which, two nights before, we had hoped to come in. The drive was clear. If Elgar had had his orders, he had not yet had time to carry them out. We darted across the gravel, slipped down the steps to the garden and hastened, Elizabeth leading, to where the walk began that led to the belvedere.

Twenty minutes later, Winter, still breathing goodwill, was leading us down to where he had berthed the car.

If our narrow escape had shocked us, the drive to Raven ministered to our minds. Woods and meadows were fragrant, the winds were still, and the Rolls seemed to skim the country through which we passed. After our two days' confinement, the rush of the soft, night air was grateful beyond relief and I could have wished the journey as long again.

Supper for three had been laid in our sitting-room, and a note addressed to Herrick was lying beside his plate.

As he read it, his face grew grave.

SIR,

I am told that you are returning to Raven tonight. A man, of the name of Max Bracher, was found by Salzburg yesterday afternoon. He corresponds to your description of the man of that Christian name. Your identification of him is desired, and I beg you will visit Salzburg without delay. When found, he had been dead for some hours, shot through the back.

Your obedient servant,
SERGEANT OF POLICE

I confess that from this time on a mediaeval vigilance ruled whatsoever we did. If we entered the Raven meadows, we took good care not to stroll too close to the woods: if we used the car, we were careful to waste no time on the neighbouring roads: if we sat out in the evening, Winter patrolled our vicinity, torch in hand: and at night, against all custom, the doors of the house were barred.

Herrick visited Salzburg against his will, and viewed the corpse of the man we had known as Max. No evidence had been discovered – against Virgil or anyone else. Even the bullet was useless, for it had spread irreparably. The same day, Thursday, Elizabeth, resting at Raven, laid her plans, I sat by her side in the meadows, and listened – and watched the woods.

The Duchess of Whelp was at Tracery, thirty-five miles from Innsbruck and ninety from where we lay. Tales out of number were told of the state she had kept, of the things she had said and done, of the efforts which had been made to obtain an invitation to enter her house. If the half were true, it is clear that for years before the War, the Château of Tracery sheltered the second Court. And now, though she shut herself up, her writ still ran; and though the 'fountain of honour' no longer played, its peaceful pool was reflecting, as never before, the vivid presence now nearly eighty years old.

"I shall go there tomorrow," said my lady. "And you, if you please, will drive me – there and back. At least, we'll be breaking a record. No one's gone uninvited to Tracery for certainly fifty years."

"With all my heart," said I. "But won't you take Winter, too? I mean, it'll look more important than if you just roll up with me at the wheel."

Elizabeth seemed to reflect.

At length –

"Perhaps you're right," she murmured, pulling the grass. "I wish I knew what to expect. I know that she visited Brief very shortly before I was born, and my grandfather knew her well: but my – my uncle has never seen her since Mother was killed."

I sat up at that.

"Are you sure that he saw her before?"

Elizabeth started, and a hand went up to her head, "My God," she breathed.

"Exactly," said I. "I'll lay he's never set eyes on the Duchess of Whelp. Your *father* saw her – and knew her: but the younger son – the 'bad hat' – was not at Brief when she came. He can't deny her visit, because he knows it took place. It was a great occasion. Brief was delighted to honour so rare a guest. *And so your uncle is bound to pretend he was there. But he wasn't* – because he isn't the man he pretends to be: and all he knows of her visit is what he's picked up from the staff."

"That's right," said Elizabeth, slowly, still pulling the grass. "What a fool you must think me for not having seen it myself."

"How can you?" I cried. "I've known the truth for a year, and you for less than a week."

"I suppose that's why I am so stupid. You can't wipe out all at once an impression of twenty years. And that's what we're up against. He's Count of Brief by prescription. To pull him down is like trying to close some road that everyone's used for ages and knows for a thoroughfare."

"Perhaps. But at least you're offering them a very much prettier way."

Elizabeth Virgil flung out a joyous laugh.

"Oh, Richard, a compliment! I must be good for you. You couldn't have said that last week."

"I know," I said, very conscious that I was red in the face. "I – I see the things, but I haven't got Herrick's tongue."

"What things do you see?"

"Your – your points," I stammered. "Your beauty. Your eyes and your mouth and your hands, and the way you move. They – they cry out for recognition: but I haven't got any words. Only please don't think I don't see them – and all the rest. Perhaps if they weren't so rare, I'd be able to – to pay them tribute: but when I see – perfection, it leaves me dumb."

With her eyes on the shimmering foliage, my lady touched my arm.

"Stay dumb, for me," she said gently. "It suits you well, and I – couldn't ask any more."

I wiped the sweat from my face.

"You always say the right thing."

"Do I?" said Elizabeth, frowning. "I'm not so sure."

But when I asked what she meant, she would not tell me, but bade me talk of Oxford and Harrow and then of the smiling manor which till I was eight years old had been my home.

At eleven o'clock the next day I stood with my hat in my hand at the foot of Tracery's steps. Elizabeth stood at their head, some ten feet up. We were waiting for the door to be opened, in some suspense. A liveried keeper had stopped us while we were yet in the drive and had been hardly persuaded to let us proceed.

At last the door was opened, and a man all in black, with knee-breeches, inclined his head.

His manner was ceremonious and very polite, but left in my mind no doubt that he did not mean to admit 'The Lady Elizabeth Virgil' or anyone else.

When he had finished speaking, I saw my lady nod. Then she held out the little packet she had in her hand. A salver appeared from nowhere...

I do not know what she said, as she laid the packet down, but after a little I saw the man bow and turn and Elizabeth cross the threshold into the hall.

At least, she was in: but, as the door was shut and I turned to the car, I confess I felt far from sure that she was to be received. And if she was not, what then? The packet contained no less than the king's great ring, with which she was hoping to gain the access she so much desired. If the Duchess of Whelp was scrupulous, well and good: but if she was not, Elizabeth would be dismissed – and the ring was gone. And 'Old Harry' might well be hostile to a girl that made bold to remind her that the bearings which Tracery flaunted were rightly hers.

I sat down on a step of the Rolls and lighted a cigarette, while Winter stood like a statue beside his charge, determined, I think, to show that he could maintain the pace which the major-domo had set.

The house was imposing, but grim, and plainly had not been cared for for several years. Massively built of stone, wind and weather could do but little harm, but rust was corrupting the bars to the lower windows and the stain of roof-water showed where the gutters were choked. The entrance-drive was unkempt, and grass was here and there sprouting between the setts of the apron which served the steps. The park, which was very handsome, was not kept up: posts and rails were rotting, and trees which the wind had felled lay still as they had fallen, the clods which their roots had hoisted stuck all with weeds.

These things I found peculiar, for rumour had it the Duchess of Whelp was rich. But I think the truth was this – that when she had closed her Court, she had determined to let its residence go. What was the setting to her, when the jewel was gone?

Nearly an hour had gone by, when the door was opened again and the major-domo appeared and began to descend the steps. Expecting some message, I rose and went to meet him, and then I saw that he was an Englishman.

As I approached, he stood still.

"Sir," he said, with a bow, "Her Grace desires to see you. If you please, I will show you the way to her private rooms."

His announcement took me aback, as well it might: but, though the summons shook me, my heart leaped up, for it meant that 'Old Harry's' interest had been aroused. And that was everything.

To my surprise, three footmen stood at the door, but the echoing hall within was that of a house whose owner had gone abroad. Furniture and pictures were shrouded and carpets rolled, but the marble floor was spotless and there was no sign of dust.

We passed up a glorious staircase, the carpet of which was gone, by draped or hooded statues and sheeted tapestry, to enter a sunlit gallery down which three four-in-hands could have passed abreast. Its range of open windows commanded the wasting park, and, when it was in commission, it must have enriched the eye. I never saw proportions more lovely in all my life and, if you except kings' houses, there can be existing few chambers so pleasant and yet so royal. At the gallery's farther end a woman-servant was standing beside a door. To her I was delivered, and at once she ushered me into a drawing-room. This was small and stiff, but, though it showed no sign of having been lately used, its furniture was not shrouded and a carpet covered the floor.

The woman, who looked very sour, addressed me in German and indicated a chair, and, when I had taken my seat, she passed to another door. As she opened this, I saw that it gave to a passage some six feet long. She closed the door behind her as though, I thought, she was happy to shut me out, and I can only suppose that I looked as much out of my depth as indeed I felt. Within thirty seconds, however, the door was opened again, and she beckoned me to approach. As I did so, I saw that a second door was now open at the farther end of the passage I had observed. Through this the woman pointed, and stood back against the wall, for me to go by. I passed her and entered the room, and the door behind me was shut.

I stood in a spacious bedroom, splendidly furnished in the Italian style. Gold leaf, and velvet and beautifully painted wood; lantern and plaque and mirror; silver, dusky crimson and mellowed green made up a stately harmony of lovely things. In their midst, commanding them all from its dais, a great state bedstead stood with its head to the wall. And sitting up in bed was Her Grace the Duchess of Whelp.

The room was full of light, and I saw her well. A highly elaborate coiffure attired her head, and a richly embroidered vesture swathed her from throat to wrist, but once I had seen her face, I had no eyes for anything else in that room. That this was painted was nothing – motley could not diminish the light of her countenance. Her cheeks were raddled, her lashes were stiff and laden, her lips were a scarlet blotch: but the visage thus overlaid was above these things. It was handsome as an eagle's is handsome – with a cold majesty of feature, heedless of the sense of minority which it imposed. Her nose was aquiline and its bridge was high: her chin was jutting: her mouth was firm to a fault: her eyes, which were grey, were piercing and very clear; and the whole of her face was very finely shaped and might have been that of a woman of fifty years. Looking upon it, I knew that I was in the presence of something extremely rare – a ruling personality, that had no need to order because it controlled.

I bowed – something awkwardly, dimly aware of Elizabeth sitting beside the bed and smiling at me to tell me that all was well.

Old Harry inclined her head.

"How do you do, Mr Exon. Come here, if you please."

I stepped to her side, and she put out a hand which was blazing with three magnificent rings.

I took the fingers in mine and put them to my lips

"That's right," says she. "I may be of bastard stock but – "

"I think you are above lineage, madam."

"Nowadays, yes," said Old Harry, folding her arms. "But it gave me a flying start. And now let's talk about you. I'm told you're a man of action, and so it seems. But you're not very quick off the mark." She tapped the papers that lay on her delicate quilt. "This Gering business. Why did you wait so long?"

"For two reasons, madam," said I. "First, for several months I was not myself. I found life hard to handle and had no brains to spare for anything else. And then I shrank from interference with a state of affairs which had been established so long."

"And then you saw Percy Virgil?"

"Yes," said I. "He's – he's not a nice-looking man."

"He'd look very well from a gallows," observed the Duchess of Whelp. She turned to Elizabeth. "What made you allow Mr Exon to carry you off?"

"That," said Elizabeth, "is what I keep asking him."

"Sex," said Old Harry, firmly. "You liked subjecting yourself to the strength of the male. It's been done before. The Sabines kicked and screamed for the look of the thing: as a matter of hard fact, they were tickled to death." She turned upon me. "And what do you mean, Richard Exon, by hiding this lady at Raven for over a week?"

Her attack was so sudden that I was taken aback.

"Madam," I said, "it seemed the best thing to do."

"Did it, indeed?" said Old Harry. "Well, God preserve us all from your benevolence. The Lady Elizabeth Virgil, for whom the cities of Europe are being surreptitiously scoured, sharing two young men's lodgings ten miles from her father's house! And who's this Herrick person? I knew a Naseby once…"

"He's one of the best," said I. "And he pulls far more than his weight. As a matter of fact, he's the present Lord Naseby's heir."

"His mother," said Elizabeth gently, "was my mother's greatest friend."

"You're not staying with his mother," snapped Old Harry. "By consenting to do as you did, you were playing straight into the hands of father and son. Supposing you'd been discovered… Brief would have seen his chance and have flattened you out. He'd have trumpeted the scandal, played the outraged father and ordered his erring daughter out of his sight. 'Never darken my doors again.' *And you would have had to go* – your cousin would have seen to that. Father fooled, police fooled, Austria fooled – because you desired a weekend with a couple of men. And ring or no ring, I couldn't have helped you at all. I used to be able to drop a soul-shaking hint, but I've never mastered the art of raising the dead."

There was a little silence, only disturbed by the sleeveless fret of a bee on a window pane.

At length –

"You should blame me, madam," I said. "That Elizabeth should stay at Raven was my idea."

"Are you proud of it, Richard Exon?"

"No, I'm not," said I. "I'm greatly ashamed."

"Good," said Old Harry. "In future stick to your last. Take action – that's your forte. But never reflect. From what I hear, you have instinct – a precious faculty. Well, be content with that – and drown your ideas at birth. And now take a seat." She touched a chair by her side. As I did her bidding, she turned to Elizabeth. "What were you going to tell me about your mother's jewels?"

Elizabeth recited the facts.

When she had done, Old Harry wrinkled her brows.

"I'm not surprised that your cousin found you *de trop*. That he's drawn and sold the gems, there can be no doubt. And that by forgery. Now the English are a tolerant lot. They'll overlook treason and fight for a murderer's life, while a healthy theft in England is nearly always worthwhile. But they've always loathed forgery – probably because they feel that it isn't playing the game. Witness, your poor father... Now Cousin Percy has committed that 'loathsome' crime. *But yours is the only voice that can send him down.* Without you, he can't be arrested, much less arraigned. With you, he is doomed... And so you had to go. The sheep must be stolen to cover the theft of the lamb. I think it likely that you would have gone any way: but if he was to have the jewels, he obviously had to get them before he put you out... I'm afraid he's an egoist. And you had him at your mercy, Mr Exon. In the dark...on a steep, stone stair... I hope you won't have cause for regret that you let him live."

I swallowed before replying.

"Madam," I said, "we English are a tolerant lot."

"I know, I know. A very charming defect. But prevention is better than cure. That's Percy's motto, you know. Never mind. You were awkwardly placed. And now do I know everything? Or have you omitted some detail which you think of no account?"

Together, Elizabeth and I went faithfully over the ground, while the Duchess interposed questions and comments, frequently acid, on what we had to relate. Finally, she glanced at a clock.

"Lunch," she said, "will be served in a quarter of an hour. For you two: in the Medici room. After that, you may sit on the terrace until I send. I must think this matter over. I don't want to let you down, but I can't make bricks without straw."

With that the door was opened and the woman-servant appeared. This, as though by magic; but she must, of course, have been summoned, and I think that a bell-push was lying beneath the quilt. As we got to our feet –

"You are very kind, madam," said Elizabeth.

"No, I'm not," said the Duchess, shortly. "As usual, I'm pleasing myself. And don't look at me like that, unless you want to be kissed. I used to be much admired – some fifty years back. But I never belonged to the class of Helen of Troy."

I saw Elizabeth stoop, and made my way to the door.

We could not talk freely at table, for never less than three men were constantly in the room. The meal was royally served, and the dishes set before us were fit for a king. All the appointments were flawless, and, ruled by the major-domo, the footmen moved and waited as though their duty had been tirelessly rehearsed.

At these things I shall always wonder, for Elizabeth told me later that months had passed since the Duchess had left her room, while no guest had been entertained for nearly two years. Indeed, I can only submit that they showed forth Old Harry's dominion as nothing else could have done. The palace was out of commission, its mistress was out of sight: and yet, at a nod from her, the machinery sprang to life, to move with all the precision of practised vigilance.

Coffee was served upon the terrace, above an Italian garden, run to seed. And there we were left to ourselves – and the lizards that stared and darted over the mouldering stone.

"She deserves her fame," said Elizabeth. "I know no more than you what line she's going to take: but whatever she does, I haven't wasted my time, because I have seen and talked with 'Harriet the Great'."

(Here let me say that that surname does her justice as can no periods. A few men and women have borne it, since Time was young. If she had had as fair fields, I have no doubt that she would have borne it, too.)

"I wish," said I, "she was not confined to her bed."

"She isn't," said Elizabeth, swiftly. "She stays there because she likes it. She told me so. She said she had crowded so much into fifty years that she never had time to digest 'the brilliant burden they held'. And now she is doing that. She goes leisurely through her diaries, considering in detail the play which, because she was leading, she never saw."

"And she never gets up?"

"Never. She says that the mental exercise keeps her perfectly fit and the more she rests her body, the clearer her brain becomes."

I felt rather dazed. There were more things at Tracery than were dreamt of in my philosophy.

"Her English," I said, "is better than that of an English judge."

Elizabeth nodded.

"And she's right up to date," she said. "She's a wireless set by her bed, and books and papers from England come to her all the time. She has agents in London, New York and Paris, whose only business is to keep her informed. Say Shakespeare's right and 'all the world's a stage'. For fifty years she was playing a leading part. Well, now she sits in a box and watches the play."

"Talk of yourself, Elizabeth."

My lady laughed.

"As you saw, she was sweet to me. And her brain's like mercury. When I came in, 'Why you and not Brief?' she said. I gave her the statement at once. She read it through in silence. Then – 'I beg your pardon,' she said. 'It seems you are Brief. No need to ask why you're here, but who opened your eyes?' I told her all you had done. 'And here's a man,' she said. 'Don't let him go. I may or may not help you: but such a man's little finger is thicker than my old loins.' "

Before I had time to expose this ridiculous estimate, the major-domo was approaching – to give me the shock of my life.

"By your ladyship's leave, Her Grace will receive Mr Exon without delay."

Elizabeth smiled and nodded, and, begging her to excuse me, I got to my feet.

Two minutes later I stood before Old Harry, as a sheep before her shearers is dumb.

The piercing eyes held mine, as a magnet the steel.

"Mr Exon, I have formed of you a very pleasant opinion, and I am usually right. But I must request your assurance upon one point. That is that you are aware that you cannot possibly marry the Countess of Brief."

The bedroom went black about me, and the blood surged into my face. And I felt as though something had taken me by the throat.

Somehow I answered thickly.

"I am well aware of that, madam."

"Good," said Old Harry, agreeably. "I thought as much, but I simply had to be sure. And now come here and sit down, and I'll do the talking until you've got your breath." As I took my seat, her hand went on to my shoulder and held it tight. "Always remember – those things cannot be helped. I loved a commoner once, and he loved me. But there are some bars, Richard Exon, more rigid than those you loosed. So we both of us did our duty. He bowed and went, and I married the Duke of Whelp. And, all things considered, it turned out extremely well... And you are the only person to whom I have ever told that – not because no one else would believe me (though that is a fact), but because I have met no one else for whose sake I felt disposed to open an ancient wound."

I believe that I thanked her there, but I cannot be sure. I was like a man sunk in deep water, whose senses are out of hand because his soul is possessed by a frantic instinct to rise.

I had harboured no hopes, of course. But, because I was only human, I had made me a dream to play with – a pretty dream. And now, as one takes from a child a toy that may do him harm, the Duchess of Whelp had taken away my dream. Though I knew she was right, the knowledge did me no good. As a child, I could have burst into tears – and very near did. 'From him that hath not shall be taken away even that which he hath.'

Old Harry was speaking again.

"I have no other questions. Fate, that great producer, has cast you for one of the parts in this highly intimate play, and I am far too wise to question her choice. Besides, I think it's a good one – to date you've done very well. So I'm going to treat you as an equal – 'the play's the thing'.

"Elizabeth, as you know, has invoked my help to dispossess her uncle of the birthright which he stole from her father some twenty-one years ago. Her request is a natural one, for it is her bounden duty to do her best to bring this parricide down. But, while I am generally bound to respond to her call, I am not bound to make a fool of myself. If she likes to wish for the moon and comes crying to me, I have every right in the world to send her empty away. Do you agree, or don't you? Not that I care a curse, but I may as well know."

"I agree with you, madam," said I. "The request must be reasonable."

"Very good. What is her request? Not to reach her the moon, but to help her uproot a tree which is more than twenty years old. 'All right,' say I. 'It certainly cumbers the earth and it ought to come down. Where are your tools?' " She slapped the quilt with her palm. "Mr Exon, she *has* no tools. And neither have I.

"You're a very strong man, Mr Exon. I'd have liked very much to see you break into Brief. But could you with your bare hands uproot a tree which was more than twenty years old?"

"Madam," said I, "if Elizabeth Virgil asked me, I'd have a hell of a try."

Old Harry sighed.

"I suppose you would," she said slowly. "But you know as well as I that you'd make a fool of yourself. And can you fairly require such devotion from me?"

At her words my heart leaped up, for they showed that she had accepted the fact that I was in love and did not propose to deny me such crumbs of comfort as I could pick out of that state.

"Madam," I said boldly, " 'the play's the thing'."

"Perhaps it is. But I'm damned if I'm going on in a knock-about turn. *Whelp and Exon, Comics.* I'm much obliged, but I'm past the tramp-cyclist stage."

I threw back my head and laughed till the tears came into my eyes.

"That's better," said the Duchess of Whelp. "But please observe that I have to debase my coinage to make you smile."

"Madam," said I, "I have yet to learn that a sense of humour is depreciatory."

"Good for you," said Old Harry. "And now let metaphor go. For me to move in this matter would be to fail: and for me to fail in this matter would bring me into derision, if not contempt." As I made to protest, she held up a sparkling hand. "I don't expect you to agree. You'd cheerfully sell my soul to buy your pretty darling an easy hour. But what I say is true, and, though you will not admit it, you know it as well as I. Very well. Now listen to me. *I am going to move in this matter, cost what it may.* And this, not because I am bound, for nobody can be bound to bring themselves into contempt; but because, if I do not do something, Elizabeth, Countess of Brief, is going to lose her life."

Before this blunt prediction, the thanksgiving which I had ready, died on my lips: and I think that I must have turned pale, for the Duchess surveyed me grimly and then went straight to the point.

"I seem to have shocked you, Mr Exon."

"Naturally, madam. I – "

" 'Naturally' my foot," snapped Old Harry, and flounced in her bed. "It isn't natural at all. It you weren't a fool, Richard Exon, you wouldn't have to be shown what an infant in arms would remark."

"Madam," said I, "you told me not to reflect."

"I didn't say 'Shut your eyes.' I didn't say 'Look through the obvious, as though it didn't exist'."

I made no answer to that, and after a pregnant pause the Duchess went on.

"In her cousin's sight, the removal of Elizabeth was always to be desired. Once he had forged her name, her removal became expedient – I think that's clear. But in view of what has occurred in the last seven days, her removal is now *essential* to Percy Virgil's health. A week ago she could have sent him to prison for seven years: today she can send him to the gallows for the murder of Max. Why? Because she – and nobody else – can switch on that current which makes all evidence live. *Motive*. Prove the theft of the jewels, and you prove the abduction: prove the abduction and you prove the murder of Max…" The sweat was out on my face, but still Old Harry laid on. "Do you see now, Richard Exon? Have I chipped the scales from your eyes? Now do you see why I deplored your omission to kill that man when you held his life in your hands? Because, the instant he knows that his victim is safe, the dog will return to his vomit and use his utmost endeavours without delay to put your darling to death."

I can set down the words she spoke, but I cannot present the sinister note she sounded or the dreadful air of conviction she lent to her prophecy. Enough that she shook me so much that, without knowing what I did, I made to get up; but she laid a hand on my arm, to bid me sit still.

"There, there, Richard Exon," she said; "don't take it so hard. We are not going to let it happen. Between us, we shall be able to curb the power of the dog. And don't go and brood on your failure to read sharp practice at sight. My acquaintance with evil is very much wider than yours, and I have known men *and* women beside whom Percy Virgil is almost a philanthropist. I need hardly say that all were far too clever to run any kind of risk, and that I have nothing to prove what I know to be true. Wilful murder is by no means uncommon in this respectable world, and if, at some given signal, its victims could rise from the dead, you'd be surprised at the number of loving tombstones which their ascent would displace. But that's by the way. Just don't lose sight of two things – first, that any day now Virgil is going to turn into a desperate man; and, secondly, that if you come into collision, you must not expect him to keep to the Queensberry rules. Oh, and one thing more. All that has passed so far is between you and me. Elizabeth is to believe that I have come into this business because I desire to honour my ancestress' bond."

"May I tell Herrick, madam?"

Old Harry wrinkled her nose.

Then –

"Yes," she said. "He should know. If he resembled his uncle, he wouldn't be 'one of the best '."

"Lord Naseby dislikes him," I said.

"*Ça va sans dire*. To find favour in Naseby's eyes, you must be sanctimonious and servile and reap where you have not sown. He demands, but never supplies, and he still has family prayers. But I understand he's failing."

"Herrick gives him another three years."

The Duchess picked up a tablet and made a note.

"I'll have that checked," she said, and laughed at the look on my face. "My agents are paid to find out what I want to know. Some people, when they retire, devote themselves to the study of bygone days; each to his taste, of course, but I've always preferred a live ass to a decomposed lion. For me, the creation took place some sixty years back, and while I respect the ages that went before, the present is the dunghill on which I shall always scratch.

"And now to business.

"Elizabeth must stay here – no doubt about that. You will return to Raven, to fetch her things. Nothing of hers must be left there, and everyone living at Raven must forget her visit as though it had never been. Very well. Tonight I shall write to Brief." She picked up a pencilled sheet. "And this is what I shall say.

"I have the pleasure to inform you that the Lady Elizabeth Virgil is now at Tracery, happily none the worse. I am loth to part with her – I wish I had known her before – and since her place is at Brief, she has persuaded me to restore her to you myself. This will entail a visit: but the occasion warrants a breach of the rule I have made, and you may expect us on Tuesday at five o'clock.

"I had invited to stay at Tracery a Mr John Herrick, whose uncle I used to know. He is staying at Raven, by Dever, not far from you. Since I cannot now receive him, I shall be obliged if he and his friend, Mr Exon, may be invited to Brief for the length of my stay.

"Now I think that will do very well.

"You see, Brief can't refuse to do as I ask: and so we shall all be together within the enemy's camp. Brief will be ill at ease, because he will have to pretend to be the brother I knew. And Virgil won't be at his best, not only for reasons we know, but because to entertain Herrick will undoubtedly shorten his life.

"I've set the stage, Richard Exon: and on Tuesday at five o'clock, the curtain will rise. But I can't give out any parts, because I have none to give. The performance will be improvised, but it shouldn't be dull."

That I was staggered, I must most frankly confess. At most I had been expecting that the Duchess would give me some orders and, possibly, hint at the line she was going to take. Instead, she had laid before me a vivid line of action – bold, clean-cut and sweeping, to be put into force at once. I think the truth is that my powers of conception were strained. The nut to be cracked was so hard that she had not had time enough to lay any plan: yet there was the plan before me, consummate and unexceptionable.

Old Harry continued slowly.

"We have no choice in this case, but to take the bull by the horns. Sooner or later, Elizabeth must go back: and if Brief is to be unseated, we are not going to bring that off without coming to grips. Besides, a change of air will do my digestion good. And now you be off, young man." I got to my feet. "See your darling first and send her to me. How long will it take you to get to Raven and back?"

"Madam," I said, "I can do it in less than five hours."

The Duchess glanced at the clock, which said it was a quarter past two.

"Then do it in six," she said, "and dine here at half-past eight. Bring Mr Herrick with you. What are you going to say to that very beautiful girl?"

"Madam," I said, "I shall quote from the Queen of Sheba. 'Behold, the half was not told to me'."

Old Harry smiled. "I like your style," she said gently. "Partly because you always mean what you say." She put out her hand for mine.

"Try to look upon her as a picture – a glorious museum-piece. Find her exquisite, Richard: but glaze her – rope yourself off. Start doing that now. It'll cost you something, of course. But you'll find it a good investment...before you're through."

"Madam," I said hoarsely, "I'll engage you never did that."

The piercing eyes grew sightless.

"I know," said Old Harry, slowly. "That's why I hope that you will."

7

Love Upon the Terrace

The festival held that evening in Tracery's Medici Room was one of such intimate splendour of matter and mind that, though I subscribed to it, when first I awoke the next morning, I wondered if it was not a dream.

I sat between two Old Masters – on the left of the Duchess of Whelp and the right of the Countess of Brief. Each glowed with the sterling quality of a forgotten age. Lost arts made up their being. Sheer beauty lived with kindness: sheer brilliance beamed with goodwill. And each admiring the other was thus exalted. Their natural royalty was duly served. Powdered footmen in scarlet livery stood behind every chair: gold plate winked upon the table: the choicest fare was perfectly presented.

And there I will leave an event which neither Herrick nor I will ever forget, for that evening we two hobnobbed with the stuff that queens were made of in olden days.

That Herrick found instant favour, I need not say. Indeed, Old Harry and he were as good as a play, for, as I have said before, his address was beyond compare, and I think that each of them whetted the other's wit.

When dinner was done, Herrick and I were left with orders to 'join the ladies' in ten minutes' time: and when that had gone, we were led to a glorious salon, whose sixteenth-century tapestries filled the eye. These were so very lovely and were so cunningly lighted and cleverly hung that you had the rare illusion that you were not confined by walls, but were standing on some high place, commanding a living landscape of which the depth and detail bewildered sight. (I afterwards learned that they were beyond all price; that they had been woven in Flanders of threads of gold and silver, as well as of silk and wool; and that they had been designed by a master, to please a king.)

Though the evening was warm, a fire of logs had been lighted upon the hearth: before this the Duchess was resting upon a mighty *chaise longue*, and Elizabeth was standing beside a jamb of the fireplace, one of her beautiful hands on the chiselled stone, regarding the leisurely flicker that hovered above a hillock of rose-grey ash.

As the door closed behind us –

"I have ordered your car," said Old Harry, "for half-past ten. That gives us just half an hour, which should be enough. I've one or two things to say, and I'll say them first.

"I think we all know where we are and where we shall be next Tuesday at five o'clock. On no account try to conceal that we have already met. That way madness lies. We have all met here tonight – for the very first time. Let no one be ill at ease. Except for Richard Exon, I don't think anyone will."

"Oh, madam," protested Herrick.

"Don't interrupt," said Old Harry. "Besides, you'd be at ease with a gaggle of Elders discussing the wrath to come."

I very near laughed and Elizabeth covered her mouth.

"If you feel uneasy, Richard, always remember at once that though Brief is doing the honours, you are Elizabeth's guest. And that, I think, should bring your confidence back. You will take your man, Winter, with you, and I shall take three servants to look after me. One will be Parish – that excellent English page whom you have already seen. Should need arise, we can communicate through them, with all convenience. Tell the police that you have been invited to Brief, as you understand, to meet me. That will set you above all suspicion, such is this snobbish world.

"One thing more.

"As luck will have it, Elizabeth's mother's jewels were held by the firm of goldsmiths whom I have always employed. Bauble and Levity – you probably know the name. She has, therefore, written to them to say that by my advice she will have the gems reset and desiring them to be ready with new designs against her coming to London in six weeks' time. That letter will send the ball flying: and since she gave this address, the reply will come to this house and will go on to Brief by hand, in my private bag.

"And now can anyone think of anything else? Because, if they can, let us have it – for better or worse. We shan't see each other again until we strut on to the stage."

There was a little silence.

"Very good," said Old Harry. "And now I want to see Mr Herrick alone. Take your leave of me, Richard, and then make the best of the terrace, until Mr Herrick appears. Elizabeth will go with you."

I stepped to her side.

"Madam," I said, "I have much to thank you for."

"I don't know about that. Never mind. I've much enjoyed your visit – and that's a thing I can say to very few guests."

"Thank you. Madam." I put her hand to my lips. "I hope you're not very tired."

"Tired be damned," said Old Harry. "I never felt so fit in my life."

"Till Tuesday, madam."

The Duchess smiled and nodded, and I followed Elizabeth out of the handsome chamber and, presently, into the air.

As though Nature were on her mettle, the world seemed to be without end and the terrace was magnified. The moon, which was low in heaven, was whiting the flags with silver and slanting a print of the parapet down their length; and the sleeping country beyond had the look of a spreading woodcut, from which all imperfection was done away.

Elizabeth led the way to the head of the steps.

"It's all your doing," she said.

"Which is absurd," said I. "She's mad about you."

"My dear, you gave her the lead. I had a claim upon her. How could she fail me, when you, upon whom I had none had done so much?"

I shook my head.

"You must thank yourself," I said. "I saw you – and that was enough. And as with me, so with her. The king's ring got you inside: but, once you were in – well, supposing you'd asked for the moon, she might have told you off, but when she was through, she'd have sent for a pair of steps."

Elizabeth laughed. Then she slid her arm through mine.

"I wish I was going with you I've been so happy at Raven: and if this morning I'd dreamed that I shouldn't come back, I – I wouldn't have gone. It may have been out of order, but I know I'd jump at the chance to do it again. I've...much enjoyed...my 'weekend with a couple of men'."

"They'll miss you terribly, Elizabeth."

"Sit in the meadow tomorrow – I'll think of you there. Close to the stream – by yourself: between lunch and tea. And, if I can, I'll sit here – at the head of the steps. Oh, and please be very careful and always go armed. Remember, he knows where you are, and the woods about Raven are thick."

"I promise," I said. "And on Tuesday..."

"On Tuesday I'll see you again. And on Wednesday we'll ride before breakfast – that's natural enough. Besides, it'll be my joy to entertain you as a guest."

"I'll never be easy," I said, "when you're out of my sight. Here I know that you're safe: but at Brief…" I drew in my breath. "Can you trust your maid? I think she should sleep in your suite."

"Perhaps you're right. I'll see what Old Harry says."

"I'd be easier, Elizabeth. You see, by day I can always be within call. But by night I can't. And if you want me to sleep – well, you'll do as I ask."

My lady lifted her head to the lambent sky.

"You don't look back," she said, "do you – when you've put your hand to the plough? You're not going to rest till – till you've carried me out of the wood?"

"Men don't lay down their honours before their time."

"And then?"

"They lay them down," I said slowly: "and go their way."

There was a little silence.

"What way shall you go, Richard?"

I drew myself up.

"I don't know. Perhaps John Herrick will help me. We might do something together, until Lord Naseby dies. But I'll always be at your service. You'll only have to call me. I'll always come."

"Why do you say that, Richard?"

"Because you have made me your servant – for as long as I live."

"I don't want you to be my servant."

I laughed at that.

"Then you shouldn't have your eyes, or your mouth, or your beautiful ways. You shouldn't move as you do, or throw a smile over your shoulder, or push back your hair from your temples with one of your lovely hands. And you shouldn't have your nature – which makes a man want to pay tribute with all his heart."

"And what does he get – in return?"

"He's paid in advance," said I. "That very question shows that you don't understand. To have to do with you is to run into debt – your debt. And at once one's instinct is to do what little one can to pay you back."

Elizabeth raised her eyebrows.

"I'm afraid you're an idealist, Richard. And that's a mistake, my dear. Red Lead Lane should have shown you... But then the complete idealist never learns. If it makes you happy to set me up in a niche, why then you must have your way. I'll smile upon you from there. And sometimes, when you're not looking, I might climb down and be a good-looking girl, with the usual human passions, a weakness for animals and a definite love of dress." She plucked at her frock. "Can there any good thing come out of Salzburg? My dear, you wait. If you like the look of me now, you'll get up and walk at Brief."

"There spoke Old Harry," said I: "but not Elizabeth."

She whipped her arm out of mine and started aside.

"What ever d'you mean?"

I set my hands on her shoulders and turned her round.

"That you are a work of nature and she is a work of art. And you cannot play on her piano, and she cannot play on your pipe. I think you only did it to – to make me alter my focus and see that you're not the nonesuch I think you are. But it only upsets me, my lady, and doesn't do any good. I know you've got failings – you must have, because you're of flesh and blood: but you're rather exceptional, – 'The heaven such grace did lend her, That she might admired be'. Well, you must let me admire you in my own way."

All right," said Elizabeth, meekly. But don't bring me garlands, Richard. I couldn't bear that.

"You wicked girl. You – "

"That's better. And there's John coming. Say goodbye nicely. Quick."

She had put up her beautiful mouth, and I had stooped and kissed it before I knew where I was.

So much for Old Harry's counsel. So much for the voice within me that told me that she was right. So much for the knowledge that I was hastening to that terrible valley of torment, where hearts are broken in pieces and the light of the eyes is put out. Indeed, from that time on, so far as I was concerned, the future cared for itself. For me, the wind was with me, the tide was full; and though I knew I must shipwreck and could see that coast of iron upon which I must come to grief, I gloried in my present condition, found myself the favourite of Fortune and rejoiced as a giant to run my desperate course.

Though I have not said as much, to please Elizabeth, Herrick and I had gone armed for exactly a week; and a pistol had been purchased for Winter, because we had only two. Approaching and leaving Raven, we used to sit with these drawn, for, if we were to be ambushed, the road which ran down to the farm especially favoured attack: and though, of course, it was clear that if we were fired upon, we should be hit or missed long before we could use our arms, by having them drawn we should at least be ready to make some sort of reply.

It was half-past one in the morning before we once more entered this dangerous zone, and, remembering Old Harry's words, I found myself thanking God that Elizabeth was not with us and would not have to run such a gauntlet again. Thus thinking upon the matter, I presently grew quite sure that we were to be attacked, and, since I was driving, I made Herrick take my pistol because; for once in a way, he had left his behind.

He did so reluctantly.

"And at what do I fire?" he said. "At the spot where the rude noise came from before I was plugged? Before I have time to reply, we must be out of range. I mean, that's our only chance. We can come back after they've gone and have a smell round, but this is a place to come first to – or not at all." As I slowed for the first of the bends, he continued ruefully. "Of course, I wasn't meant to carry a gun. It spoils the set of my coat and all day long it gives me a series of shocks. And I think the swine likes warmth: if I don't watch it, I find it nursing my groin... I hope to God Brenda's all right. So as not to forget it, I left it out on my bed. Let's hope she's had the sense to leave it alone."

Winter lifted his voice.

"I don't think she'd touch it, sir. I showed her mine last night and I warned her off."

"Good," said Herrick. "All the same, she'd have to touch it, if she was to make the bed..."

Our alarms were without foundation.

We were not fired upon, and Raven was fast asleep. And since we were very tired, we shared a bottle of beer and stumbled upstairs.

I had put on my pyjamas, when Herrick opened my door.

"What d'you make of this?" he said. "The firearm has gone."

"Gone?" said I, staring.

"Gone," said Herrick. "As I told you just now, I left it out on the bed. Well, the bed's been made: so, of course, it had to be moved. But it's not in the room."

"It must be," said I. "You've missed it."

"Come and see," said Herrick, and led the way.

For full five minutes we sought it, and sought it in vain.

At length –

"Brenda must have it," said I. "The thing's not here."

"I don't think that's likely," said Herrick, "in view of what Winter said. And yet I can hardly believe that Percy Elbert the Good would steal it away. And tell me another thing. Why do these crises arise, when one is so drunk with sleep that one can hardly stand up?"

With that, he sank heavily down on the foot of his bed.

As he did so a deafening explosion made me jump out of my skin, and, in one most frantic convulsion, Herrick leaped upward and outward, as though propelled by some spring.

"My God," said I, and ripped the quilt from the bed.

Twelve inches from the foot of the bedstead, a broad-arrow ruck in the blanket declared that *below* the blanket something had moved.

I turned to Herrick.

"Are you all right?"

His hands clapped fast to his seat –

"Well, I'm still the same shape," said Herrick, "if that's what you mean: but you can't sit down on a land-mine and be as good as you were."

Someone was running on the landing.

Then Winter appeared in the doorway – and Brenda wide-eyed behind him, with one of her hands to her throat.

"Nobody's hurt," said I. "Mr Herrick's pistol went off. Where did you put it, Brenda? I mean, when you made the bed."

"On the chest of drawers, sir" – pointing.

"I see," said I. "And what time did you make the bed?"

"At six o'clock, sir. As a rule I make it at nine: but, as you were out to dinner, I made it before."

"And then?"

"I visited my cousins at Monein, and spent the evening with them."

"Well, that's all right," said I. "You go back to bed. Let your father and mother believe that we fired by mistake."

"I will do that," said Brenda: "but please may I know the truth?"

"It's simple enough," said I. "As soon as you'd left for Monein, somebody entered this house and came up to this room. They took Mr Herrick's pistol, which you had laid over there, and put it into his bed. Before they put it in, they put down the safety catch. And they laid it with its mouth to the pillow – that ruck shows that: on firing, the pistol kicked and shifted towards the foot... Now they've very light triggers – these things. Mr Herrick touched it off by sitting on the edge of the bed. But if he'd got into his bed in the ordinary way, and had touched it off with his foot – *as somebody meant him to do...*"

"I think," said Brenda, quietly, "that the sooner that man is in jail, the better for all of us."

"I entirely agree," said I: "but how can we prove he was here this afternoon? More. If he were asked his movements, I'll wager that he could prove he was fifty miles off."

Herrick was inspecting the bed.

"The muzzle," he said, "is now pointing rather that way. If, therefore, we stand on this side and loosen the sheet..."

We did so gingerly. Then we lifted the loose sheet and blanket, turned them over and let them fall clear of the bed.

The weapon lay as he said,

Between trigger-guard and trigger a piece of cork had been wedged, so that all the play of the trigger was taken up. It follows that the cork, which protruded beyond the guard about three-eighths of an inch, became the pistol's hair trigger, the slightest touch upon which must certainly fire the thing off. Indeed, I shall always wonder how Percy Virgil – for, of course, it must have been he – had contrived to arrange the bedclothes without mishap, for when Herrick sat down on the bed, he did not sit down on the pistol by fully eight inches or more, yet the draw of the sheet on the cork had fired the weapon before he was fairly down.

The sheets were scorched, and the path of the bullet was plain, for the under sheet was ripped and, when we had moved the pillows, there was a hole in the panel which made the head of the bed.

"Thank you very much," said Herrick. "Supposing I'd...got into bed. Fancy being drilled from below. You know, I'm afraid dear Percy must have a nasty mind."

Using great care, I picked up the pistol and put up the safety-catch. Then I freed the cork and laid the two in a drawer.

"It's our day out," I said, "and Percy Virgil's day in. I mean, he's clean out of luck. This morning Elizabeth left her wristwatch behind."

"On the landing table," cried Herrick, and clapped a hand to his mouth.

"It's all right," I said. "He wasn't here before six. And, as luck will have it, I saw it – at half-past five."

After so full a day and in view of what was to come, we were thankful to have a weekend with nothing to do: for all that, I must confess that, had I not been sure that the Duchess would be annoyed, I would have driven to Tracery every day – not to assure myself that my lady was safe, for of that I could have no doubt, but because I was mad to see her and hear her call me by name. Instead, I sat in the meadows and played with the dream which the Duchess of Whelp, in her wisdom, had taken away, which the Countess of Brief, in her sweetness, had given me back. And because I was foolish I wrote her a little note, which all the world might have read, which I posted myself at Gabble on Saturday afternoon.

Here I should say that out of evil came good: the attempt upon Herrick's life had cleared the air. We had thought it likely that some such attempt would be made, and, while we were not uneasy, our senses did constant duty against some surprise. But now the attempt had been made, and the danger was past – for Virgil would know that, whether he won or lost, his 'throw' could not be hidden or made out an accident, and so would be sure to give Raven a very wide berth.

Herrick wrote to Old Harry on Saturday afternoon.

MADAM,

I have the honour to tell you that Exon and I reached Raven this morning at half-past one. And that, without incident, I am bound, however, to confess that my young and something downright companion, for whom I share Your

140

*Grace's good-natured contempt, possesses an instinct which
I would give much to enjoy. But I, of course, should turn it to
good account. Approaching the farm, he smelt danger: he has
since admitted so much. D'you think he could tell me so?
D'you think he could make my brain free of this highly
important fact? He preferred to withhold it, madam. He
preferred to offend me – and, as you know, I am one of the
mildest of men – by insisting upon precautions I could not
take and by fidgeting in his seat – a vulgar practice, of which,
I may say, I have spoken to him before. I have said he smelt
danger, madam: but because we had not been killed on the
road of approach, our friend dismissed the matter and
pitched his precious instinct into the draught. And now listen
to this. When I was changing yesterday afternoon, I laid on
my bed a pistol – which I forgot to take up. Before retiring, I
sought for this dangerous thing – at first, casually, and then,
since it was not apparent, with an uneasy diligence. I mean,
a loaded automatic is not like a bunch of sweet peas, and if I
am to sleep with one, I like to know where it is. Madam, my
desire was granted. I presently found the thing. I found it by
the process of exhaustion: because I was so fatigued, I sat
down on the edge of my bed. This very simple action caused
it to fire itself off, for its trigger had been made very light –
by someone who knew his job. It was, in fact, in the bed...
Now beds are made to get into, and not to sit down upon. If,
then, I had used that bed as beds are meant to be used, I
should not now have the honour of writing to you, for the
bullet passed through my bolster and split the panel beyond.
All this I tell you, madam, because you were kind enough to
charge me to care for my skin. It shows that your judgment
was sound, and, it shows that, the bolt being shot, I have
nothing to fear – at any rate before Tuesday, when we shall
meet again. I propose to inform the police this same
afternoon. Unless little Percy wore gloves, the pistol might
well have yielded his horrible fingerprints: but Richard had*

pawed it all over before I had time to think. Not that I was deranged. My self-possession was bottomless. As for my companion, who was present when the outrage took place, his make-up is out of order. Things which would disconcert Caesar, appear to fortify him. For me, to be honest, the world had come to an end – my end. Before I had collected my wits, he had resolved the phenomenon and spiked the gun. I think he throws back to some one of those blockish knights, who could neither read nor write, but made history instead – and that, while wearing a suit which weighed ten or twelve stone. Probably he was born under a morning-star.

Madam, I send you our duty – and beg that you will believe that yesterday was a day which we shall never forget. We are well aware that we were only received as friends of the Countess of Brief: but the very great honour remains, and to that you added a kindness which must have touched anyone's heart.

Please give Elizabeth my love: and tell her that Raven is gloomy even at noon, because the light of our eyes has gone to Tracery.

Believe me, Madam,

Your most obedient servant.
JOHN HERRICK

On Saturday the police came to Raven, and we reconstructed for them what had been so nearly a crime.

As they were leaving –

"Sirs," said the sergeant, "one day he will go too far, and will pull up the sluice which will let all our evidence go. And then he will be overwhelmed. To arrest him now would be futile. He bears a very big name, and his word would be taken before yours, in the absence of definite proof."

"I entirely agree," said Herrick. "In fact, I was in two minds whether or no to report this latest affair. You see, we were frightfully tired. Dining out's all very well, but when the house you're dining at's ninety miles off…"

"Ninety miles?" cried the sergeant.

"Well, how far is Tracery?" said Herrick. "If you go by Goschen…"

"*Tracery?*"

Herrick surveyed the sergeant in some surprise.

"Tracery," he said. "We dined with the Duchess of Whelp."

The sergeant appeared to have lost the power of speech. At length –

"I beg your pardon, my lord. I – "

"I'm not a lord," said Herrick.

The other waved his statement away.

"I – I had no idea," he stammered. "If I had known – that first day…" He broke off there and put a hand to his head. "If Her Grace were to learn that one of her friends had been subjected to – "

"Her Grace," said Herrick, swiftly, "would also learn how highly the friend in question thought of the police."

The sergeant flushed with delight.

"Your lordship is very good."

"Not at all," said Herrick. "Not at all. And now don't you rush this business. We both agreed just now that the time wasn't ripe. And if I am content to wait – well, I'm pretty closely concerned. In fact, may I leave it like this – that before you take any action, you'll let me know?"

The sergeant gave his assurance with all his might and, after further civilities, took his leave.

As we turned to the house –

"Of such," said Herrick, quietly, "is the kingdom of earth."

On Monday three letters arrived.

One came from the Duchess of Whelp.

DEAR JOHN HERRICK,

I very much hope that this letter will find you alive. But you were so obvious a victim that I have been kicking myself for letting you go.

I considered and rejected your suggestion that I should express a desire that Virgil should be at Brief. The man will be there, because he would know no peace if he went away. He will suspect our relation violently. Had I desired his – presence, this suspicion would have been confirmed.

I don't care what time you're invited – be there at four. And stand no rot till I come. From that time on, the contingency will not arise.

Tell Richard to be his dear self and on no account whatever to try to pretend.

Elizabeth continues to do me good, but, though she is sweetness itself, I know that her heart is at Raven, with her young men.

A perusal of those pages of my diary which deal with my visit to Brief in 1912 has been instructive and should prove valuable. All the same, I would give a great deal for some heavier stuff. It is one thing to twist a man's tail, but it is by no means so easy to break his back.

Believe me,

Yours very sincerely,
HARRIET WHELP

One came from Elizabeth.

MY DEAR RICHARD,

I have learned quite a lot about you – some things, perhaps, which you do not know yourself. You'll never guess who from. Parish. His sister was your mother's maid. And twice he visited Usage, whilst she was there. He remembers you on your pony and your father riding to hounds and the rookery beyond the stables and how everyone worshipped your mother and heaps of things.

The Duchess is kindness itself and speaks much of you: but I miss you very much and shall be very glad to see you again. But I wish I was going to Raven, instead of to Brief. Looking back on our time there, I see how precious it was. I have never let the world slip before, and if I am never to be allowed to let it slip again, then I do not want to become the Countess of Brief. I hope you are being careful, as you said you would be. If anything happened to you, I don't know what I should do.

> *With my love,*
> *ELIZABETH*

One came by hand from Brief.

The Count of Brief presents his compliments to Mr John Herrick and begs to express the hope that he and Mr Richard Exon will make it convenient to become his guests tomorrow at six o'clock, to meet the Duchess of Whelp and to remain at Brief during Her Grace's pleasure.

Herrick read this aloud, and fingered his chin.

"Ice for two," he said shortly. "I suppose it could have been ruder, but the blood you wring out of a stone is usually thin. And when we roll up at four, he'll go blue in the face. As for Percy the Good, he must be half out of his mind – a victim raised from the dead and two witnesses coming to stay. Let's send him a wire signed 'Max Bracher', asking to be met at the station at half-past three. You know, this play has its points. It may be melodrama, but you must admit that the situation is pregnant – if nothing more."

"I'll be glad when it's over," said I. "He's wicked enough in cold blood, but he's going to be red-hot with his back to the wall."

8

A Stalled Ox and Hatred Therewith

"How good of you to come early."

Herrick and I looked round – from one of the magnificent Bouchers which hung in the hall of Brief.

Percy Elbert Virgil was standing six paces away.

"For that," said Herrick, slowly, "the warmth of our invitation must be our excuse."

Virgil raised his eyebrows and took out a cigarette.

"My uncle will see you later. Till then you must put up with me."

"We'll manage somehow,"' said Herrick. "I don't remember you here in 1912."

The other frowned.

"Allow me to warn you," he said, "not to refer to that visit when my uncle is here. As you probably know, in 1914 his father and wife were both killed and his only brother, my father, met with a hideous fate. And these three terrible blows all fell within twenty-four hours. From that day to this he has never so much as mentioned what went before. For him the past is buried – in holy ground."

"Is it indeed?" said Herrick. "I'd no idea. And I don't think his daughter has. She never said – "

"His daughter? When did you meet her?"

The queries flamed. That Herrick had drawn first blood was as clear as day.

"At Tracery," said Herrick, calmly. "We dined there on Friday night."

Virgil stood still as death.

Then, as though released from some spell, he turned to a table beside him, struck a match and lighted a cigarette.

"Well, well," he said lightly. "And how are you proposing to get me down?"

The sudden, impudent question hit me between the eyes, but Herrick replied as coolly as if a child had come up and asked him the time.

"Well, we rather thought of leaving that operation to you."

Virgil laughed.

"I don't know that I blame you," he said, and took his seat on the arm of a mighty chair. "It's rotten to be laughed out of court. Have they found Max yet?"

"They found him on Tuesday," said Herrick.

"Well, that ought to help you," said Virgil, comfortably.

"I think it will," said Herrick, "before we're through."

Virgil regarded the end of his cigarette.

"You're to have the same rooms," he said.

Herrick raised his eyebrows.

"That's very nice. To be honest, I can't remember – "

"In the tower," said Virgil. "The rooms that you had last week."

His eyes were not upon Herrick, but full upon me.

"Last week?" said Herrick, staring.

"Last week," said Virgil. "On Wednesday. I wish I had known you were there."

"What makes you think that we were? Did somebody leave a pistol in one of the beds?"

I saw the man tighten his lips.

Then –

"Why were you there, Mr Exon?"

I sighed.

"Is it any good saying I wasn't?"

"None whatever," said Virgil. "Before leaving you knocked a man down. But you didn't hit hard enough – you only put him to sleep. And when he woke up, he described you, and Herrick as well."

"And yet," said Herrick, "no summons for assault has been served. You know, I can't help feeling that if you'd a rag of a case, you'd have gone to the police."

This was, of course, most true. To discredit us in their eyes, the man would have sold his soul.

Virgil fingered his chin –

"Where were you," he said, "on Wednesday, at half-past nine?"

"Elsewhere," said Herrick, shortly. "Where were you on Friday, at half-past six?"

"That," said Virgil, "is easy… Never mind. Let's look at your rooms." He got to his feet.

"Did you bring a servant of sorts? Or are you working alone?"

"I don't think he'd suit you," said Herrick, "if that's what you mean."

"Is that meant to be rude?" said Virgil.

"Intensely," said Herrick.

Virgil sucked in his breath. Then –

"As your host, I – "

"What makes you think," said Herrick, "that you are our host?"

The other's eyes burned in his head. Then, with a manifest effort –

"Come," he said thickly. "I'll take you a way that you know."

And so he did.

At the foot of each staircase-turret, there were two doors, one of which gave to the terrace and one to the house. A moment later, therefore, we followed him into the turret which gave to

Elizabeth's suite, climbed the stair and passed through her lovely rooms.

Though the fellow can scarcely be blamed for ramming down our throats his just suspicion that we had been there before, his casual intrusion into my lady's apartments made me so angry that I could hardly see straight, and when he paused in her bedroom, to put out his cigarette on an elegant silver tray, I was so much offended that I could have picked up the salver and dashed it against his face.

He led the way out of her rooms, on to the mighty landing and past the head of the staircase down which I had knocked the servant six days before.

As we went by, Virgil pointed.

"A little harder," he said, "and you would have broken his neck."

And then we had entered the tower and were climbing up to the bedroom I knew so well.

Winter was busy, unpacking. As we came in, he turned, with a shirt in his hands…

Now Winter, of course, was prepared for some such encounter as this; but Virgil was not: and the sudden, improvised meeting with the valet whom he had oppressed, who must, he knew, be itching to take his revenge, hit our unpleasant companion extremely hard. Indeed, for one or two moments, his self-possession was gone, and he seemed the prey of some nightmare, too grim to be true.

As a man who comes full on a snake, he started violently back. And then in a flash he was round and was searching my face and Herrick's with bolting eyes.

We regarded him coolly enough.

"I said he wouldn't suit you," said Herrick, complacently…

For an instant I thought that the fellow would launch an attack. As a beast about to spring, he dropped to a crouch and actually lifted his lip. Then he had himself in hand, and had turned about.

As he crossed to the window –

"I'm not at all certain," he said, "that Brief is going to suit him."

I addressed myself to Winter.

"Did you hear that remark?"

"I did, sir," said Winter, quietly.

"Repeat it to Mr Parish, Her Grace's page."

"Very good, sir."

Virgil stood very still, with his back to the room. When at last he turned, I saw he was very pale.

"My uncle will receive you," he said, "in a quarter of an hour."

Then he passed to the doorway and left us alone. Two things were now clear, and Herrick at once sat down and wrote the Duchess a note.

MADAM,

Before we had been here ten minutes, Virgil took care to warn me not to remind his uncle of anything which had happened before he became Count of Brief. This, I submit, goes to show that Virgil is aware of the truth.

The presence of Winter appeared to shock him so much that I am sure that he regards him not only as a personal enemy, but as a witness, to be used against him, if and when he is charged with the theft of the jewels.

Yours to command,

JH

This note we gave to Winter, to give to Parish at once. Then we washed our hands and made our way back to the hall.

We were not sent for to go to the Count of Brief. In fact, we did not see him, until he passed through the hall, on his way to receive the Duchess, whose car had entered the drive. This, I suppose, by design – so that Herrick should have no time to awaken such sleeping dogs as the Count desired to let lie.

I shall never forget his appearance, or how startling to me was his coming across the hall, for, except that he was stouter and, seemingly, younger in years, he might have been his poor brother, come back to life. The voice was the voice of Gering, the eyes were Gering's eyes, the manner was Gering's manner, the gait was Gering's gait – and he had a trick of holding one arm behind him that I had seen Gering use a thousand times.

If he was ill at ease, he never showed it, but used us both cavalierly, as though to confirm the impression his letter conveyed.

"Which is which?" he demanded, and gave us no time to reply. "Oh, this must be Herring. The Duchess mentioned your name. If you want anything, ask the steward – he knows the rules of the house. And now you'd better come with me. She will expect to see you upon the steps."

With that for welcome, he led the way to the courtyard, as though he were late.

A little bevy of servants were standing beside the steps – with Bertram, the steward, before them, wand in hand. On the other side were standing Parish and Winter and two waiting-women in black.

As I came out with Herrick, Parish came forward at once, to pay his respects.

I put out my hand for his.

"I'm looking forward," I said, "to a talk with you."

As he took my hand –

"I shall be honoured, sir, whenever you please."

I turned to see the Count staring – and Percy Virgil beside him, poking his head. Then the Count said something in German at which the two of them laughed.

Herrick's voice rang out, as the crack of a lash.

"We know the Duchess' servants, because we know Tracery. Can you say as much, you two?"

151

His words might have been a spell. Everyone in the courtyard seemed suddenly turned to stone. Bertram stood open-mouthed, with a hand halfway to his head, and the others stared straight before them, not seeming to breathe, Only the Count and Virgil turned slowly as red as fire, and at this full-flavoured moment, I heard the crunch of gravel beneath the wheels of a car.

Since this meant that the Duchess was come, the tense situation was less relieved than submerged, and all eyes were turned to the archway which led to the drive.

A liveried groom appeared, backing…

Then a long limousine turned slowly into the courtyard and moved to the foot of the steps – and there were Elizabeth smiling and the Duchess of Whelp leaning back, with the air of a Lord Chief Justice up on his Bench.

The chauffeurs sat still, uncovered, while a footman opened the door and the Count stood bowing and waiting for the Duchess to put out a hand.

In silence Old Harry surveyed him. Then she spoke clear and loud.

"There is something different about you. We're both of us older, of course, but it's deeper than that. The flesh is Esau's flesh, but the spirit… " White to the lips, the Count looked ready to swoon. "It's very strange. I should never have said you were Brief."

Somehow the man made answer.

"In twenty-four years, madam – "

"No, no, it's not that. The leopard grows old, but he never changes his spots. Never mind. Here's your daughter back. She has escaped – this time: but I think you should warn all your servants, within and without, to expect another attempt – well, any time now."

With that, having set two balls rolling before she had fairly arrived, Old Harry got to her feet and stepped out of the car and, declining the arm the Count offered, walked up to the head of the steps. There she stopped and looked round.

"Ah, Richard," she said. "And John Herrick, I'm glad to see you again."

We went to her side at once, and she gave us her hand to be kissed – and then, but not until then, Elizabeth left the car.

The Count was not there to greet her. (He was in fact attempting without success to present 'my nephew, Percy' to the Duchess of Whelp.) But as her foot touched the ground, the servants went forward with Bertram, to welcome her home.

It was a moving scene, for they were all bowing and bobbing and one of the women was crying and another was holding Elizabeth's hand to her breast – and poor Bertram had dropped his wand and was down on one knee, with the hem of the coat she was wearing pressed tight to his lips. I never saw devotion so honest in all my life, and the Duchess was plainly pleased, for she smiled and nodded approval and, wholly ignoring Virgil, addressed the Count.

"Since when was blood thicker than daughters?" was all she said.

Then she turned, to enter the hall, where Parish was somehow waiting, to lead her up to her rooms.

The reception was over, and we were alone in the hall, when, as though from nowhere, a maid appeared at our side.

"Her ladyship begs that you will take tea in her suite."

"At once?" said Herrick, rising.

"At once, sir. If you follow me, I will show you the way."

She waited for me to rise, and then, with a delicate deference, took the lead.

Her demeanour was point-device: her appearance, beyond reproach: she breathed efficiency. She was dark and by no means ill-favoured, and I would have said discreet, but for a curious expression about her lips – Leonardo da Vinci could have caught it, for the woman was not smiling, and yet the smile was there.

I followed her thoughtfully, because I knew who she was. And that was Elsa – Elizabeth's personal maid.

She led us the way we had gone some forty-five minutes before – that is, by the staircase-turret Elizabeth always used; and, as we went, I paid what attention I could to the doors which shut the turret from the rest of the house. Of these there were three – one which gave to a lobby upon the ground floor, one which gave to the picture-gallery upon the first floor, and one which opened directly into Elizabeth's bedroom upon the second floor. These doors, which were small but massive, could be neither bolted nor barred, but below each old-fashioned latch was a good Yale lock. The bolts of these locks were not shot, but were at present held back by catches within the locks: but, once the catches were down, none could have passed the doors unless they had been admitted or possessed the appropriate key. (I have made it clear before now that the turret had also a door which gave to the terrace without, that this door had a Yale lock, but could also be barred.) All the locks were within the turret, except the last: and that was in Elizabeth's bedroom.

Her sitting-room door was open, and as we entered the bedroom I heard Elizabeth's voice.

"I have said that, because of my fall, I cannot remember what happened for several hours: that, after that, I was cared for by people I did not know and that, by their advice, I sought the Duchess of Whelp. I may say that these people knew you and that, though they had not been engaged to, er, care for my health, nobody could have been kinder – or more insistent that I should not return to Brief."

"If you think," said Virgil, as I walked into the room…

Elizabeth turned and smiled.

"Do sit down," she said. "The inquest is nearly done."

In some agitation, the Count of Brief got to his feet, and Percy surveyed us with murder in both of his eyes.

" 'If you think,' you were saying," said Elizabeth.

"Thank you," said Percy, calmly. "If you think you can get away with a tale like that – "

"D'you mind getting out of this room?"

There was a pregnant silence.

Then I walked to the door to the landing and opened it wide.

The Count of Brief glanced at his watch,

"My God, I'm late," he said, and fairly ran out of the room.

" 'Adjourned', not 'done'," said Percy, and with that he turned on his heels and followed the other out.

As I shut the door –

" 'Such men are dangerous'," said Herrick, and put on Elizabeth's hat...

For a quarter of an hour we talked. Then she and I left for the stables, and Herrick went to the tower.

But long before then, my inventory was complete.

The door to the landing had a Yale lock, but no bars.

There was no mark upon Caesar, and if his legs had been tender, he now was perfectly sound. The grooms had noticed nothing when he came in. Two other good-looking hunters were each let out of his box, and Elizabeth bade me choose one "for tomorrow at seven o'clock." And then she gave her orders, and we went down to the garden and up to the belvedere.

There was that about her which turned this into a bower.

Sitting sideways, half on and half off the grey of the parapet, backed by the living green of the jealous boughs, a stave of the evening sunshine touching her lovely hair, she seemed to have found her true setting for the very first time: yet this was a fanciful notion, soon to be falsified, because wherever she went, her surroundings appeared to become her as never before. I cannot pay her a finer compliment.

155

For all that, sitting there on the stone, for me she embodied for ever those pretty princesses that live in the fairy tales, that lean from turret-windows and gallop down forest-glades, and I found myself the youth that was seeking his fortune, to whom the princess was gracious – because the great tradition must be observed.

"How d'you do, Richard Exon?"

I took her hand and kissed it.

"The better for seeing you."

"Does that mean that you have missed me?"

"Yes," said I. "At every hour of the day."

Elizabeth nodded contentedly.

"I like to hear you say it," she said…

I wrenched my mind from her beauty to other things.

"Was that Elsa who fetched us?" I said.

"It was."

"Are you sure of her? I'm not mad about her, myself."

Elizabeth laughed.

"My dear, you see a robber in every bush. Elsa is a maid in a thousand – and true as steel."

"Is she going to sleep in your suite?"

She nodded.

"By your request."

"I – I didn't specify Elsa," said I, uneasily.

Elizabeth knitted her brows.

"Richard, be reasonable. You've seen her for less than two minutes: and I have known her well for nearly four years. And if anyone is to sleep there, it must be she. If I were to choose someone else, I might as well say to Elsa 'I don't trust you.' "

"Yes, I see that," I sighed. "All the same, you will lock your doors?"

"All five," said Elizabeth.

"Where are the keys?"

"There's only the one you know – the one you brought me on Friday, with the rest of my things. That's a master key and fits all five of the locks."

There was a little silence.

Then –

"I wish we were at Raven," I said – and spoke as I thought.

"Ah, Raven," said Elizabeth, softly, "with the low of the cows in the meadows and the leap of the fish in the stream – and Winter in his shirtsleeves, cleaning my buckskin shoes. But Brief is too high and mighty – I think that it always was. And Tracery, too. I was not meant for such things."

"Yes, you were," said I. "You were born to the stalled ox – but not to hatred therewith... If this belvedere was at Raven, you'd think it a paradise. And what could be more lovely than the Golden Ride at sunrise? Or the terrace at Tracery under a westering moon? Served without hatred, the stalled ox is splendid fare: but a dinner of herbs would be ruined, if Percy sat at the board."

A hand came to rest on my shoulder.

"You say I was born to all this. Did I seem out of place at Raven?"

"You could never seem out of place. But – well, Raven is Brenda's home. She was born and bred to Raven, as you were to this."

"And my happiness does not count?"

"My dear," said I, "it's all that I'm thinking of. But I...have been through the mill. The flesh makes certain demands – according to the condition to which you were born. Think of the winter at Raven – and then at Brief. You take for granted a thousand important things. I did that once...in a very much smaller way. Red Lead Lane was a nightmare: it is a nightmare today. But if I had been still at Oxford, a weekend at Red Lead Lane would have been an amusing experience..."

"I wish I'd been there, with you both. And all the time I was here, being waited on hand and foot. And sometimes you went hungry, whilst I was being fed by a chef who gets five hundred a year." She stood up there, and took my lapels in her hands. "I owe you money, don't I?"

"I suppose you do," said I, "but it's not worth talking about."

"Well, I'm not going to pay it back. I'm proud to be in your debt. I'd like everyone to know it. What I *really* owe you can't be reduced to pounds: if it could, I could never pay it – and you know that as well as I. But this I *can* pay: but I won't. I asked you to lend me money, and now I won't pay you back. You've piled such mountains between us that let this lift up his head – a sordid, little molehill of forty p-paper pounds."

Before this outburst, I stood like a man transfixed, with the breath of her lips on my face, and her eyes, two pools of starlight, reflecting a tiny image I knew was mine.

So for one hungry moment…

Then she clapped her hands to her face and burst into tears.

I would like to be shown the man that would not have gathered her weeping into his arms – and have done his poor best to comfort such beauty in such distress. And for me her hairs were numbered…

Be that as it may, I know she was in my arms, and the world was rocking about me, and stars that I could not see shot out of their spheres, to make another heaven.

I do not know what I said: I think I did no more than say over her name: but, after a little, she wiped the tears from her eyes and put an arm round my neck.

"D'you love me, Richard?"

"Yes," I said. "I cannot tell you how much."

"And will you always love me?"

"Always, my darling."

"And, after this, you will treat me as your equal? And not kneel down and look up, with your eyes on my face?"

"I – I will try to, Elizabeth."

"And you will not do me honour? John Herrick may kiss my hand: but you and I – Won't you ask me if I love you, my darling?"

"I – I'm afraid to, my sweet," I faltered, and held her close.

"Oh, Richard, I've made so much running. I made you kiss me on Friday, and time and again I've given you lead after lead. Yet no one could call me forward, who'd seen the look in your eyes. You've cried out that you love me with them a thousand times. You told me the truth, my darling, the moment you knew it yourself – when you'd broken into the tower, and I was up at the window and you were holding on to the cage. But I loved you before that."

"I loved you when first I saw you – I know that now."

"If I hadn't been knocked out, I could say the same. It was because I loved you that I let you carry me off. And that's why I stayed at Raven, instead of returning to Brief."

I felt rather dazed. The whole thing was out of order – to put it no higher than that. I had, of course, known that she liked me, and, if I am to be honest, I believed she had let me kiss her because she knew that I loved her and what it would mean to me. But I had never dreamed that she loved me… And now here we were, with desperate issues before us and life and death and fortune flung into the scales, and she and I in the toils of a passionate love affair, which both of us knew was hopeless, which nobody else must suspect.

On a sudden impulse, I picked her up and set her down on the parapet where she had sat before: and then I stood before her, holding her hands in mine.

"Listen," I said. "This is all wrong, and you know it – but I don't care. If you are mad, I'm human. If I'm given my heart's desire, I cannot throw it away. But I will not have you injured by – your extravagance. And so we must keep our secret at any cost."

"Yes, yes, I see that. This other stuff must be dealt with – for better or worse. And then…"

"If Old Harry consents, I will ask you to be my wife."

The beautiful eyes grew wide.

"Since when has the Duchess of Whelp – "

"Since Friday," said I. "You have no father or mother: by doing as you have done, you have set her up in their place. For your sake, she has left her retirement and taken the field: she could do no more, if you were her only child: and you cannot take such services from such a personage, and then deny her the rights of a patroness."

"What d'you think my father would say, if he were alive?"

"I know what he'd say," said I, "if he were the Count of Brief."

Elizabeth sighed.

"You do make things hard, don't you? If you were a racehorse, my darling, you'd have to run in a hood. Still, at least I've managed to get you on to the course. And it's bound to be a walk-over – if only you don't run out."

"I'll never do that," said I.

But I did not say that, as both of us very well knew, fence we never so wisely, I must be disqualified. Instead, I stooped and kissed her exquisite mouth, and then drew her up to her feet and into my arms...

"Why do you love me, Elizabeth?"

"Because you are strong and gentle and like the things I like. Because you are natural. Because you are Richard Exon, and I cannot help myself. And now you tell me."

"Because there is no one like you. Because you have the look of a queen and the way of an Eve. Because your airs and graces are those of the dawn and the dew. Because, with it all, you are human. Because you lift up my heart."

The softest light came stealing into her eyes.

"I like the last reason best."

And there again a feeling of unreality rose as a wave, and I wondered if it was true that Elizabeth Virgil was actually in my arms, if her eager, parted lips were truly so close upon mine, if it was indeed my image that hung in her peerless eyes. Then the wave sank down unbroken, and I knew that these things were facts.

I believe I began to tremble.

"I have no words," I said hoarsely. "I can only say that I love you with all my soul."

Elizabeth put up her hands, to frame my face.

"I ask no more," she whispered, and drew down my head to hers.

As though inspired by the Count of Brief's evil genius, Old Harry saw fit that evening to wear such a mask as made the blood run cold. Her right hand and her mirror, between them, had taught her terrible things. She had so painted her face that she made me think of some chieftain, arrayed for war, and had tired her head with ear-rings – two monstrous, pear-shaped diamonds that dangled as lustres do, and shuddered brilliance with every movement she made. These things, with her splendid features and piercing eyes, would have dismayed an opponent before she had opened her mouth, and, when she came into the room, I must confess to a feeling of great relief that I was to fight with her and not upon the opposite side.

Here let me say that the game which she played was so cunning that I was soon out of my depth: add to which that she spoke in German which I could not understand. But, since I later knew all, I will set down directly what happened, because my own reactions have nothing to do with the tale.

Old Harry had had Herrick's note. She, therefore, laid herself out to entice the Count on to the ground which Virgil had said was forbidden, three hours before. In a word, she set out to make him put a rope round his neck – a seemingly hopeless task...but not to the Duchess of Whelp, for she turned the rope into a garland, and, after a little, he put the pretty thing on. She handed him memories and then demanded them back; she said he must see her diary; she made the desert of danger bloom with goodwill; arm in arm, they wandered over its borders... By the time that the entrée was served, the Count was most deeply committed – and Virgil, whom I was watching; could hardly sit still.

And then, without any warning, Old Harry let fly. Above our subdued conversation, her voice rang out.

"*What became of George Eliot?*"

The table was round, and I was facing the Count, so I saw him well.

A servant was presenting a dish, but, because of this startling query, his master had no mind to spare and the man stood beside him unnoticed – except by everyone else.

Even at a literary luncheon, the question, so suddenly put, might well have disconcerted a wiser man: as it was, its striking irrelevance hit the Count over the heart.

He stared upon the Duchess, who had coolly returned to her plate, as though she had asked him whether his soul was saved: then he lifted his eyes to Virgil's – to read an interpretation which brought the sweat on to his face.

He shot a glance round the table, and a hand went up to his mouth.

Old Harry looked up from her plate.

" 'What became of George Eliot?' I said."

Somehow the man made answer.

" 'George Eliot', madam? Now let me see..."

The Duchess stared.

" 'George Eliot'. I think the edition we had – "

"Edition," cried the Duchess. "*Edition?* What ever d'you mean?"

There was a painful silence.

The servant presenting the dish stood up and looked round for guidance: but Bertram, who had come to his help, was staring upon his master with saucer eyes. The latter wiped the sweat from his brow.

"My memory," he said, "is uncertain. You have revived it, madam, to some extent, but – "

"You remember our visit to Palfrey, where the pictures were going to be sold. And your father saw one of George Eliot..."

Her victim leaped at the bait.

"Oh, now I have you, madam. The picture, you mean. For the moment – "

"*Picture?* Is one of us mad? I asked what became of George Eliot." She threw a glance round.

"Is there nobody here to support me...when I say that that is something which Rudolph of Brief should know?" Her eyes came to rest upon Bertram. "Steward, I know your face. Were you here when I came?"

In some emotion, Bertram inclined his head.

"I was here, your Grace."

"Who was George Eliot?"

"His lordship's pet spaniel, your Grace."

"By God, so he was," mouthed the Count. "To think I'd forgotten – "

"So *what* was?" said the Duchess. Her victim clawed at the cloth.

"The dog, madam. The – "

"George Eliot was a bitch," said the Duchess. And then, "What became of her... Brief? What became of Rudolph's pet spaniel...that never would let her master out of her sight?"

I shall always remember that moment that held so much and shall always see the three faces of those concerned. Old Harry's, keen and relentless, seemed cut out of painted stone: the Count's was a mask of wet grey, with lines that give the impression of having been drawn with blue chalk: and Bertram's was tense and bloodless – the face of a man who is waiting to hear some monstrous suspicion smothered at birth.

Twice the Count tried to answer, and twice he failed.

At the third attempt –

"Madam," he croaked, "I have told you that my memory – "

"What became of George Eliot, steward?"

"His lordship shot her, your Grace, because she was going blind."

"Himself? His favourite dog?"

"He would let no one else do it, your Grace. And no one, except his lordship, knows where she lies."

The Duchess returned to the Count.

"D'you remember it now?"

Somehow the man made answer.

"I remember…that I shot her…myself."

Old Harry lunged.

"In that case, you can tell me her colour."

The silence which succeeded this challenge dragged at the nerves, and I was really quite thankful when Virgil, in desperation, put in his oar.

"Madam, you are dealing with matters which my uncle has fought to forget."

Old Harry raised her eyebrows.

"That explanation is one which I am not prepared to accept. I'll tell you why. *It's too easy*. There's something very wrong here – and I'm glad that I came." She turned to survey the oarsman.

"Why are you here?"

"Madam," said Virgil, "this was my father's home."

"I know that better than you. I asked you why you were here."

"I have no other home, madam."

"Indeed," said Old Harry. "Where is your father now?"

"My father," said Virgil, "is dead."

"When did he die?"

"At least ten years ago, madam."

"In that case, he's been resurrected before his time. I must get into touch with him. I know he was living in London a year ago."

The Count of Brief leaned forward.

"Madam," he gasped, "this is very painful to me."

"Then it shouldn't be," said Old Harry. "Mistakes have been made before now, and I'm not at all certain your brother wasn't an innocent man."

Virgil whipped into the breach, before the Count could reply.

"In that case, madam, there's only one thing to be done. May I have my father's address?"

"I'm afraid," said Old Harry, "your filial affection must wait. I'll deal with this matter myself. And when I have talked with your father, I'll let you know. I expect he, too, has fought to forget the past. But he may have been – less successful… However, we'll very soon know. I'll write to my agent tonight." She returned to the Count, whose head was shaking a little, as that of a very old man. "He will ask your brother two questions, and send his answers to me. The first will be this – *What was George Eliot's colour?*"

The Count half-rose from his chair.

"Madam, I protest."

"Protest and be damned," said Old Harry. "Whelp is not Whelp for nothing, and I was a friend of your father's before you were born."

"But what can that prove?" cried the Count. "If he tells you George Eliot's colour, what can that prove?" His voice rose into a scream, and he smacked the cloth. "That can prove nothing, madam…nothing at all – except that he can remember what I have contrived to forget," and, with that, he sank back, breathing hard, with the air of a man who knows he has made a mistake and yet must needs go on, because he cannot retire.

"Quite so," said the Duchess, "quite so. But the second question will be much harder than that. *Where is George Eliot buried?*" She set her arm on the table and dropped her chin to her palm. "If he answers that, I think that that will prove something…and prove it up to the hilt." With that, she left the Count and sat back in her chair. "And now let's change the subject. Richard, I beg your pardon for speaking in German till

165

now. Elizabeth, dear, that's a highly becoming frock. But then you'd distinguish sackcloth. What does John Herrick think?"

"Madam," said Herrick, "she'd get away with linoleum, if you ask me. And I always thought that I was a Caroline poet: but now I'm Elizabethan. I've got a sonnet to her collar-bone half-done."

"John," said Elizabeth, firmly, "throws back to the cap and bells."

Old Harry smiled.

"And Richard to some Crusader – that's clear as paint – while you, of course, beyond to The Golden World. And now let's return to the present. What do you do, Percy Virgil? Or are you just – decorative?"

His eyes like slits –

"Madam," said Virgil, "I make the most of my time."

"That," said the Duchess, "is a very beautiful phrase. And I hope you know what it means, for I'm damned if I do."

Percy Virgil swallowed.

"I have many interests, madam."

"That sounds very well," said Old Harry.

"What may they be? Do you visit the sick at all?"

"I travel," said Virgil, thickly.

"What in?" said Old Harry. "Or don't you earn any bread?"

"I – I can't say I do," said Virgil.

"Well, well," said the Duchess, softly, "each to his taste. But I'd rather push button boots than batten upon a bounty that wasn't mine." She looked across at Herrick. "How's that for alliteration?"

"Truly Virgilian, madam. And I'm glad you believe in 'B'. It's a valuable consonant."

Old Harry leaned back and laughed, till the tears came into her eyes.

I glanced at the Count.

The man was sitting up straight and was staring directly before him, but not at me. It was plain that his eyes saw nothing that eyes can see, that Apprehension possessed him, body and soul. And this, I think, was natural, for the Duchess had hit very hard. She had publicly forced the cupboard in which his skeleton stood and had hung the sword of vengeance over his head. And this, after twenty-two years...

I glanced at Bertram, the steward.

He had returned to his place, four paces to the left of his master, from which he could watch the table and intercept the servants who moved to and fro. But he was not watching the table. His eyes were fast on the Count. And that, too, I think, was natural, for his father had been steward before him and he was the third generation to serve the house; and servants of standing like that are more jealous of seigniory's rights than are the seigniors themselves. And now, after twenty-two years...

As I returned to the Count, he seemed to take hold of himself: a shiver ran through his limbs, and a hand went out to his wine: and then he was glancing about him, as though to take up his place. But the look on his face was haunted, and he might have been twenty years older than when he sat down.

Virgil was addressing Elizabeth, who sat between Herrick and me.

"You seem to know your neighbours remarkably well."

My lady looked right and left.

"I'm glad of that," she said. "I shouldn't like people to think that we weren't on good terms."

"You need have no fear," said Virgil, and fingered his chin. "And yet I remember a time when you found a far longer acquaintance not long enough to warrant the calling of Christian names."

"So do I," said Elizabeth, calmly. "The man was a friend of yours. He was also a rich, French Jew – entirely and utterly leprous, body and soul. He had to go in the end, because no woman-servant would enter his room."

"Who invited him here?" said Old Harry.

"Madam," said Virgil, "my cousin is prejudiced."

"It seems with reason. I asked who invited him here."

"My uncle was good enough, madam, to do as I wished."

"In his daughter's teeth? You might be the son of the house."

"An impression, madam, I hope very soon to correct. If you'd give me my father's address, I would ask your Grace to excuse me and leave tonight."

"A very natural instinct – to fly to his side. But I fear you might exceed your instructions: whereas I can count on my agent – "

"To do as you say?"

"To the letter," replied Old Harry. "And he's such an efficient man. And now let's return to the guest of whom we were speaking just now. Why did you wish such a charmer invited to Brief?"

"Madam," said Virgil, "he was a friend of mine."

"Does he still enjoy that honour?"

With goggling eyes –

"Where my friends are concerned," said Virgil, "my cousin is hard to please."

"That I can well believe."

"Madam, I will be plain. I do not accept my cousin's estimate. Porus Bureau had his faults, but – "

"So have we all," said the Duchess. "But Porus Bureau doesn't seem to be clean in the house. But that's not the point, which is – that your cousin is the mistress of Brief. When she pronounced him repugnant, why did he stay?"

Virgil swallowed.

"She could have requested my uncle to ask him to leave."

"I did," said Elizabeth, quietly. "I asked you both, the morning after he came. I told you what had occurred – that during the night he had tried to get into my room."

A frightful silence succeeded these moving words, and Herrick told me later that I went white to the lips.

Old Harry looked at the Count.

"Is that within your memory?"

The Count of Brief swallowed.

"We – I thought her mistaken, madam. I said so at once. I explained that one must be quite sure, before taking the serious step of asking a guest to leave."

"What made you think she was mistaken?"

"I – I formed that impression, madam."

"So you've said. I want to know why."

The Count of Brief writhed in his chair.

"Her – her tale was incredible, madam. I decided that she had been dreaming. I – I think so still."

Elizabeth lifted her voice.

"When I tried to shut it, the man put his foot in my door. But he couldn't keep it there, because his slipper was soft: and when he withdrew it, he left his slipper behind. I showed it to you the next morning, to prove my case. If you wanted further proof, he was lame for three days."

There was another silence – of great intensity.

Then –

"The explanation," said Virgil, "was always perfectly clear. Bureau was strange to the house and mistook his room."

"That's – that's right," said the Count, somehow.

The Duchess surveyed them in turn.

Then –

"Quite so," she said grimly. "In fact, what I don't understand is why the Lady Elizabeth wasn't put into the street. I mean, you were three to one – three swine to one pearl. Uncle and nephew and *nephew's paying guest*...and she was only the daughter of this distinguished house."

If the words were savage, Old Harry lent them the harshness of frozen iron. The winter wind whistled in her accents, her tongue was a sharp sword: and I was not surprised to see the Count cower before them and actually put up a hand, as a man who will ward off a blow. And though Virgil sat still as death, for the first time I saw the glint of fear in his eyes. And I did not find that surprising, for the Duchess had made it quite plain that she owed the Count no duty, because he was not her host.

Some sweet was served – in a silence which nobody cared to break.

Then Old Harry spoke in German.

"John Herrick, relieve the tension. You know how to tell a good tale."

"Madam," said Herrick, "command me." He put a hand to his head. "A few minutes ago the conversation turned upon remembrance – a precious faculty. By that my story shall hang…"

(Here I should say that Herrick's story was heard by every soul in that room, for the Duchess had taken her spoon, yet did not begin to eat; and while we, at table, sat waiting for her to begin, the servants had nothing to do, because the course had been served.)

"There was once an English vicar, a very forgetful man. Now all of us sometimes forget. I forgot my pistol on Friday afternoon. But he was much worse than that. He would set forth to keep an engagement and, while he was on his way, forget why he had gone out. He would frequently enter a shop and, ere he was served, forget what he came in to buy. And sometimes in winter, when the heaven was dark and he was rising early, as parsons do, he forgot he was getting up, but supposed he was going to bed, took off the clothes which he had that moment put on and then retired, as though it were night and not day. But, with it all, he was so gentle and charming and had a nature so sweet that his flock forgave his failing with ready hearts, smiled at his errors and said it was 'Parson's way'.

"Well, one beautiful summer morning, he could not resist the call of the countryside, and, after his early breakfast, he set out afoot to prove the lively beauty he loved so well and draw from it a sermon such as no books could give. For the following day was Sunday… As though upon air, he roamed for mile upon mile, and his heart was lifted up, because he had eyes to see and ears to hear. For him, the praise of larks fell down from heaven, the flower-starred fields were living tapestry, brooks ran with precious magic, and the greenwood was a shining chapter out of the Book of Dreams... Of course he forgot all else: and of such was his communion that he forgot all time. In fact, it was past two o'clock, and he had covered the best part of fifteen miles, when he climbed a stile in a hedgerow, to find a man in the road, with a watch in his hand. And the man was watching a chauffeur changing a tyre – or, rather, trying to change it, for the car had detachable rims, and, because of the heat of the day, the metal had expanded and the rim had seized on to the wheel.

"At once the Vicar perceived the state of the case. The man, who was wearing full dress, was clearly due at some function, for which he feared to be late: the chauffeur was needing assistance to pull off the rim: but the other dared not give it, because of his clothes.

"Without so much as a word, the Vicar went down on his knees in the dusty road – not to pray, but to add his strength to that of a fellow man. And after a moment or two, before their united endeavours, the rim gave way... The rest, of course, was easy, but the Vicar continued to help till the work was done. Then at last he straightened his back, to find the other beside him, silk hat in hand.

" 'Sir,' said the man, 'I never can thank you enough. And since you have done me a service which I can never repay, I beg you will do me the honour to be my guest. I am to be married this day at half-past two, and I should not now be happy if you were not there.'

" 'My very good friend,' said the Vicar, inspecting his state, 'you know very well that I am not fit to appear.'

"This was true: he was not even wearing clerical dress.

" 'Whose fault is that?' said the other, and ushered him into his car.

"Now, though, for the moment, he did not know where he was, so soon as they moved, the Vicar got his bearings, only to find that they were approaching the village of which he was priest. At the sight of the distant spire, his memory suddenly stirred.

" 'Dear, dear,' he cried. 'I'd forgotten. I shan't be able to come. You must set me down at that village. I've got a wedding myself.'

" 'At that village?' cried the other. *'But that is where I'm to be married – in ten minutes' time.'*

"The Vicar smiled his rare smile.

" 'Make it twenty, my friend,' he said gently. 'You must give me time to change.'

"So they brought one another to church – the priest and the groom, for, had they not met as they did, neither the one nor the other could have arrived."

There was a moment's silence.

Then the Duchess of Whelp shook her head.

"Too good to be true," she said, "as I'll lay the Count will agree."

"Madam," said the Count, "I am with you. And who ever heard of a – "

"God in heaven!" cried Herrick, and started up to his feet.

His eyes were upon the Count, and the Count was staring back, with the eyes of a beast at hay.

So for a long moment…

"What then?" said Old Harry, sharply.

Herrick put a hand to his head.

"But he's denied it," he cried, and looked dazedly round. "And I was there – at the wedding. I saw them arrive."

"What of that?" said the Duchess. "He wasn't."

His eyes again fast on the Count –

"*My God*," said Herrick, "*I don't believe that he was. And yet the bridegroom's name was Rudolph of Brief.*"

Two hours had gone by, and Winter was telling his tale. This in Herrick's room, the middle room of the tower. (This had not been a bedroom the week before: but now it was changed.)

"The first thing I knew, sir, a servant came running in, to say his lordship had fainted and his valet was wanted at once. Well, that told me you were off, and very soon after, Bertram the Steward comes in, as white as a sheet. He asks the older servants to come to his room, an' when he was gone, a footman begins to talk. I couldn't get all he said, but I made out her Grace an' Mr Herrick 'ad put it across the Count. There's a chauffeur there speaks some English, and so I got on to him. 'What's the trouble?' I says. 'What's anyone done?' An' then he starts off..."

"They've got this much clear, sir – that there *was* another brother an' he was a twin: that 'er Grace and Mr Herrick keeps on referring to him: that his lordship keeps getting caught out, because he don't seem to see that they're mixing him up with his brother in all they say. *But they can't understand why his lordship is so much upset.* 'Why can't he see?' they keep asking. 'Why don't he tell them they're mixing him up with his twin?' Of course, the Steward's got it – you ought to have seen his face. An' Mr Parish has rammed a point or two home. But they all know there's something wrong, an' they all think her Grace has come here to put it right. It seems she said something like that. And they've got Mr Herrick's story about the forgetful priest: but they think that when he said 'Rudolph' he must have meant 'Ferdinand'."

"Oh, give me strength," said Herrick, and threw up his hands.

"If I may say so, sir, you 'aven't no call to complain. They've got the truth in their hands, but, except for the Steward, they're holding it upside down."

"And what will happen," said Herrick, "if ever they turn it round."

"Shocked to death, sir," said Winter, "if you ask me. I think they'll walk out on him, sir, from bottom to top. They're a very 'ouse-proud lot. An' another thing – in their eyes her Grace can't do no wrong."

There was a little silence.

It was clear that we had won the first round, and won it well. It was also clear that Old Harry was going for a knock-out, because the pace she had set could not possibly last – for one thing only, her threat to produce poor Gering was one which she could not fulfil. And again it was clear that Old Harry's judgment was good, because a win on points would be useless to us. The Count of Brief had to be floored – or be made to throw in the towel. But if he contrived to stand up for the first few rounds, the man was safe.

Now had he known it, the man had nothing to fear, because his brother was dead. Old Harry had seen that at once. Only the production of Gering could send him down. *But fear of the production of Gering reinforced by a taste of the exposure which Gering's production must bring, might make the man throw up the sponge.* That, then was Old Harry's line, and it cannot, I think, be denied that she had begun very well. The Count was badly rattled. But I could not lose sight of one thing. And that was that *he had a second who knew no law.*

Indeed, this was how I saw it – that the Duchess of Whelp was fighting the Count of Brief, because the fall of the Count would set Elizabeth up: but Virgil was fighting his cousin, because, if he brought her down, the fall of the Count would not matter, because he – Percy Virgil – would then be bound to succeed.

"Well, well," said Herrick. "And who ever heard of two guests abusing their host at table until he's carried away and then getting down to his brandy and having a rubber of bridge? You know, it's blasphemous – I don't believe the Borgias ever did that. And I'll lay li'l Percy's got earache. 'Three swine to one pearl.' "

I forget what answer I made, but I know I sent Winter to bed and, after two or three minutes, went up to my room. But not to sleep: for the 'pearl' was out of my sight.

I had seen her into her suite twenty minutes before. I trusted to see her come out in a little less than eight hours. But I had no faith in Elsa, and – Virgil had his back to the wall. Had there been but one door to her suite, I would have slept across it – and let the world believe me another Porus Bureau. But there were four doors to her suite, and one was outside. I could not so much as watch them: Argus himself could have watched but one at a time.

I took off my coat and lighted a cigarette...

As I threw the match out of the window, somebody knocked at my door.

I was at the oak in a flash, to find Winter standing without, with a key in his hand.

"I forgot to tell you, sir." He entered and shut the door. "You gave me this key, and told me to lock up the Rolls – her doors, I mean. But I 'aven't been able to, because this isn't the key."

" 'Isn't the key?' " I said, frowning, and took it out of his hand.

"It isn't, indeed, sir. I tried it again and again."

"But..."

And there I stopped dead – with my eyes on the key I was holding between my fingers and thumb.

Winter was right. This was not the key of the Rolls. Although she did not know it, Elizabeth Virgil had the key of the Rolls. I had handed it to her on Friday, with the rest of her things. It was now, perhaps, under her pillow. *But this was her master key...that fitted all five of her locks.*

9

Into the Mouth of Hell

Whilst I changed, I gave Winter his orders. These were, in short, to pass the night on the landing, watching the door which gave to Elizabeth's suite.

"If anyone tries to enter, put your torch on his face and hold him up. The door may be opened for him; but I don't like Elsa's face, and he's not to go in. When you've got him, lift up your voice and shout my name, and I'll be with you before you know where you are. I shall be in the staircase-turret, watching the other door of her ladyship's rooms."

"And if you want me, sir?" said Winter.

"I'll call her ladyship. She'll let you through her suite and on to the stair. I don't think anything will happen, and, but for Elsa, I'd tell you to go to bed. But it's thanks to me that she is inside that suite, so it's up to me to see that she does no harm."

And there I remembered Elgar, the man for whom Virgil had called when we had escaped from the tower. I had learned from Elizabeth that he was Virgil's chauffeur and was as much trusted by his master as he was distrusted by everyone else at Brief.

But when I mentioned his name –

"He's away just now," said Winter, "with Mr Virgil's car. There's a knock in the engine or something they can't get right."

"So much the better," said I, and spoke as I thought.

And that, I think, shows how ill-equipped I was to deal with a man of Virgil's capacity, for I should at once have suspected the absence of his chauffeur and car. But I am ashamed to say that it did not occur to me that, if there is work of a certain kind to be done, the lugger will take an offing, instead of staying in port. Be that as it may, I read the danger signal as being a piece of good news: then I took up my pistol and torch, and we left the tower.

To post Winter took but a moment; and then I was treading the steps down which I had knocked the servant six days before. My shoes were rubber-soled, and I made no sound, but, as I have said before, the well of the staircase was lit, and the first floor, to which I was going, was very much better illumined than was the landing above. Still, there were shadows enough, and I kept to them.

As luck would have it, I knew the whole of my way. I was not going down to the hall: I was bound for the picture-gallery, where we had gathered that evening, before dinner was served. This lay upon the first floor – a fine, long room, and its range of windows was broken into three bays by two of the staircase-turrets with which the castle was served.

And the first of these, I knew, was Elizabeth's own – I had seen her come out of its door at a quarter past eight.

Using the greatest caution. I left the magnificent staircase and stole to the gallery's doors. Happily, these were open, but here the darkness was thick, so I put to the doors behind me and drew my torch. And there my luck went out, for the torch was dead.

Now I could, of course, have gone back: but, since Winter needed his torch, it meant going back or sending him back to my room: so I made up my mind to go on, because, though I should have liked it, I could tread upon Virgil's toes without seeing his face.

The gallery seemed broader than I had thought, but at length I was touching the curtains, which had been drawn. At once I turned to the left, for now I had found the windows, I had to do no more than follow their line along. And because I had my bearings, perhaps I moved with less care than I should have shown. In any event, I had almost come to the door, when I brushed against something unwieldy – and knocked it down.

Now when a man who is trying not to be heard knocks over a chair or a table, it shortens his life. But when he knocks over a harp...

Not only was the crash appalling, but every string of the instrument sounded its liquid note. Indeed, as I stood there, trembling, I thought that the dulcet announcement would never die, and when at last it did, I should have been glad to die with it, because in all my life I never felt so much abashed. Discovery was, of course, inevitable. I had not only waked the household: I had declared where I was: for the harp, like that of the giant in *Jack and the Beanstalk*, had lifted up an unmistakable voice.

I wiped the sweat from my face and waited for the sound of men running and voices raised – a second Porus Bureau on his way to my lady's rooms. Virgil, no doubt, would come thrusting – to rub my nose in the desperate mess I had made. I began to try to prepare some halting explanation which was not beneath contempt...

I do not know how long I stood still, but as the moments went by, yet nobody came, I began to dare to believe that I was to be spared. The silence which I had shattered was absolute as ever: no faintest indication of movement came to my ears. And at last I knew I was saved. For some extraordinary reason, no one was coming to answer the call of the harp.

Expecting to be discovered and put to shame, I had, of course, relinquished my delicate enterprise: but now there was plainly no reason why I should withdraw, provided that on my way back, when my watch was done, I set up the harp again by the light of the dawn. So I ventured to hold on my course, feeling my way before me and moving, as may be believed, as nicely as any cat.

Before I had covered six feet, I touched the door of the turret to which I was trying to come…

Now I had expected the staircase to be in darkness: but the moment I opened the door, I knew that a light was burning beyond the oak. For a moment I found this strange. Then I remembered that I had left lights burning on the staircase within the tower and decided that the practice was natural where dangerous steps were serving a private room.

I took the key from the lock, stepped across the threshold and closed the door.

I was now in a little, stone passage which ran through the castle wall and gave directly on to the turret-stair: the wall being four feet thick, the passage was four feet long, for the turret adjoined the castle, yet was complete in itself. An electric light was burning where passage and stairway met, thus lighting the steps up and down as well as the passage itself.

I leaned against the wall and heaved a sigh of relief. Harp or no harp, I had gained the position I sought, and Winter and I between us commanded Elizabeth's suite. If…

And there I heard a girl laugh…a stifled, mischievous laugh…to tell me she knew I was there.

It was Elsa, of course. I knew that. She must have heard the harp fall and have left Elizabeth's suite to see what the matter might be. And then she had seen the door open and, probably, me come in. She was just out of sight, up the stair: and she had been waiting there, to see what I would do.

There was only one thing to be done.

"Is that you, Elsa?" I said, and stepped to the curling stair.

Looking up, I saw her standing, point-device as ever, back to the wall.

Then somebody standing behind me laid me out.

The first thing that I remember was Percy Virgil's voice.

As I lifted my head, he spoke, and a gag was clapped into my mouth – a pad of sweet-smelling silk, which I afterwards found was one of my lady's chemises, fresh from some drawer. When I tried to sit up, I found that my hands were not free. My wrists were strapped tight together, behind my back.

I was still too dazed to make any useful effort, so I laid my head back on the stone and closed my eyes, determined to stay where I was till my strength and my senses came back, for though I could not think straight, I knew that I needed them both as never before. For a moment I seemed to be swaying, although I was lying still... Then somebody made me sit up and pushed my head forward and down... Then water was poured on my head and down the back of my neck...

It was that that cleared my brain, and though my head was aching, from that time on I was healthy in body and mind.

I lifted my head and looked round.

I was still in the passage, just clear of the turret-stair. Percy Virgil was sitting on the stair, a step or two up. And a man who I knew must be Elgar was standing in the passage beside me, pitcher in hand.

Percy Virgil picked up my pistol, looked at the safety-catch, weighed the thing on his palm, and slipped it into his coat. Then he glanced at his wristwatch and fingered his chin.

"You are very convenient, Mr Exon. I should have got you later, but probably only after an ugly scene. And I do so dislike being crossed... But now you've avoided all that, and, what is more, you have made my path very smooth. You see, my cousin is going. The Lady Elizabeth Virgil is leaving the castle tonight. That was always understood – not by you, or that silver-tongued fairy, the Duchess of Whelp. But it *was* understood by me – as soon as I heard that my cousin was coming back. You see, I don't want her here. I really made that plain about ten days ago. But some people won't take a hint... Well, now she is going for good. She will never come back. Where Max went wrong I don't know: but this time I'm making sure – I was in her bedroom tonight before she came up. Indeed, my arrangements were perfect – as I shall show. And yet, with it all, I had a sort of feeling that when tomorrow arrived and the Lady Elizabeth Virgil was not in her room, I should be roused from a slumber I really required and once again charged with abduction and things like that. There would have been no shadow of proof. Elsa would have heard nothing. No car would have left the castle. And the Steward himself would have said that if I had gone out by night I could not have come in. You see, for two days now I have had no key. Everyone knows that I lost it on Sunday night. I assure you, the castle's been ransacked... To no avail, of course, because – *here it is...* So I *can* get in, though everyone knows that I can't. But tomorrow I shall throw it away... Never mind. I should have been suspected, indeed, I think it likely that you would have been very rude. But now you won't be there to be rude: and what is still more to the point – well, I won't say I shan't be suspected, but even the painted lily will find herself stopped from making a charge."

The man stopped there and leaned forward, with glittering eyes.

"My luck came in, Mr Exon, when you knocked over that harp... We were going, Mr Exon. I'd had a talk with my cousin, Elsa had received her instructions and Elgar was on this stair And then you knocked over the harp... And so I held everything up and waited for you. I mean, it was worth it, Mr Exon – from my point of view.

"*Now* what will they find tomorrow? Not one, but both of you gone... Abduction? Well, hardly. They don't abduct people like you. What about an illicit elopement? A passionate flight? Oh, that's absurd... Wait a minute. Consider that beautiful scene in the belvedere? This evening...at sunset, Mr Exon. Yes, you were watched – by a most reliable man. And then the key to her bedroom...that a lady gave to her swain? And then the dressing case...which Elsa is packing now? Elsa – there's a good girl. She will speak to her own reactions – with tears running down her cheeks: how she and you fought for her darling and how her entreaties were foiled by the way of a man with a maid. Aunt

Sally may put up a show, but she won't be able to face these basic facts. And I hardly think she'll lay them before the police. I mean, they might miss the idyll and get the blurb…"

He got to his feet and yawned.

"Go and get her ladyship, Elgar; and tell Monna Lisa I'm not going to wait all night. If she can't pack a dressing case – "

"It is ready," said Elsa's voice, as Elgar went up the stair.

"You see, Mr Exon," said Virgil, "the way to win in this world is to go all lengths. It's simpler, swifter and safer – every time. Think what I should have been spared if I had taken that course ten days ago. But there… One lives and learns. Take my two, er, assistants, for instance." He threw a glance up the stair. "I can count upon Elsa. She's wanted in Bristol for abortion – a very bad case. But on Elgar I have no hold: so, though he does not know it, he hasn't got long to live. I think he will be run over – I'm not quite sure. All lengths, Mr Exon, all lengths. If you'd gone all lengths in the tower six days ago… It's a dangerous place, that staircase, at any time…and you're pretty strong…and I didn't know you were there. I'm afraid you're not bold enough. He who strikes and runs away, Lives to die another day. And here they come."

He picked up a length of cord and then stepped over my legs and out of the way. The next moment Elgar appeared, with Elizabeth over his shoulder, as though she were wounded and senseless and he was bringing her in.

"Put her ladyship down," said Virgil, making a knot in his cord.

Elgar unshouldered his burden and set it down on the steps…

So far I have said nothing of the rabble of thoughts and emotions that had command of my soul. It was a case of mob rule. Passion, regret and hatred; apprehension, incredulity, despair swept to and fro within me, quarrelling amongst themselves. If I arrested one, the others fell upon me until I let go; and I seemed to be the prey of some supernatural nightmare which had followed me out of its darkness into the light.

For this half-mad condition, there can be no doubt that my impotence was to blame. I am a strong man, as men go: but Virgil's casual discourse had borrowed for me the strength of some demigod. Had I been free, I would have shown him – I would have torn his throat from his neck...and have broken Elgar in pieces...and cast the two into the drive...if – I – had – been – free... And I was so nearly free. Only my wrists were bound – fast strapped together with leather, *behind my back*. For all my strength, I could do nothing. The gun was spiked.

Then my eyes met those of my lady, and order came back to my soul.

'Canst thou not minister to a mind diseased?'

I can never describe the magic that hung in her steady gaze. Before it, the rabble melted, the mob dispersed, and my plight became an adventure, which I was sharing with her – a very insignificant business, because that we were together was so much more important than anything else. Percy Virgil and all his works seemed suddenly pygmy stuff: the man was a fretful puppet, fit for contempt, strutting before high heaven to make the angels smile. But we were invulnerable. We had armed each other forever five hours before...and that, with an armour no other could ever pierce.

I tried my best to tell her that all was well. And I think that she understood, for the rarest smile stole into her lovely eyes... And then I came back to earth, like a giant refreshed.

She was gagged and bound, as I was. But her ankles were tied together, as well as her delicate wrists. Cord had been used to do this sacrilege. She was clad in a blue cloth dress that I did not know – no doubt to bear out the suggestion of sudden flight. Her beautiful hair was tumbled, but that was all.

Virgil was speaking again.

"You will have observed, Mr Exon, perhaps with hope, that while we have bound my cousin's, we have not bound your feet.

I will tell you why. Because she is light to carry, but you are not. And so you will walk – to the car. Now, lest you should abuse this freedom, I'm going to put you on a lead." He held up his cord. "One end – this end will be fastened about your waist: and the other about my cousin's most excellent neck. You see? I have made a slip-knot…the knot that they hang people with. So that any irregular movement which you may see fit to make will put to inconvenience your, er, heart's desire. In fact, if I were you, I should emulate Mary's lamb. Not that it matters – if you like to choke her yourself. But I've really made other arrangements – a shade less exacting, I think. But I'll leave it to you to judge." He looked up at the light and sighed. "Poor Porus Bureau. If he were here, I don't know what he would say. The French are so emotional. And he wanted her very badly. He'd say I was smashing a bottle of very good wine…that might have given pleasure to others, though it doesn't appeal to me. But there you are. If Max hadn't messed things up…" He glanced at his watch. "And now I think we should be moving. Thanks to you, Mr Exon, I'm a little behind my time. But we haven't got far to go, and I ought to be back in an hour and a quarter from now."

With that, he stepped across me and set the loop he had made about Elizabeth's neck. Before my horrified eyes, he drew this tight – not tight enough to choke her, but so tight that the loop could not lie, as a necklace does, but stayed where he had put it against her throat. Then he and Elgar, between them, got her on Elgar's back.

Somehow I got to my knees and so to my feet, and without a word he fastened the end of the cord about my waist.

I saw Elsa standing above, with a dressing-case in her hand… Then Elgar began to go down, and I turned in behind him, weak-kneed for fear of stumbling and coming down and being unable to rise because my hands were tied.

Not that it mattered, perhaps. But I – I did not want to choke my darling myself.

As we went down to the terrace, I remembered Elizabeth's coming that afternoon – the pomp and circumstance and the homage the servants did: and now she was leaving, after a stay of eight hours, gagged and bound and helpless, with a halter about her neck.

It was this reflection that showed me the truth of what Virgil had said – *The way to win in this world is to go all lengths*. The man was right. It was manifestly simpler and swifter: direct action always is. *But it was safer, too* – because it was the way of a monster, and we believe in monsters no more than we do in giants.

Virgil was playing the monster: and that, as calmly as though he were playing bridge. In other words, he was doing the incredible thing. If I had not seen and heard what I saw and heard that night, I would not have believed the truth though one rose from the dead. *And so no one else would believe it* – that Elizabeth Virgil and Exon had been haled out of the castle and put to death by a man who, six hours later, was taking his early tea with a cigarette.

I confess that I had no hope: but that was because there was no hope to be had. Percy Virgil's demeanour had murdered hope. His quiet, confidential manner, his easy air, his natural way of speaking precluded doubt. In all he had said in the turret, he had conveyed the impression not so much of predicting the future as of relating the past. He had revealed no plan, but a *fait accompli*. The cards were upon the table. The game was done.

I cannot clearly remember our leaving the staircase-turret and passing into the air, for the cord was none too long and I could think of nothing but keeping it slack, but I know that the moon was not up, that Virgil was moving behind me, that Elgar turned to the right and stepped out for the entrance-drive.

185

Perhaps ten minutes went by – it may have been less, but I know we had passed the point from which Herrick and I had surveyed the castle at dawn, when I saw in the shadows ahead the shape of a car.

This was open and low – it proved to be Virgil's own car 'now under repair' – and Elgar discharged his burden directly over its side. It will be understood that I did not have to be told to enter myself, and an instant later I was upon the back seat, with Elizabeth Virgil beside me, so far as I could hear, drawing regular breath.

I suddenly realized that I was streaming with sweat...

The dressing-case was set at our feet and Virgil and Elgar got in. For a moment the self-starter whirred... Then all was silence again, except for the purr of an engine in excellent trim. Virgil sat back in his seat and let in his clutch...

It was as he did this, and we moved, that my fingers encountered something which did not belong to the seat. In an instant, they had it fast: and the moment I knew what it was, the hope which Virgil had murdered came back to life.

It was a small screwdriver...which Elgar or some mechanic had left in the back of the car...some eight inches long, over all...with a fine enough blade. For all I know, it may have been there for weeks, for, the seat being tilted up, it had lodged between the seat and the padding on the back of the car; and I should never have found it or known it was there, if my wrists had not been fastened behind my back.

Now, as I have said, my wrists were strapped together – not bound with cord. And every strap has a buckle, and every buckle a prong.

When a man or a beast is restrained by a leather strap, it is upon the prong of the buckle that such restraint must depend. Disengage the prong from its hole, and the stoutest strap will be loosed and all restraint be at an end.

My fingers were free. If I could contrive to thread the blade of the screwdriver over the frame of the buckle and under the prong...

It was a difficult business. I was working blind and my fingers had not fair play, and though I soon found the buckle, I could not reach this with my fingers and so could not guide the blade, while the movement of the car was distracting the aim which I tried to take.

Blindfold a man and give him a needle to thread – to save his life and that of the lady he loves. And jog his arm, while he is trying...striving to beat the clock. For I was up against time. Virgil was driving fast, and we hadn't got far to go.

I do not wish to labour the point, but I think I should make it clear that during that terrible drive I endured such vexation of spirit as sends a man out of his mind. Had there been nothing at stake, the thing I was trying to do would have maddened a better man. It was one of those finical jobs that make a man lose his temper and throw down his tools. He may be the most patient of workmen, but this is a matter of luck. And when luck has made game of his efforts for two or three minutes of time, he has had enough of kicking against the pricks. God knows I had more than enough: but because of what was at stake, I had to go on.

Again and again I was on the edge of success, and then the car would lurch and I would lose prong and buckle and sometimes my balance, too. And once the blade was in place, but, before I could drive it home, a wheel dropped into a pothole and shook it out. I could have screamed with the rage of a thwarted child...

And then, at last, the blade slid under the prong...

What happened I do not know, for I never examined the strap, but I know I was trying to lever the prong from its place and the buckle was turning with it and spoiling my game, when, all of a sudden, the strap went slack on my wrists and I knew I was free.

Now my impulse was to do murder, and do it at once: break Elgar's neck and then choke Virgil to death: and but for Elizabeth's presence, I think that I should have done that – and as like as not lost my own life, when the car, which was travelling fast, crashed into a tree. But Elizabeth had to be saved. And so I did nothing at all but shake the strap from my wrists and keep my hands behind me and use my brain.

At once I saw that the first thing for me to do was to free myself from the cord which put my lady in peril whenever I moved.

With my eyes upon Virgil and Elgar, I felt for the knot at my waist. This I found and untied. Then I made a bow-knot in its stead, which I could undo in a flash whenever I pleased.

Then I saw that, for better or worse, I must not launch my attack until the car was at rest, for if, in the struggle, the car were to leave the road, Elizabeth, bound hand and foot, might fare very ill.

And then I remembered that Percy Virgil was armed.

This showed me that, come what might, I must deal with him first: else, whilst I was dealing with Elgar, he might very well put me out.

And there, without any warning, our lights were 'dipped' and Virgil reduced his speed…

Till now I had been too much engaged to observe our way, and now I could see next to nothing from where I sat: but the road was rough and winding, and though there were trees on the right, there were none on the left. Wheresoever we might be bound for, I judged we were nearly there, and I held myself all ready to strike the instant we stopped.

I sometimes think, looking back, that I should have done what I could to loosen Elizabeth's bonds; but her hands were bound before her, and not behind, and I found it so important to hide from Virgil and Elgar the fact that my hands were free that I dared not make the movements which I should have had to make. Be that as it may, I did nothing but bide my time – and measure the distance from me to my enemy's back. Had I been directly behind him, I should have been better placed, but I remember reflecting that a neck which cannot squarely be broken can always be wrung.

I have said that the night was dark, and since we were sunk in some valley which ran north and south, we were denied the glow which heralds the rising moon. Still, I could see some six feet – and that was more than I needed to do what had to be done.

And there, as though in reply, the car passed over some rise and then swept into surroundings of which I shall always think as the mouth of Hell.

In a flash the world was transfigured.

The air, which had been sweet, became the breath of corruption – reeked of decay: the sudden chill of a morgue displaced the pleasant cool of the summer night: the steady purr of the engine changed to a snarl and the darkness became so thick that I could not have seen my hand in front of my face. Then I knew that we were on cobbles, and, when I lifted my head, I saw the lines of three ridge-poles against the sky. We were in the great court of some mansion, long uninhabited.

(Here I should say that, by rights, the lamps of the car should have helped: but they were so deep and so trained that their light was concentrated, as that of a torch, and neither the beams which they threw nor the apron of light which they spread did anything more than hold the eye, when it found them, and so increase the darkness they did not actually touch.)

Now what possessed Elgar to do it, I do not know; but, as the car came to rest and I rose to my feet, the man slewed round in his seat and dropped down a hand for Elizabeth's dressing-case. As he heaved this up, it struck me under the knees and, because I was rising and was neither up nor down, the blow made me lose my balance and sent me backwards into the seat I had left. Since this was low and tilted, I as good as fell on my back, and before I could rise again, Percy Virgil was out of the car, on the opposite side.

Not that I saw him – the darkness was far too dense. And so, at least, I knew that I had not been seen. But I knew where he was, for I heard him using my name.

"The, er, cemetery, Mr Exon... It's better known as Palfrey – the place which Jezebel mentioned at dinner tonight. Nobody ever comes here, because it is said to be cursed. But, blessed or cursed, it has a magnificent well... Ninety feet deep, Mr Exon. And fifty-two feet of water – I measured it yesterday... And its parapet is of white marble – at least, it used to be white – and it has three statues about it...statues of men in armour, leaning upon their swords. How's that for a sepulchre? I wish you could see it, Mr Exon. I'm standing beside it now. Elgar, you see, has gone to borrow some stones...to go into the dressing-case. As anchors go, it wasn't quite heavy enough..."

By now my door was open, and I was half out of the car, with Elizabeth in my arms.

You see, we shall lower that first: and that will be attached to my cousin's feet. And then we shall lower her: and as she's already attached, that will bring us directly to you."

I was on the cobbles now and was stealing the way we had come. I never found it so hard to turn my back on a man: but Elizabeth had to be saved before anything else.

"And so, you see, Mr Exon..."

And there I saw Elgar approaching, against the dusk prevailing without the court.

For a second I hesitated. Then I laid Elizabeth down and twitched the cord from my waist.

And then I went to meet Elgar, who could not see me... And, as I went, I ripped the gag from my mouth.

He must have found the case heavy, for when I was almost upon him, he laid it down for a moment, to rest his arm.

As he straightened his back, I took the man by the throat...

It was a curious business and seemed to belong to the stage or the cinema's screen, for whilst we two stood silent, Virgil, a little way off, was addressing the empty car. I could not hear all he said, but his tone was as careless as ever and once he laughed. But Elgar could not laugh. He never struck me. From first to last his hands were tearing at mine. They might as well have torn at the cobbles beneath our feet. So for, perhaps a full minute... Then his knees sagged, and his arms fell down by his sides

Still gripping his throat, I lowered his weight to the ground. Then I cracked his skull on the cobbles and let him go.

The sound was slight enough, but Percy Virgil heard it – and found it strange.

For an instant there was dead silence.

Then –

"Is that you, Elgar?" he cried – and brought my heart into my mouth.

I had meant to approach him forthwith, as Elgar would have approached him, bearing the dressing-case. But now Elgar's failure to answer would tell him that something was wrong, and, once his suspicions were roused, it. would be but a matter of moments before he discovered the truth. *And my lady was still within range...*

In a flash I had whipped to where I had laid her down. As I stooped –

"Mother of God!" screeched Virgil – and told me he knew we were gone.

My hands encountered nothing. *Elizabeth was not there.* Being bound, she could not have moved, yet *she was not there.* For an instant my heart stood still: and then I saw that, because of the darkness, I must be a foot or so out. I felt to the right...to the left. I took a pace forward, and stepped on a rotten stick. Its snap declared my presence and I shot a glance at the car. I could, of course, see nothing – except the beam of its lights. Virgil was quiet as death. Death... *The man was armed, and*

Elizabeth lay hereabouts. Hereabouts, but where? I fell on my hands and knees and began to crawl, sweeping the cobbles before me with one of my hands. It was just about here – I knew it. More to the right, perhaps... No? Then I must have passed her... I made my way back. As I went, I cast to and fro – frantically. And then my hand brushed something – the sole of her shoe. My heart leaped up to heaven...and then fell down into hell. It was not her shoe. It was that of the man I had killed – from whose side I had set out to find her a moment ago...

What that discovery meant took a year from my life: for it meant that before the darkness I was a broken reed, and when I looked to the head-lights to get my bearings afresh, their beam was gone.

10

I Am Hoist with My Own Petard

I shook the sweat from my eyes and tried to think what to do. And since my thoughts were frenzied and mostly poisoned by the knowledge of what I ought to have done, I will not recite them here, but will state what, upon reflection – if, indeed, you can give it that name – I set out to do.

I set out to find Percy Virgil.

The man would not look for his cousin. He would assume, with reason, that she was out of his range – for the moment, at any rate. But he knew that I was still there, because of the snap of the stick. And if he could find Richard Exon before Richard Exon found him, he might even yet save the game because he was armed. I did not have to be told that he was standing or moving, *pistol in hand*. And if he was moving...and if, as he moved, he discovered Elizabeth Virgil... He would not have to fire: he need only tighten the halter about her neck: and then pass on in silence in search of Richard Exon, who left his helpless darling to care for herself.

I stifled a groan and felt again for the corpse. Then I picked up the lines of the ridge-poles against the sky. And then I began to steal forward to where, I believed, was the car.

I wish that I could describe the blindness that ruled that court. God knows what disorder of nature provoked such gloom, but the place was steeped in a darkness which I had never conceived. I can well believe Palfrey was cursed, for I never yet heard of shadows to which the eye of man could not accustom itself. But here I could see no better than I had seen when I first drove into the court. And when I say I might have been blindfold, I say no more than the truth.

Now I had seen Elgar coming because he was silhouetted against the dusk which was keeping the world without. And since I had no wish to offer to Virgil the target which Elgar had offered to me, I dropped to the cobbles and once more began to crawl.

To say that I watched and prayed means nothing at all. I moved like any shadow and listened with all my might. Elizabeth's life might depend on my hearing the enemy move, and I made the slowest progress because my own advance was bound to embarrass my ear. I tried to keep the direction I hoped was right by glancing up at the ridge-poles from time to time, but the court was so broad that they gave me but little help, and after a minute or two I could be sure of nothing except that I was not heading away from the house. This horrid uncertainty sent me half out of my mind. The thought that, for all I knew, I was actually creeping by inches *away* from the car pricked me into a frenzy which I could scarcely control, and more than once I almost made up my mind to get up and run to where I believed it to be.

And then I heard Virgil move.

The man was away to my right, and his foot had touched something that stirred – I think, perhaps, a flinder of broken slate.

I shall never forget that almost imperceptible sound that stood up out of the silence to make me a finger-post, for it was so slight, yet commanded the balance of life and death.

With a hammering heart, I turned at once to my right, no longer pausing to listen, but using the utmost care to deny to Virgil the cue he had given to me.

Before I had covered six feet, my outstretched hand met something that did not belong to the court. It might have been a silk tassel…

And then I knew I was touching Elizabeth's hair.

I could have wept for relief…

Now had I not been sure that Virgil was near, I would have picked her up and run for the woods: but he must have heard me moving and almost at once have seen me against the dusk, and then we should have been at his mercy, because he was armed. And so I determined that we must both stay where we were, unless and until something happened to make it less dangerous to move.

To show her that it was I, I smoothed her hair and held her hands tight in mine. Then, very gently, I eased the knot from her throat and lifted the cord from her neck. That done, it seemed best to bestride her, as though I were a man in some battle bestriding his fallen chief, for so, if Virgil came up, I stood more chance of saving her precious life: and when I had strained my ears, but had heard no sound, I put down my hands and began to unfasten the cord which was binding her wrists…

Her blessed hands were free, and her fingers, as though to thank me, were fast upon mine, when something moved upon her, directly below my face. It was a sliding movement upon the breast of her frock, for I was standing across her, with my back to her feet. As it moved, I felt her stiffen; and so I knew it had nothing to do with her; and when I put down a hand, I found that it was the halter which had been about her neck.

As I touched it, it moved again – and told me the truth.

Percy Virgil was feeling the other end.

For once my brain worked quickly.

Virgil had found the cord and knew what it was. And now he was testing it – *to see if both ends were free*. If I gradually took the strain, he would believe it still fast to Elizabeth's neck, and would lead himself up to his quarry, hand over hand. Up to his helpless quarry? *Up to his doom.*

I took the loop in my hand and set out to play my fish…

He came with a rush at the last, and, with both of his hands on the cord, he had no chance.

Before the man knew where he was, I had his wrists.

His hands were empty. No doubt, when he found the cord, he had put his pistol away. Be that as it may, he was finished. The snake was scotched.

Of course he fought like a madman. And I – I laughed in his face. It was he that had lent me a strength which was not of this world. I think, if I had pleased, I could have torn his arms from their sockets and tossed them across the court.

I let him fight in silence, and when he was spent, I spoke to Elizabeth, lying two paces away.

"Stay where you are, my lady, and take out your gag."

She answered at once.

"It's out, and my feet are free. You haven't forgotten Elgar?"

"I've dealt with Elgar," I said. "Can you make out the mouth of the court?"

"I think so. It's lighter there."

"That's right. Can you manage to walk? Or are your ankles too stiff?"

"I'm quite all right," she answered. "I'm standing now."

"Then listen," said I. "I want you to leave the court. When you're clear of it, wait for me. I may be a little while, because of this cursed dark: but – "

"Let me stay here, I beg you."

"No," I said firmly. "I can't have you on in this scene."

"Richard, I'm frightened. Supposing – "

"Only one thing can help him now. And that is your disobedience to what I say."

There was a moment's silence.

Then –

"Very well," said Elizabeth, shakily.

"Let me hear you move," said I.

I heard her turn and start moving towards the mouth of the court.

"Come," said I to Virgil. "Let's look for the sepulchre."

With that, I turned him about; without loosing his wrists. While I think that he tried to prevent me, I cannot be sure, for his efforts counted with me no more than the play of a child: but in any event, once turned, he could struggle no more, for, now that his arms were twisted, the slightest attempt to resist me entailed unbearable pain. Then I urged him before me towards where I thought was the well.

Now I meant to find that well, if it took me an hour and a half: and so, as is often the way, I found it almost at once. At least, I found the car, which was near enough – or, rather, my prisoner found it, by fouling one of its wings. Slowly I steered him round it… And so, a few moments later – we stood by the side of the well.

To be sure, I circled this, brushing the parapet's side and counting the three stone statues of men-at-arms – with Virgil always moving before me, because I had hold of his wrists. And then I turned him round and bent him over its edge…

"I'm going to kill you," I said, "because I know it's not safe to let you live. If it was safe, I'd thrash you within an inch of your life, and then call in the police and give them the inch that was left. But you have taught me tonight that, while you are still in being, your cousin will always go in danger of death. And so, for once in a way, I'll take a leaf out of your book, and go all lengths."

The man said nothing at all, but I could feel him trembling under my hand.

As I bent him over the depths, I knew he was bracing his knees against the parapet's wall, and God knows I did not blame him, for as I leaned over above him, the awful breath of the water smote my face. It was chill, yet heavy, and reeked of death and decay, and it offered so dreadful an earnest of what was to come that for one instant I flinched from thrusting a fellow creature to such a doom.

I suppose that he felt me falter, for he threw his weight on to his knees in one final, desperate effort to hold himself back.

This, to no avail. For the parapet crumbled before him, and we went down together into the well.

Now for Virgil I cannot answer, but it is a remarkable fact that, though our descent to the water can hardly have taken more than one second of time, I was able to decide quite clearly, before we struck, that, while I must do what I could to save my life, before I did anything else I must put Virgil to death. In that period I also remembered that I had ordered Elizabeth out of the court and that so she would be out of earshot if I were to call. I was actually thinking this over and was weighing the pros and cons of calling at all – for if I called and she came, she might fall into the well – when at last we hit the water, and thoughts and resolutions were, so to speak, blown to bits.

This was natural enough, if for no other reason, because I had never expected the water to be so cold. God knows what springs they were that fed that terrible well, but they proved their own descent, for the lymph of the snows that sired them ran in their silver veins: and though once, for a wager at Oxford, I bathed when ice was about, I will swear that the pool I then entered was warmer than that which was lying in Palfrey's well.

I do not know how far I went down, but I know that my lungs were bursting before I came up, and the first thing I clearly remember was scrabbling upon a wall that was coated with slime and finding a crack too small to admit my finger-tips. Then I heard Virgil rise beside me – for, of course, I had let him go – and that restored in an instant the wits I had lost.

I missed his throat in the darkness, but found his wrist: but both of us knew that the odds were now more equal than they had been in the court. With a frightful laugh, he flung an arm round my neck, and I had just time to draw breath before that hellish water once more closed over our heads. I tore away his arm, but before I could seize his throat, his arm was back on my neck. Again I cast it off and forced his wrists together into one hand; but, as we rose again, he locked his legs about mine and threw his weight down. And then I thought I was done, for though at last I had managed to seize his throat, I could not kick us up to the surface, nor spare a hand to deal with the grip of his legs. Unless I could kill him quickly... I put forth all my strength, and my fingers sank into his throat as though it were dough.

The blood was pounding in my temples and I felt that my senses were swaying for want of air, when all of a sudden his limbs and his body went slack and I knew I was free... And then I was back on the surface and was blowing like any grampus and thanking God for the gift of that tainted air.

Now whether in fact I killed Virgil or whether he drowned himself in an effort to end my life, I never shall know: but I know that the man was dead or else had lost his senses and so was presently drowned, for though he rose beside me, he never moved and I think that after a little he sank for good.

Though my case was not so bad, it was evil enough.

I was not wholly exhausted, but the struggle had sapped my strength, and I badly needed the respite I could not take. As was to be expected, the walls of the well were smooth, and though I proved them all round, dislodging slugs and slime and all manner of filth, I could find no sort of handhold to which I could cling. There were cracks in plenty between the blocks of stone of which the walls had been built, for either they had not been cemented, or else the cement was gone: but they were too small for my fingers, and there was nothing else.

All the time my strength was failing, for the deadly chill of the water was laying hold of my muscles and stealing into my blood, and though I did what I could to hold it at bay, the realization that I must very soon sink began, as an ill-mannered bully, to thrust aside my efforts to think what to do to be saved.

Indeed, I sometimes think that a wiser man than I would have faced the unpleasant fact that his hour was come and would so have allowed himself some peace at the last, but, perhaps because of Elizabeth waiting above, I would not read the writing upon the wall.

To show how desperate I was, I wasted the last of my strength in a frantic effort to find Elizabeth's key – this, with the mad idea of thrusting it into a crack and so creating a projection to which I could cling, and though, I suppose, a more utterly futile design was never conceived, as luck would have it, it actually saved my life.

To get a hand into my pocket was very hard, but the moment my fingers were in, they closed upon something which I had not known was there. And that was the humble tool which once already that night had saved two lives. It was the screwdriver, indeed.

I cannot explain its presence: but my habit has always been to some extent to care for my car myself, and, when I am at work, unless they are unwieldy, I always pocket my tools. And so, I suppose, without thinking, I did as I always do. Be that as it may, in a twinkling I had the screwdriver out and had pressed its blade into a crack perhaps some eight to ten inches above my head.

Praying that the steel was honest, I gradually let the handle take some of my weight, and when I found that it would hold me, I let it take more. But for the help of the water, it must have bent or broken beneath my weight; but the two together bore me and gave me just that respite my weary muscles required. And, what was still more important, it gave me a definite hope that, though my plight was serious, I might in the end be saved.

And then I heard Elizabeth calling my name…

For a moment I thought very fast. Then –

"Lie down," I yelled. "Lie down and crawl slowly forward. I'm down in the well, but *lie down*. The parapet's gone."

Perhaps two minutes went by: and then a fragment of mortar fell down by my side.

"Stop!" I screamed. "Stay still. You're right on the edge."

Elizabeth answered at once.

"I quite all right, my darling. What shall I do?"

I wonder how many women, so placed, would so have comported themselves. No wailing, no useless inquiries, no bubbling statements of how she came to be there… Only the eager question – 'What shall I do?'

And I was ready enough. Whilst she was approaching, I had not been wasting my time.

"Find the car," I said. "When you've found her, switch on her lights. Then back her slowly towards the mouth of the court. Her lights will show you the cord that I took from your neck. Take that and the pieces that bound your ankles and, wrists. Then back the car again till you see your dressing-case. Put that into the car, and then drive slowly forward until your lights are shining full on the well. When you've done that, come back and I'll tell you some more."

"All right."

How long she was gone, I cannot pretend to say, but she must have been very quick, for though the time passed slowly, at the moment at which I pictured her finding the case, the rim of the well above me grew suddenly bright. Then she must have 'dipped' the lamps, for the light came down – *to reveal a ladder of dogs driven into the wall of the well.*

Some wells have ladders like that, to the water's edge, and at once I left my hand-hold and, swimming beneath the ladder, stretched up my hand. But the dogs did not come so low… For all that, I was sure that they could not be far away, because a ladder is useless, unless it runs some way down.

As I returned to my screwdriver –

"Yes, Richard?" said Elizabeth, quietly.

"Tie all the cord together and add the strap. Then open the tool-box and take the tool-kit out. If there are tyre-levers there, I

201

want them most. If not, the nearest thing to them – tools that will bear my weight. And a hammer, too. Put them into one of your stockings and let them down. We've got to make thirty-eight feet. If you don't think it's long enough, you must add what stockings you have."

It cost me a lot not to add *Be as quick as you can*, for my faithful friend was tiring – bending beneath the strain; but such a charge would only have made her frantic, when all the time she was being as quick as she could.

I must confess that this time she took longer than I had hoped; but I am afraid that she suffered far more than I, for the tool-box proved to be hidden and she was beside herself before at last she found it beneath the floor.

The delay was serious, for every moment now I was growing more cold. My teeth were beginning to chatter: my fingers were growing numb: and though I did what I could by wriggling my body and limbs to encourage my blood to run, I knew that my circulation was steadily slowing down.

I thrust the reflection aside and glanced again at the glow which was lighting the ladder above…

At last a shadow appeared.

"I'm ready, my darling. Which side shall I let it down?"

"D-D'you see the ladder?"

I stammered in spite of myself.

"Yes."

"L-Let it down just clear of the ladder. Which side you l-like. *Don't lean on the parapet, whatever you do.*"

"All right. I won't."

"I'm not quite ready. I'll tell you when to begin."

With that, I pulled the screwdriver out of the crack in the wall and splashed my way to beneath the ladder of dogs. And there, with a frightful effort, I scratched away the filthy jacket of slime, in search of another interstice between the stones. I had not the strength to reach as high as I wished, and for two or three desperate moments I could not discover a joint; but at last my trembling fingers encountered the ghost of a crack and I managed to put up the blade and to push it a little way in.

I hardly hoped that it would hold me, but I could do no more: and, as I sank down and let the steel take my weight, I perceived that the circle was vicious – the circle in which I moved. My state of exhaustion demanded a handhold at once: to create such a handhold exhausted me unto death…

Then I knew that the blade was holding, and when I had rested a moment, I was able to push it further into the crack.

"Are you ready, my darling?"

"Yes. I'm ready," I said, and hoped for the best.

As will have been guessed, my primitive plan was this – to drive the tyre-levers between the stones of the well and so climb up by them to the foot of the ladder above. The objections to this were so obvious that I will not set them out: but the one which ruled the rest was my lack of strength to do more than hold myself up. Yet, something had to be done, for the icy water was gradually having its way…

I watched my lady's stocking pass out of the light of the lamps, with the levers jingling within it to tell me how far they had come, and three or four seconds later, I guided them into the pocket adorning the breast of my coat. As I felt for the head of the stocking, to cast it loose, I found that *it had been tied to a piece of flexible wire*.

At once I lifted my voice.

"That's enough. How much cord have you left?"

"About eight feet, my darling."

"What is it made of, Elizabeth?"

"Two pieces of cord, the strap and some flexible wire. The last was in the tool-box, on an inspection lamp."

I could have cried out for joy. Flexible wire will bear a considerable weight.

Again I addressed my lady.

"I want you to move the car; so that one of its wheels is directly in line with the ladder – say, five feet away from the well. Before you do this, hitch the cord round a statue, so that it doesn't fall."

"Very well."

Whilst she was doing my bidding, I unfastened the end of the 'flex'. Then with a shaking hand I got it about my body, under my arms. As I made it fast, I heard Elizabeth's voice.

"Yes, Richard? The car is there."

"Take your end of the cord and thread it between the spokes and so round the tyre. Then, very slowly, draw it as tight as you can. When you hear me shout, make it fast by taking two or three turns."

"Very well."

A moment later the 'flex' began to move.

I dared not ask too much of so frail a rope, and directly it took the strain, I called to my lady to stop; but though it could not have borne me, it held me up and, what was a thousand times better, it freed my hands. Before she was back at the head of that cursed well, I had hammered one of the levers into the wall.

Now I was not out of the wood by a very long way, but I knew that the lever would bear the whole of my weight: and this meant that, if I could manage to plant my other levers as rungs, I could emerge from the water which threatened to take my life.

After working the matter out, I called upon my lady to loosen the cord…

Somehow I planted a lever beneath the waterline.

Since I had but three, this seemed a terrible waste, but I simply had not the strength to drag myself clear of the water without some support below. And when the business was done and the slack of the cord taken up, it was all I could do to reach the first lever I drove. And there I hung, like a man cast up on some shore, who knows what still lies before him if he is to save his life and doubts that he has the strength to get to his feet and stagger landward out of the reach of the waves. For I had to set one of my feet on the lever below, and, when it was there, I had to haul myself up – a terribly difficult movement, at any time.

Stand at the foot of a ladder of seven rungs – *of which all are missing, except the second and fourth.* Then take hold of the second and mount the fourth… And I was not standing, and I was very tired.

Of course, the trouble was this – that my levers were much too close. And yet I could not plant them farther apart: for without some foothold I could not work higher up, and in my exhausted condition I could not work lower down.

It was a very near thing.

I never could have done it, without Elizabeth's help: for she handled the cord with such skill, always just taking the strain, but never taking my weight, that I depended upon her from first to last. When after a frightful convulsion I got a foot on to the lever, to hang, bent double, half in and half out of the flood: when the water clung to my body, as though reluctant to let go its lawful prey; when I made my last desperate effort to heave myself clear of its clutches and, keeping my foot on the lever, to straighten my knee; when I was up and was standing against the wall of the well, and all the handhold I had was the lever a bare two inches above my knee; when I dared to let go of this and, bracing my thigh against it, put up my hands above me, to search the wall… At these times, that poor cord saved me – and nothing else. And yet it must have broken, if once it had taken my weight.

Trembling, I straightened my back and put up my hands…*and met the last rung of the ladder shoulder-high.*

Reaching up as far as I could, I could actually grip the last but two of the dogs driven into the side of the well.

Be sure I tested the three as well as I could. Then I mounted my second lever and tested the fourth and fifth.

Though rust had corrupted them all, they seemed to be sound, and since they were very thick and were almost certainly grappled behind the stones of the well, I wasted no more time, but swung myself up.

Once I was on the ladder, I called my lady by name: and when she replied, I told her to drop the cord.

"I'm on the ladder," I said, "but I want to know where it stops."

"Just clear of the parapet, Richard."

"Stand still where you are," said I. "I'll come up and see."

It was as she said. The last of the dogs – or the first – was set perhaps six inches below the true rim of the well.

"Draw the cord tight," I said, "and then give me your end."

I passed this round my body and then threw it back.

"Put it round the wheel again and give it to me."

Again she did as I said: and again I passed it about me and pitched the end of it back.

"Now make that fast to the wheel, and then stand clear."

There was a moment's silence.

Then –

"All right, Richard," she said.

"Are you standing well back?"

"I am."

I took the five strands in my hand, and took a step up. The dogs were taking my weight, but the cord was holding me into the side of the well. I mounted step by step, and hand over hand. As my head rose above the parapet, I saw Elizabeth standing with one of her hands to her throat.

Three more steps…

Then I flung a leg over the wall and pulled myself in.

I was lying flat on the cobbles, with my head in Elizabeth's lap.

"You've paid your debts," I said somehow. "You saved my life."

"If I did, then I saved my own. But I didn't save it, my darling. I may have helped: but I think your great heart saved you, and nothing else."

I laughed at that.

"You wouldn't say that, my sweet, if you'd seen me down in that water an hour ago."

Elizabeth smiled her rare smile. Then she glanced at her watch.

"Did it seem so long, my darling? It's not quite twenty minutes since you sent me out of this court."

Whilst I was still staring, she put down her lips to mine. Then she held my head to her breast and kept saying over 'My Richard' and smoothing my dripping-wet hair. And then she kneeled up on the cobbles, which must have hurt very much, and thanked the God that made her for bringing me out of the well. And, perhaps because I was shaken and not yet myself, I lost what control I had and the tears ran down my cheeks. And, seeing this, she broke into tears herself, and the two of us wept together for joy of being together and both alive.

Ten minutes later we left that sinister court.

To the best of my belief, all traces of our occupation had been removed, and unless the well were searched, which was improbable, no one, I think, would have guessed that the haunted peace of Palfrey had been disturbed.

Elgar's body lay with his master's within the well, and the ounce of blood he had lost was cloaked with a handful of soil. Made fast to a block of stone, the pieces of cord and the strap lay fifty feet deep; and, except for the two tyre-levers, the tool-kit was once more complete. And the dressing-case rested behind us, its cargo of stone discharged.

Clear of the court, I stopped by Elizabeth's wish. Then I left the car and stripped and rubbed myself down with the silk with which we two had been gagged: then I wrung out my trousers and put them back on my legs; but I drove to Brief bare backed, "for a shirt that is soaked," she insisted, "is worse than nothing at all."

I did not argue with her, for, for all I knew, she was right: but after the chill of that water, the cool night airs seemed hot, and, wet as they were, my clothes had felt warm upon me before I had spent five minutes out of that well.

And then we set out for Brief.

It was very near three o'clock when I berthed the car in the shadows which masked the entrance-drive, for now the moon was up and was refining the country on which, as we both believed, we had looked our last an hour and a quarter before.

Ten minutes later, perhaps, we entered her staircase-turret and climbed its steps…

Now I had advised that Elsa be told to dress and to be beyond Brief's verge before six o'clock – unless she preferred to be charged with attempted murder and almost certainly sent to prison for life: but, to our surprise and relief, her bed was untouched and she was not within the suite. In fact, it was very soon clear that, because she did not trust Virgil – and there she can scarcely be blamed – she had discarded the *rôle* which she had been ordered to play, and had selected a better and surer part.

To be short, 'Monna Lisa' had fled – taking with her the best of all that Elizabeth had.

That she had behaved with discretion cannot, I think, be denied; for, had Virgil returned, and not we, he would have been forced for his own sake to cover his creature's retreat. Though he would have raged in spirit, he must have subscribed to the fiction that she had gone with Elizabeth, when she eloped – the devoted maid, attending her erring mistress upon her clandestine flight, *and bearing an excellent suitcase, laden with precious goods*. Unsuspected, far less pursued. she would have passed out of his ken on the wings of the wind he had sown – and left him to reap any whirlwind that happened to rise… There can be no doubt that Elsa was very shrewd.

In fact, her disappearance suited us very well, for we had our secrets to keep, and such a wolf in sheep's clothing was far better out of our way: and though the things she had taken were worth a good deal, their loss but served to remind us of what we had saved that night.

I made the most of the bathroom before I did anything else; but, of course, I had no dry clothes and, though I begged for my shirt, Elizabeth would not allow me to put it on. Instead, when I reappeared, she put a flask into my hand and bade me do as she told me or else go off to my bed. Since some things remained to be settled. I let her have her way, but I could not help thinking of the strictures which would have been passed, if the Duchess of Whelp had suddenly entered the room.

I suppose that one treasures for ever the gift of forbidden fruit: but I know that as long as I live I shall never forget the short, most intimate scene which brought to an end the drama in which we had played that night. Less than an hour before, I had been fighting for life in Palfrey's terrible well: and now I was in Elizabeth's exquisite bedroom, sitting, with a flask in my hand, on the foot of Elizabeth's bed, while Elizabeth stood to her pier-glass, putting her hair to rights.

Her clothes were stained and torn and one of her legs was bare – for that had furnished the stocking which she had sent down the well. Her delicate ankle was bruised, and the wrists she had raised were marked, for the cords had chafed her skin; but bruises and stains and tears could not at all diminish the startling splendour of body which she had been given at birth, and for the five-hundredth time I wondered how Virgil had dared to lay hands upon something so perfect and irreplaceable. Indeed, I can only suppose that a man who will plan and commit such hideous and cold-blooded murder as he did his best to do, is ruthless to a degree which most of us cannot conceive, for, though he was her cousin and had been familiar with her for a number of years, her beauty was such as custom can never stale. (And that is not my opinion and that of nobody else, for the Duchess of Whelp and John Herrick have many times said the same thing, but have put it far better than I.)

Then I met her eyes in the glass and the two of us smiled, and I saw myself beyond her, looking like any miner, about to begin his toil.

"High time I was gone," said I, and got to my feet.

Elizabeth spoke over her shoulder.

"As a matter of fact, I love to see you there. When we're married, you must always sit there when I'm brushing my hair."

Old Harry's words rang in my ears, and I turned away.

I must request your assurance upon one point. That is that you are aware that you cannot possibly marry the Countess of Brief.

For an instant my spirit rebelled.

She owed me her patent. I, Richard Exon, had made her the Countess of Brief. And we had faced death together. We had entered the mouth of Hell and had turned round and come back together into the rolling world. And now I was in her bedroom at…half-past three of a morning, stripped to the waist…and she was before her mirror, brushing her beautiful hair… And yet I could not be her husband… I could be haled up to Pisgah, to view the promised land. And then, when I had viewed it and seen how fair were its fruits, I could withdraw from my view-point and go my ways.

And then I remembered Old Harry's other words:

Always remember – these things cannot be helped. I loved a commoner once, and he loved me. But there are some bars, Richard Exon, more rigid than those you loosed. So we both of us did our duty…

'We both of us did our duty.'

I put the flask to my lips and when I had drained it dry I put it back in the cupboard from which she had taken it down.

"What about tomorrow?" I said. "I mean, if we can, we'd better keep out of the wet. Not that I care. If the police knew I'd bumped him off, they'd put their arms round my neck. But I can't hear anyone knowing that you were involved... And yet – "

"My darling, what are you saying?"

I turned to meet Elizabeth's startled eyes.

Then she laid down her brush and came and put her hands on my shoulders.

"Can you get what I'm saying, Richard? Or are you all in?"

"I'm all right, my beauty, but I'm too tired to make plans."

"I'll make them for you;" she said; "and now listen to me. When you leave this room, you must go by the way that you came. That is, by the picture-gallery. There you must pick up the harp – I'll help you do that. And then you must pick up Winter and enter the tower. And so to bed. At seven Winter cancels the horses – you gave him that order last night, by my request. He calls you again at nine: but, because there is no one to call me, I sleep till ten. Then I find that Elsa has gone: and after a little I find that she's taken some of my things. But you don't even know that – *because neither you nor your servant were out of the tower all night.*"

"Yes, I've got that," I said.

"It's vital, Richard – *vital*. If we say *anything*, we've got to say *everything*. And, except for Old Harry and Herrick, no one must ever know what happened tonight." She raised her eyebrows there and gave a little shake of her head. "I don't know what stuff I'm made of, but it hasn't upset me at all Neither was fit to live – quite apart from the fact that you did it in self-defence. But the fact remains that you've been the death of two men...and one of those men was the cousin with whom I have been brought up... My darling, listen to me. *It simply must not be known that the man whom I am to marry put Percy Virgil to death.*"

"Yes, I see that," I said somehow. "All right. I'll keep my counsel, and Winter will hold his tongue." I put my arms about her and held her close. "Kiss me good night, my lady. The dawn will be coming up, and I want you to get to bed."

As I kissed her mouth, she took my head in her hands...

"Oh, Richard," she breathed, "I can't bear letting you go. I've got to, of course – the conventions must be observed. You're here by accident: and so you must go away. But it seems so natural and right for you to be here. After all, how many brides have known their bridegrooms so well? Tonight we stood together beyond the world, breast-high in the river that runs between life and death. And that has bound us together more tightly than any service or any plighting of troth. Supposing I was engaged to be married to somebody else. I might have meant to go through with it, although I loved you. I mean, such things have been done. But I couldn't go through with it now – not after tonight. I should have to tell him straight out that we had been joined together by God Himself and that I had become your woman and you had become my man."

I dared not trust my voice, so I kissed her lips again: then I drew her head on to my shoulder, because I did not want her to see the look in my eyes.

What she had said was most true. We had been joined together as lovers are seldom joined. And yet we should never be married, because Old Harry would never give her consent. And I – not she – *must have* Old Harry's consent.

I had passed my word to the Duchess of Whelp. Unless I had passed my word, the Duchess of Whelp would not have lifted a finger to help Elizabeth's cause. But, once I had passed my word – well, no one could have done more than the Duchess of Whelp. *I had received full value against my bond.* And so my bond must be honoured – at any cost.

I threw a glance round the bedroom through which I might pass again, but to which I should never belong: I saw the flash of the bathroom which I had used that night for the first and last time…the eiderdown on which I had sat, but never should sit again…the pier-glass which never again would show me Elizabeth brushing her sweet-smelling hair.

I dropped my lips to that hair.

"Good night," I whispered. "Good night, my beautiful girl."

I let her go, slipped into my sodden coat and laid my shirt over my arm. Two minutes later we stood in the picture-gallery.

By the light of the staircase-turret, I set up the eloquent harp. Then I turned to her standing beside me, picked up her little hand and put its palm to my lips.

"Sleep well, sweet-heart." I whispered.

"And you, my dear. Look. I'll keep my door open until you get to the hall."

So she lighted me on my way…

When I came to the head of the staircase, I purposely bore to the left, and an instant later a torch was flashed into my eyes.

"Well done, Winter," said I. "And now we'll go back to the tower. That's enough for tonight."

In my room I gave him his orders. One of these concerned the suit which I was so glad to take off.

"Let no one see you do it, but, when you can tomorrow, conceal this suit in the Rolls. And the next time I send you for petrol stop in some lonely place, cut my name out of the jacket and burn the lot."

"Very good, sir," said Winter, blinking. "And – and what about this?"

"My shirt? Oh, that doesn't matter. Hang it out on – "

And there I stopped dead.

He was not holding my shirt.

What he was holding was one of the dainty chemises with which I had rubbed myself down.

11

The Fall of the Curtain

I had told Winter to call me at nine o'clock; but, tired as I was, I woke at a quarter to eight, and after trying in vain to go back to sleep, I presently threw in my hand and began to get up.

My state of mind was uneasy.

I could not reach my lady, because I had given her back the key of her suite. Yet, since I had her chemise, my shirt must be in her bedroom. If she found it, well and good. But if some servant found it…

In fact I need not have worried, for about ten minutes to nine a manservant came to my room, bearing a note and a parcel addressed to me.

"From his lordship, sir," he said, and bowed himself out.

With starting eyes I read the following words:

MR EXON,
I have the honour to return you the shirt which you dropped this morning on leaving my daughter's suite.

Perhaps you will make it convenient to leave the castle at once.

BRIEF

I remember that I stared at the paper as though it belonged to some dream. Then I sat down and put my head in my hands. And then I stood up again, because something had to be done.

As I made for the door, this was opened and Winter came into the room.

"Find Mr Parish," I said: "and ask him to come here at once."

As it was, I was more than half dressed, and as I got into my jacket, the Englishman entered the room.

"Parish," I said, "how soon can I see her Grace?"

"Perhaps at ten, sir: but certainly not before that."

I glanced at my watch. The time was five minutes past nine.

"Very well, I must see the Count. I don't think he'll want to receive me, but if you can get hold of Bertram, perhaps you can bring it off."

"I'll manage it, sir," said Parish. "Do you wish to see him at once?"

"Immediately."

"Then come with me, sir," said Parish. "I think I know where he is."

I thrust the note into my pocket and left the room.

The respect with which Parish was treated by the servants of Brief was very nearly as deep as that they were pleased to accord to the Duchess herself, and before two minutes had passed I was ushered unannounced into an elegant library.

As the door closed behind me –

"What the hell does this mean?" said the Count, getting up to his feet.

I answered him slowly enough.

"It means," I said, "that we are to clear the air."

"I'll see about that," said the man, and made straight for the bell.

"I strongly advise you," I said, "not to try to have me removed. If you do, you will force my hand: and so, Lord Ferdinand Virgil, cut your throat."

215

I saw the shaft go home. My use of his proper title hit him beneath the heart. If more revelations were coming, better that they should come whilst we were alone. For all that, his eyes were burning… I was Richard Exon, and not the Duchess of Whelp.

As a servant answered his summons, he turned on his heel…

I watched him curiously.

There was a moment's silence.

Then –

"Your lordship rang?" said the servant.

The other spoke over his shoulder.

"Yes," he said thickly. "Has – has Mr Percy returned?"

"Not yet, my lord."

"Desire him to come here the moment he enters the house."

"Very good, my lord," said the man, and made himself scarce.

As the door closed behind him –

"I do not think," I said, "that your son is going to come back."

Lord Ferdinand started about.

"My *son*? Is this blackmail?"

"It's not even bluff," said I. "But listen to me. I say I have reason to think that your son is not coming back. In view of what I told him last night, I think he will find it convenient to disappear."

The man was staring as though I were not of his world.

"Of what you told him? *Who are you?*"

The question flamed.

"I'm a plain-clothes man," said I, "and I'm working for Scotland Yard."

I watched the blood flow out of the fellow's face…

At length he moistened his lips.

"Does the Duchess know this?" he said.

"No," said I. "Nobody knows – except the Austrian police."

I saw his mouth twitch at the word.

216

"Why – why the Austrian police?"

"Because I could not arrest you, without their leave. It's a question of extradition. You broke your bail in England twenty-two years ago."

"So you say. But – "

"You arranged your flight with your brother. He booked your passage for you and went alone to the station, taking your tickets and money to see you off. And, when he was gone, you went – to Paris, instead. And the police mistook him for you…and sent him down. That's twenty-two years ago, and he's done his time: but the charge against you remains, Lord Ferdinand Virgil, and I have been sent from England to…clear things up."

His fingers were plucking at his trousers, as those of a dying man will pluck at his sheets.

"What d'you mean – clear things up?"

"I'll tell you plainly," said I. "Because of the mistake that was made, another warrant must issue – as a matter of form. Before that warrant can issue, a further information has to be sworn. I am here to complete that information… Thanks to what happened last night, it is very nearly complete."

"And then?"

"Then I shall return to London. And when the warrant is issued, I – shall – come – back."

There was a deathly silence.

Then the fellow turned round and made his way to a chair. I saw that he went heavily, as a man that is tired.

After a little he spoke.

"Why do you tell me these things?"

I took out the note he had written and held it up.

"Because of this letter. It seems that one of your people saw me leaving the Lady Elizabeth's suite. I had to convince you, therefore, that I was there on duty – and nothing else."

He let out a laugh at that, and the blood came into my face.

217

"If you doubt me," I said, "I can prove it. I'd a man outside her door the whole of the time."

"A man?" he cried, starting up.

"A man," said I. "Don't think I'm working alone. The man in question is playing the part of my servant: he's really a sergeant out of the CID."

He quailed to the words, as a beast will quail to the whip. And then, as a beast will turn, he was showing fight.

"So you say," he snarled. "So you say. You prate of warrants and duty and – where's your badge?" His voice rose into a scream. "Show me your badge, you – "

"It's in my dispatch-case," I said " – with other things. Would you like to know the duty which took me into her suite?"

"What then?"

I raised my eyebrows.

"I wanted a word with her maid – a girl of the name of Elsa… She's wanted for abortion in Bristol. Perhaps you didn't know that."

And there, when I stood to lose it, I won my game – with a shaft that Percy Virgil had set in my hand: for I saw in his father's eyes that he knew the truth about Elsa…and how could I have known it, unless I belonged to the police? 'The evil that men do lives after them.' The son had delivered the father into my hand.

Lord Ferdinand's head was shaking.

As he felt for his chair –

"I swear that I didn't. I swear – "

"You needn't worry. You won't be accused of that. But that isn't nearly all. I didn't go just to see Elsa: I wanted to see your niece. For one thing, I wanted to speak of her mother's jewels."

The fellow's head stopped shaking, and a hand went up to his mouth.

"What – of – her – mother's – jewels?"

"This," said I. "Your son, Percy Virgil, stole them six weeks ago."

Lord Ferdinand sat very still, with his mouth a little open and his eyes staring over my shoulder at something which was not there. That he had not known of the theft was perfectly plain, and I shall always believe that his son had 'double-crossed' him in that disgraceful affair.

I went on steadily.

"The jewels were in London, in Bauble and Levity's hands. Your son produced to that firm his cousin's 'authority' to hand them over to him. Then he sold them to a broker named Inskip. The deal was put through in Surrey – at dinner, in a country hotel. I saw it done. I was sitting two tables away."

The fellow sat back in his chair, with a hand to his throat.

"You say that he's gone," he said.

"Both he and Elsa have gone. You see, I had instructions to give them their choice... That is sometimes done – if the injured party consents. It – it tends to avoid a scandal... I gave them both until dawn to be clear of Brief. And both have availed themselves of the chance which they had. Personally, I think they were wise: and I must confess that Elsa got back on me, for she packed a suitcase whilst I was engaged with your niece, and, when she went, it went with her... But that's by the way. In fact, this is all by the way, for I have so far said nothing of the most significant duty I did last night: *I proved your brother's statement that he is the Count of Brief.*"

My words brought him up to his feet.

"I defy you," he mouthed. "It's a lie." He clawed at the air. "There is no proof. Because some old doddering servant imagines vain things – "

"I am not a doddering servant and I have no memories. Yet I can prove the statement your brother makes. I was sent to see if I could prove it – I told you just now. I was sent to complete the information...upon which the warrant will issue, the day after I get back."

"Then prove it – prove it to me."

219

"With pleasure," said I. "The Lady Elizabeth Virgil is twenty-four. She is also the next in line. If you are the Count indeed, *why have you never shown her the secret of Brief?*"

Beside this, my other blows were so many flicks on the face. Before my eyes, Lord Ferdinand seemed to shrink; and he took a step back and then sideways, and put out a hand to find something on which he could lean. All the time he was gazing upon me, as though I had uttered some spell which had paralysed the resistance which he had intended to make – and so, I suppose I had, for I had told him something of which he had never dreamed, which ought to have been written upon his heart.

His fingers encountered a table, to which they clung.

"The – the secret?" he breathed.

"Yes," said I. "The secret. The secret of Brief. Only the first-born is shown it – or ever has been shown it, for more than five hundred years. If you are the Count indeed, then tell me the tale of the secret and what exists in that chamber which no one would ever find. Tell me the names there written and show me the secret steps... But, first of all, tell me this – how is your brother aware of these mysteries, unless he is, as he says, the Count of Brief?"

To my surprise, he made answer.

"I – I cannot tell."

But he spoke as a man in a trance, with a dull, emotionless voice, and I knew that his spirit was broken, because I had shown him something against which he could not stand.

"Listen to me," said I.

He lifted his head.

"Following your brother's directions, I found the way to the chamber eight hours ago. I took his daughter with me: and now she knows for herself the secret of Brief. Both of us, therefore, can swear that we have seen with our eyes what your brother said we should see...which means that, as I warned you, the information is very nearly complete."

Though I heard no sound, I saw his lips frame the words. "Very nearly."

"Very nearly, my lord, I have proved all your brother said, except one thing. *He declared that if I were to ask you to tell me the secret of Brief, I should ask you in vain.* And so... I ask you...to give me one single detail...of what your father revealed to his first-born son."

The man was trembling, and the sweat was out on his face.

"My b-brother," he quavered. "I think, if I could see him... I mean, without his statement the – the warrant could not issue...and could not be – "

"He has made his statement," I said. "I have a copy upstairs."

"But my son is free. Statements were made in his case, but he has gone free. You said that you had instructions – "

"If the injured party consents."

"That's what I say," cried the man. "My brother would never subscribe to my – to proceedings against his father's son. I – I know he wouldn't Exon. He wouldn't bear malice like that. And then the scandal... You said yourself that, rather than have a scandal – "

"Your son has gone," said I. "There can be no scandal there. Percy Elbert Virgil has disappeared."

"I – can – disappear."

I raised my eyebrows.

"Your case is far more serious than that of your son. You've forged and lied and stolen for twenty-two years. And an innocent man has served the heavy sentence which should have been served by you for your first offence. I was able to tell your son that, if he made himself scarce, the case against him would be dropped. Without authority, I cannot say that to you. For your brother, I can answer. If he is allowed to do so, I know that he will withdraw. But the Crown may not allow him to take that course."

"But you can advise them, Exon." The man was cringing – at last. "You can say you've spoken with me and you think it's best. I'm not as strong as I was, and I shan't live long: and – and it's no good im-imprisoning someone in failing health."

He was panting now, and his eyes were half out of his head; yet he did what he could to wreathe his face into a smile, as though to do me pleasure and make me his friend.

"I can make no promise," I said, "until I have reported to those who sent me here. The case is too grave. But I'll tell you what I will do. If you will indorse the statement your brother has made, I'll take it to London tonight and recommend my people to let you go. To be honest, I don't think they'll do it, but – "

"How soon will you know?"

"On Friday. And on Sunday I shall be back – with or without the warrant for your arrest. This is upon condition that you indorse the statement to which I refer. Otherwise…"

"Yes?"

"In view of what you have admitted, I shall lay an information at Gabble without delay. That will ensure your detention until the demand for your extradition is made."

"But if I sign…"

"I can make no promise," I said. "I'll take the statement to London, and do what I can. You can take it or leave it, my lord. Sign, and I leave for London. Don't sign, and I leave for Gabble – within the hour."

The fellow was biting his fingers, with his eyes on my face. The signing stuck in his gullet, as well it might. And then he threw in his hand…

"All right," he said. "Give me the statement… And you'll do your best for me, Exon. I'm – I'm not as young as I was."

I stepped to the bell and rang it.

"I want my…servant," I said…

With a shaking hand, Lord Ferdinand wiped his face: and then, still holding the table, he made his way round the oak and took his seat in a chair. When my summons was answered, one hand was shading his eyes and the other was toying with a paper that lay on a blotting-pad.

"I want my dispatch-case, Winter."

As the door closed, Lord Ferdinand spoke again.

"Will – will he go to London with you?"

I shook my head.

"He'll take me to Innsbruck this evening, spend the night there and be back tomorrow at noon."

"I see."

He said no more, but I saw him pick up a pencil, as though to write. Then he seemed to remember my presence and laid the pencil down.

Winter re-entered the room. As he gave the case into my hand –

"I shall want you again," I said, "so wait within call."

"Very good, sir."

As he left the chamber, I held a paper up. "The statement," I said. "A copy of the first of the statements your brother made. The second does not concern you, because it only deals with the secret of Brief."

The man half rose from his chair, but I bade him sit still. Then I stepped to his side and laid the paper before him, for him to read…

I am glad to record that in the next three minutes that black-hearted parricide paid a part of his debt.

As he read, I saw him writhing, and the sweat fell down from his forehead, to blur the ink.

It was a frightful indictment.

My twin-brother was under arrest, on a charge of forgery.

It was perfectly clear that, if Ferdinand stood his trial, he would be sent to prison for several years.

My brother fell on his knees…

He had put this into my pocket – to gain his terrible ends.

So he and I changed places.

He took my father's title and all that was mine, and I was sent to prison for seven years.

My daughter became his daughter, my life became his life.

And Ferdinand was careful. He even denied my cheque for five hundred pounds. He said that I had forged it…

Twice, while he read, he dropped his head to the table and cried aloud, and when he had done, he fairly burst into tears and laid his head down on his arm and sobbed like a child.

To me, it is a terrible thing to see a grown man break down and weep as he used to weep in his mother's arms, for it means that his heart has thrown back to the age of innocence, to which, because he is adult, his mind can never return, of which he can have no comfort, because he is now too old. But, if I am to be honest, it did me good to see so vile a being in such distress, for the pitiful statement before him revived for me the full horror of Gering's life and death

So I changed my name and sought work – I had to have bread.

Gering was earning his bread in Red Lead Lane, while his brother was paying his chef five hundred a year.

I drew the statement from under his sprawling arm. Then I picked up a pen and wrote…

When I had done, I called Winter.

"Fetch Mr Parish," I said.

Lord Ferdinand started up, lifting a visage that made even Winter blench.

"Parish? Her Grace's page? What has he –?"

"To witness your signature. I shall witness it, and so will my man. But Parish is independent, and – "

"No, no. I never consented to any such thing."

"As you please," said I, and folded the statement up. "Turn out the car, Winter. I want to be at Gabble within the hour."

"Very good, sir," said Winter, and turned.

"No, no. Not that," cried the other, and savaged his thumb.

"Parish or Gabble," said I. "It's for you to choose."

After a frightful struggle –

"To witness my signature only. You'll cover the statement up?"

"Yes."

"Very…well."

I turned again to Winter.

"Fetch Mr Parish," I said…

Whilst we waited, he got to his feet and went to a glass and generally did what he could to pull himself into some shape, and I looked out of the window, with folded arms.

As he came back to the table –

"What name did he take?" he said. "I – I saw the initials 'M G'?"

"He is known as Matthew Gering," I said.

To my surprise, he nodded.

"I thought as much," he said slowly. "I thought as much. That was the name of a tortoise…we used to have. And he always used to pretend that he was a prince – transformed. And he used to say spells above him…in the hope of changing him back. … Of course, we were very small then…" With a sudden, savage movement, he brushed the vision away. Then he dragged his chair to the table and snatched up a pen. "He was always the dreamer," he snarled. "Where d'you want me to sign?"

I made no answer at all, but when he looked up, he saw the look in my face… And I think this sobered him, for he laid the pen down again and made no further movement, except with his eyes.

Five minutes later, the thing was over and done.

The damning endorsement is lying before me now.

*I have read this statement through from beginning to end,
and I hereby confess that all that it says is true.*

FERDINAND ELBERT VIRGIL

for twenty-two years supposed to be Count of

BRIEF

*Signed of his own free will
On the 22nd of July, 1936
In the presence of us:
Richard Exon
Samuel Parish
George Winter*

As Winter laid down his pen –

"That's all," I said, "thank you." Parish inclined his head and turned to the door. "You can take my dispatch-case, Winter, and – pack my things. We leave for Innsbruck together at four o'clock."

"Very good, sir," said Winter, obediently.

I blotted the precious indorsement and folded the statement up. Then I put it into my pocket and faced the man I had bluffed.

"You've done your part," I said, "and I shall do mine." As one who is listening intently, he kept his eyes upon mine and greeted every phrase with a nod of his head. "I will recommend that you be allowed to disappear – to go, to change your name, and never come back. As I've told you, I don't think they'll do it" – a hand went up to his mouth – "the punishment doesn't matter: it's a question of righting a wrong. And that is why I think they'll insist that the case must proceed. But I shall know on Friday: and on Sunday I shall be back." I hesitated. "If I were you, I should put your things in order, for whether – "

In evident apprehension he cut me short.

"They wouldn't pursue me, Exon? They wouldn't do that? You'd tell them I wasn't worth it..."

SHE PAINTED HER FACE

He laid a hand on my arm, and I shook it off.

"They wouldn't try to find you," I said, "so long as you kept out of sight."

"Even if they hadn't – No, no. Never mind. Tell me this. I've – I've saved a little money...that Percy knows nothing about. Not very much – very little. It's in a bank in England, under another name."

His head was going again. Plainly, the thought of penury hit him hard.

"If the estate is in order, I expect they'd let that go."

"Quite so," he said, "quite so. Besides, it's so very little..."

"A man can live," I said grimly, "on thirty-five shillings a week. That was your brother's wage for seventeen years."

He winced at that. Then he took his handkerchief out and wiped his eyes.

"Very sad," he said, "very sad. If only I'd known... You'll tell them I'm failing, won't you? You'll ram it home?"

Consumed with disgust and indignation, I turned on my heel...

As I opened the door, I looked back – to see his outstretched hand whip back to his side. As though I had noticed nothing I left the room.

I have no doubt at all, that before the door had closed, he had picked the timetable up.

As I took my way to the tower, I laid my plans.

I had to leave Brief at four – no question of that; for, though we had the game won, it was highly desirable that 'the Count' should take the departure which he had planned. If he fled, to avoid arrest – as, at present, he intended to do – he would indeed disappear for good and all, and would never more be heard of, because he could not take such a risk: but if he had reason to think that he had been bluffed, though now we could force his hand, he would stand upon the order of his going and would certainly be a nuisance for as long as he happened to live.

And so 'the plain-clothes man' must 'leave for London' at four.

And there I stood still in my tracks, for all of a sudden I saw that *here was my chance to do what sooner or later I had to do – that is to say, to walk out of my lady's life.*

As I saw it, I think I aged, for while my whole being revolted from a plunge ten times as awful as that into Palfrey's well, I knew in my heart that I must take it, because such a chance would never occur again.

Disappearance was in the air, and – my work was done. The play was over. Though nobody knew it but I, the curtain was down: and so I was free to be gone. An epilogue was to follow, but I had no part in it. I had been offered a part – a very shining *rôle*, for which I had lately rehearsed. But I could not take the part. And since I cared for no other, it was plainly best to be gone.

> 'If it were done when 't is done, then 't were well
> 'It were done quickly.'

The famous words settled the matter. My mind was made up.

I glanced at my watch. The time was a quarter to ten. Once my decision was taken, I could have wished that the time was a quarter to four…

I had already determined that no one must know what had happened till after 'the Count' had fled: and now I perceived that all that I had to do was to leave a note for the Duchess, to be delivered as soon as my victim was gone.

I entered my room, to find Winter, suitcase in hand.

"Leave the packing for the moment," I said. "I'll tell you when to begin. I want you to send off a wire."

I sat down and wrote it out – addressed to myself.

"Turn out the Rolls and take this to Gabble at once. And on the way back you might get rid of that suit."

"Very good. sir. Excuse me – you know Mr Virgil's not here."

"So I've heard," said I. "I rather imagine he's gone while the going is good."

"That's what they're saying downstairs, sir. I can hardly believe it myself, but they've got the idea in their heads he won't never come back. 'Rats leavin' a sinkin' ship' is what one of them said. An' when I asked what he meant, 'You wait an' see,' he says. ' 'Er Grace ain't here for nothing – not after last night.' "

"That's the style," said I. "And now you get off with that wire."

"Very good, sir. And breakfast is served – in the morning-room. It's been ready since half-past nine. Mr Herrick's gone down."

Old Harry looked round.

"And now…" she said – grimly enough.

Luncheon was over and coffee had been served in her suite. For the first time for fifteen hours Elizabeth, Herrick and I were alone with the Duchess of Whelp.

She was plainly out of humour, and I had an uneasy feeling that she knew more than I was prepared to tell.

Herrick climbed on to the altar, moistening his lips.

"Madam," he said, "quite frankly, I'm out of my depth."

"That," said the Duchess shortly, "I am quite prepared to believe. But I am made otherwise. I don't know what it means to be out of my depth and I've never yet seen the flood that I couldn't ford. The trouble here is – there's no flood. I ought to be knee-deep in water, and here I am on dry land. Where's that dangerous felon Virgil? And why does my host keep his room? If he's ill, he's breaking a record: for never before has indisposition denied me the courtesy due to my state." She slapped the arm of her chair. "What's the use of an empty pit, when you're out to bait bears?"

"They say," began Herrick…

"I mistrust that phrase," snapped Old Harry. "It suggests that the source of your news wells out of the servants' hall. So please understand that, however refreshing and rare you may find its waters yourself, no one has ever yet dared to commend them to me."

Herrick inclined his head,.

"I should have known better, madam."

"You should. Never mind. Are there any hard facts I don't know? Facts, not gossip, mark you. The enemy has retired. I'm not at all deceived, for this is a fight to the death – but I want to know what he is doing and when and where he is going to reappear."

"*Cherchez la femme*," said Herrick. "What of the maid?"

Old Harry looked at my lady.

"You heard what he said," she declared. "Why the devil don't you tell us the truth?"

Elizabeth glanced at the door.

"That's quite all right. Godolphin is standing outside and she knows no English at all."

My lady took a deep breath.

"Last night an attempt was made to put me to death. My maid admitted my cousin into my suite. Richard came to my help – and walked into a trap. But by his wit and courage he saved us both... That is why my cousin and Elsa have disappeared."

Herrick's face was a study, but the Duchess of Whelp merely nodded and then picked up her cup and drank what coffee was left. As she set it down –

"That's more like it," she said. "I mean, that is credible. I knew your life was in danger, yet what could I do – except trust in Richard Exon? Courage and wit be damned – I'll lay his instinct saved you, and nothing else." She, turned upon me. "Did you take my advice this time? Or did your better judgment impel you to spare his life?"

"Madam," said I, "he is dead."

"Well done," said Old Harry. "Well done. But you shouldn't drop shirts about, when a lady lets you out of her bedroom at half-past three."

Elizabeth started and clapped a hand to her mouth.

"Madam," I said, "I see you've received a note."

"Yes," said the Duchess, "I did. And I'll make you a present of this – I dismissed its contents at once, as being untrue. But when I heard that Elizabeth's maid was gone – well, I knew there was something behind them and hoped for the best. And now what about you? I understand you had a note? Why didn't you, er, act upon it?"

"Madam," said I, "I preferred to hope for the best."

The piercing grey eyes held mine.

"Did you indeed? Now I should have gone to see the writer…at once."

I knew that Parish had told her as much as he knew.

"Madam, forgive me. With great respect – I've a delicate hand to play."

"How long shall you wait?"

"Till tomorrow morning, madam. No longer than that."

"It's up to you," said Old Harry. "And there goes another record. Never before have I used that disgusting phrase. But I'm under the weather today, and it's – devilish eloquent." She threw a defiant glance round – to see Herrick open-mouthed, with a hand to his head. "And what's the matter with you?"

"Everything," said Herrick. "A very little more, and I shall burst into tears. I'm not only out of my depth. I'm floundering about in the water under the earth." He covered his eyes. "I am given to understand that, whiles I slept last night, certain action took place. Men came and went in – in violence: and, unless my ears have betrayed me, one will return no more. Very well. Out of that soul-shaking fact, two burning questions arise – to pierce the scum now floating upon my brain. I mean, I'm no 'Scourge of God', but I am a practical man…"

"Go on," said Old Harry, twinkling.

"Well, the first is this. I hardly like to ask after Elsa's health, but – "

"I believe it to be excellent," said I.

"I'm much obliged," said Herrick. "And that brings me direct to the second. Virgil has been bumped off. *Was Elsa in on that deal?*"

"No, she wasn't," said I.

"Thank you very much," said Herrick. "That's all I wanted to know. Of course, if, upon reflection, you should feel disposed to divulge any further, er, reactions which bear upon the matter in which I believed I was concerned – well, I shan't refuse to listen. But pray, don't put yourself out. Besides, I expect you're busy. A murder a day keeps the doctor away. What time are you taking the Count for a drive?"

"Leave him alone," said old Harry. "If I can wait, so can you. Richard Exon has taken the bit in his teeth – I saw as much the moment he entered the room. And there it can stay for me – till he's ready to let it drop. He'll take his fences all right. But don't forget this – a man can't say very much, when he's got the bit in his teeth."

I never was so grateful for any words, for, true or no, they showed an understanding of which I stood in great need. Craft is not my strong point, and the effort I had made that morning seemed to have tired my brain. Then again, though success seemed certain, 'the Count' was still in his seat, and I was forever fearing that something or other would happen to make him change the decision to which I was sure he had come. Above all, my own decision to disappear hung, like some loathsome monster, upon my neck, insisting upon my attention and gleefully indicating the several lovely features of the paradise I was to lose. Had I been cross-examined, or even been asked to relate what had happened the night before, I should, I believe, have burst out and disgraced myself, for the present was so overwhelming and the future so very bleak that to deal with the past was like going into training when you are condemned to death.

And there the maid Godolphin came in with my telegram.

Crawley's case fixed for Friday he counts upon you.
                                        FORSYTH

"My God," I said, and got to my feet.

Elizabeth stifled a cry, but the Duchess sat perfectly still. As for Herrick...

"I must go to London," I said. "I must leave for Innsbruck at once – at least, as soon as I've packed. I must catch the evening train."

Elizabeth let out a cry.

"Richard!"

"My dear, I've no choice. Six weeks ago the servant I had before Winter was charged with theft. I had always found him honest and I said that I'd swear as much whenever he stood his trial. And his case has been fixed for Friday... I can't let him down. But I can be back on Sunday." I turned to the Duchess of Whelp. "Will you excuse me, madam? I must make certain arrangements. I shall ask you to see me again before I leave."

"You are excused, Richard Exon."

I bowed and went.

Whilst Winter packed, I wrote the best letter I could.

MADAM,

By the time that you read this letter, I am very nearly sure that 'the Count' will have disappeared. Whether he has or has not, you will know the best use to make of these documents. I told him that he would be arrested unless he made himself scarce and that Virgil had 'disappeared' under fear of being changed with the theft of Elizabeth's jewels. Elsa is 'wanted' for abortion: when she knew that I'd found

that out, she may have thought it better to find a new place.
I think that's all. I'm rather worried about the servant who
saw me drop my shirt. Perhaps you could straighten that out,
for you can do what you will with the servants of Brief. Of
course I'm not coming back. It's better so. I mean, there's no
more to be done, and as I can neither 'glaze her' nor 'rope
myself off', it wouldn't be fair to her to make matters worse
than I have.

> *Madam, I have so much to thank you for,*
>> *Your obedient, affectionate servant*
>> *RICHARD EXON*

With this I enclosed two documents.

One was the statement, indorsed by Lord Ferdinand, and the other the death certificate of Matthew Gering.

Then I sealed the envelope up and addressed it to the Duchess of Whelp. And then Winter fetched Parish again and I gave it into his hand – and made him swear to hold it till ten the following day.

At half-past three I saw the Duchess again.

She spoke to me very kindly and said that my lady had told her of our 'most unpleasant experience' the night before and hoped that I was no worse for my struggle to save my life. After that she wished me good luck 'in the matters you now have in hand' and said she should look for my coming in four days' time. And when I kissed her hand, she lifted me up and held my face against hers and thanked me for 'plucking our darling out of the jaws of death'.

Then, though I knew my way, she called Godolphin and told her to show me out; and, before I knew where I was, I was passing through the state of the bedroom which Brief reserved for persons of royal descent. Thirty seconds later I stood in the picture-gallery…

Elizabeth turned from a window and came to my side.

"Come and sit down, my darling." She put her arm through mine and led the way to a seat. "You look so tired and shaken, and though God knows you have cause, it isn't like you. And now you're going straight off – to travel day and night to London and back. Oh, I wish I was going with you. I shan't know a moment's rest till I see you again."

"I'm all right," I said somehow. "I'll get a good sleep tonight."

"Will you write me a letter tomorrow? I'd like to hear. Only a little letter – to say that you had a good night. I don't want to know anything else – I promised Old Harry I'd ask you no questions at all. But it worries me so to see you unlike yourself and to think you must make such a journey at such a time."

"I promise I'll write, my darling. But you mustn't worry – really. There's nothing the matter with me. I'm only tired."

With that, I made to glance at my wrist, but she caught my hand.

"I know the time," she said gently. "I'll tell you when you must go. We've ten minutes more together... The Rolls is out on the terrace and your luggage is down."

'Ten minutes more.'

My brain seemed to sway and stagger, as a man that is heavy-laden crossing uneven ground. There was so much to be said: yet I could say none of it, because she must not know that this was the end. And yet, how could I leave her without a word? Somehow I must contrive to say one or two things which, when she later remembered, would show her that Richard Exon had been trying to take his leave.

"It – it hurts me to leave you," I said. "And I wouldn't have left you – nothing on earth would have made me – if I didn't know you were safe. But now I know that, and – well, I gave my word, my darling, and so, you see, I must keep it – at any cost."

Her beautiful fingers tightened upon my wrist.

"Of course. Poor Crawley. Do you think they'll listen to you?"

"I shall try to make them. And now let's talk about you. I do not want you to worry – I shall be quite all right. Now don't forget that, my beauty, because I mean what I say. If you feel like fretting, sit at Old Harry's feet. She's wise – she's terribly wise, and she has an understanding which doesn't belong to this world. You told me once that you'd come to lean upon me. Very well. I'm going away. The moment I've gone I want you to lean upon her. If you don't, you'll feel left – when I go off in the Rolls. And I don't want you to feel left."

"How can I feel anything else? Half of me's going to London – the better half."

"You won't, if you stick to her. She's a sort of Rock of Ages. If you don't want me to worry, you'll do as I ask."

"Richard darling, of course I shall lean upon her. And she upon me – until our idol comes back. We're, both of us, silly about you. When I told her about last night, the tears ran down her cheeks. 'He's thoroughbred,' she kept saying. 'He was beaten all ends up: and yet he won through – for his great heart wasn't broken: and a thoroughbred's never beaten until you break his heart.' And so you needn't tell me to stick to her. We shall spend our time talking about you, until you come back."

I put a hand to my head. Matters were bad enough, and I seemed to be making them worse.

"You put it too high," I said slowly. "Don't magnify what I did. I had a chance and I took it, but more than once I nearly did everything in. And you got me out of that well – no doubt about that. Never mind. We can't argue now: But let's – let's both try and pretend it was only a dream, some of it bitter and some unforgettably sweet… You know, dreams are like that. And if we try hard enough and really make believe, it'll come to seem like one and we shall ask ourselves if these things really happened or whether the dying leap of some falling star just brushed our lives with brilliance…and held us up to the peephole of immortality."

"Richard! What are you saying?" Her beautiful brows were knit and a startled presence looked out of her glorious eyes. "Oh, my dear, I don't like you to go like this. What happened last night has changed you. You're not yourself. And since then – oh, I don't want to know, but I'm sure that something's upset you... You're always so calm and stable: but now Richard Exon's on edge."

The worst was happening: something had to be done.

With a superhuman effort, I braced myself for the part which I could not play. Somehow I *had* to play it – for both our sakes. She simply must not know that this was the end.

I got to my feet and drew her into my arms.

"My sweet," I said, "if I seem to you unnatural, that is because I am trying to play a part. I am trying my best to pretend – to make myself believe that I do not mind taking my leave. If you cannot help me to this, then my resolution will crack and I shall not go. After all, I've a fine excuse – 'I have married a wife, and therefore I cannot come.' And the man I promised to speak for can go to hell...

"Now I never realized how much it was going to cost me to keep the promise I made. It is costing me so much that I dare not consider the price, because, if I did, I know that I shouldn't pay it – and yet it's got to be paid, if I am to keep my word. So I'm trying to make believe.

"Now, of course, it's utterly hopeless to pretend that I don't mind going and leaving you here. I might as well pretend that I liked being down in that well. So I've made up my mind to pretend that, when I run into Innsbruck, I'm running out of some dream. After all, it's been rather like one – for me, I mean. Raven, Tracery, Brief: and the Duchess of Whelp – and you. Who ever saw anyone like you outside some dream? Who ever saw such beauty of face and form? What hair ever smelled so sweet? What temples were ever so lovely? What hands were ever so cool? And what queen ever spoke so gently, or told a man that she loved him, or put up her darling mouth – except in a dream? So I'm going to pretend I've been dreaming...for if I've been dreaming, I don't have to leave you behind. My dream, my shining wonder, will always be here – in my heart.

There can be no separation. No miles can lie between us, because you are not of this world. When I'm crossing the Channel, I shall hold you as close in my arms as I'm holding you now. Day and night you'll be with me – always: sleeping and waking, I'll have my cheek against yours." I threw back my head and laughed. "I shall be so rich I'll be almost afraid to come back, because that will mean the rendering up of my dream."

"Dropping shadow for substance," she smiled. "Perhaps you won't like me so well."

Then she laid her head on my chest and I laid mine against hers. And so we stayed, while the merciless sands ran out – and the blood ran with them, out of some hole in my heart.

Some clock struck four, and I felt a tremor run through her before its knell.

Once more I braced myself.

Then I put my hand under her chin and lifted her lovely head.

"Goodbye, Elizabeth Virgil."

"Goodbye, my love."

I kissed her lips.

Then we let one another go, and I turned and walked out of the gallery, down to the hall.

One minute later the Rolls was clear of the terrace and was whipping up to the woods that neighboured the entrance-drive.

I remember next to nothing of the journey we made that night.

A petrol-pump, highways and mountains and the growl of a frontier-guard; a bridge, all white in the moonshine, and then the glare of my head-lights fading before the dawn – these things make up the nightmare through which I drove, with Winter asleep beside me against his will.

I know that at ten the next morning we came to Basle, and, because I could go no further, I drove to the hotel at which I had lain for two nights three weeks before.

From there I wrote to my darling – a halting, pitiful note, in which I tried to make out how rich we must always be, because we had picked our flower when it was in full flush, so that now it could never wither or run to seed.

That evening we left for Strasbourg, and, after driving all night, embarked at Calais for Dover the following afternoon.

It was as I walked the deck and saw the cliffs of England taking their ancient form that it first occurred to me that when I stepped ashore I should come to the end of my plans. My one idea had been to retrace my steps and to put the sea between me and my heart's desire: but now, in a few minutes' time, I should have achieved this purpose and since life had to be lived, I should have to take thought for the morrow and, plainly, decide what to do. For a moment I knitted my brows... But either because I was tired or because, to be honest, I did not care what I did, the effort seemed not worth making, and I let my thoughts fly back – to a slim figure standing alone...in an echoing picture-gallery, full of the lenient splendour of afternoon sun.

The steamer had berthed, and I was standing amidships, watching my fellow-passengers hasten ashore, when I found a man standing beside me, with a hand to his hat.

"Mr Exon, sir?"

He was a commissionaire, and he had a note in his hand.

"That's right," said I.

He gave me the note at once.

Within was a type-written sheet.

The Duchess of Whelp presents her compliments to Mr Richard Exon and begs that, as soon as may be, he will present himself at Tracery, where he will hear of something to his advantage.

With a hammering heart, I stared at the messenger.

239

"How did you know," I said, "that I should be coming this way?"

"I didn't, sir," he said simply. "There's a man with a note for you at each of the ports. Every boat from France has been met for twenty-four hours."

12

I Look Out of a Window

"No, you don't, sir," said Winter, stoutly. "I don't care what's in the wind. I promised her ladyship I'd make you look after yourself... I 'aven't done nothing so far – because of the look in your eyes. But now that's gone, thank Gawd. An' if you won't rest here a day before startin' back – well, I've got the Rolls locked and I'll chuck the keys into the sea."

So it came about that nearly four days went by before, after sleeping at Innsbruck, I saw the chimneys of Tracery rising against the blue.

Heavy rain must have fallen the night before, for woods and pastures were green as I had never seen them, and the countryside was glancing before the smile of the sun. All the fragrance of earth and her fruits was lading the lively air, and the mountain-tops were making a mock of distance and hoisting their lovely detail for all the world to see.

As twice before, I entered the wasting courtyard and berthed the Rolls: but before I was out of the car, the doors of the mansion were opened and Parish was descending the steps...

Five minutes later I stood before the Duchess of Whelp.

She was dressed in grey, as usual, and was sitting at ease in a salon, the open windows of which gave on to the mouldering splendour of terrace and park: as usual, by painting her face, she had done her best to disfigure her splendid countenance, and, as usual, its noble features and her majestic air were turning their motley into a robe of state: on a table, beside her, lay papers – among them my letter and the statement which had been indorsed.

As the door closed, she looked up, and after a moment or two she put out her hand.

I went forward and kissed it at once.

As I straightened my back she spoke.

"Come for your cake, have you?"

"Madam, I have obeyed the orders you saw fit to send."

She pointed to a chair.

"Sit down." I did as she said. "I was right when I said you had taken the bit in your teeth: but it never occurred to me you were going to bolt."

"Madam," said I, "I did as – "

"I know. You acted for the best." She raised her eyes to heaven and let out a sigh. "You must get out of that habit. No need to tell you to act. You are a man of action. 'He hath done all things well.' But you must not act – *for the best*. That hideous qualification has been the ruin of many a great career. Besides, your judgment is filthy – I told you so. The very first time you came here, I said to you 'Never reflect.' And then you go off and do it. The dog returns to his vomit. And I actually helped you to – to that disgusting repast. 'Leave him alone,' I said. 'He's got the bit in his teeth.' " She drew in her breath. "Bit in your teeth! If only I'd known, you'd have had a flea in your ear."

"Madam," said I, "with respect, I shall always believe I was right to do as I did."

"Without speaking to me?"

"Yes, madam – because I had nothing to say. It was understood between us that, when I had done what I could, I should 'bow and go.' "

"Quite so," said Old Harry, "quite so. But you needn't have gone like that."

"Madam," said I, "the water was up to my chin. That night when – when Elsa fled, we were more or less pitchforked into each other's arms. Had I stayed – "

"Why didn't you come to me and tell me the truth?"

"And ask to be let off – in view of what I had done? Forgive me, madam, but I don't think you'd have done that."

"No. I shouldn't,' said Old Harry. "I should have come and *demanded* the hand of the Countess of Brief." I started at that, but she took no notice at all. "And if my demand had been questioned, I'll tell you what I should have said. I should have said, 'Look here. That she loves me is nothing: that I love her is less. But I've saved her life twice over and damned near lost my own, I've made one man cut his throat and I've killed two more... And if you imagine I've done all these parlour tricks to keep her nice and warm for somebody else, then, by God,' I'd have said, 'you've made a mistake in your man.' "

I stood up and folded my arms.

"Madam," I said, "I'll see you. Take it as said."

Old Harry regarded me straitly.

"This, to me, Richard Exon?" was all she said – but the words were sharply spoken and stung my ears as a lash.

Such rank injustice was more than my blood could stand.

"And this, madam. Your wisdom is infinite, and you can draw distinctions which I cannot comprehend. You speak of 'judgment' and 'instinct' as if the one was black and the other white. But I can see no difference between the two. In all I have done in this matter, I have acted as I thought best: and when I left Brief last Wednesday, I was acting according to my lights. You saw fit to call me back...

"Five minutes ago I told you a thundering lie. I said that I had come in obedience... Madam, I did nothing of the kind. I came to receive your permission to marry the Countess of Brief. Had your note not promised me that, you might have called me until you were black in the face...and I would never have answered, much less have come. And now, if you please, I should like to have my cake."

"Well, I'm damned," said Old Harry. " 'Black in the face'. Never in all my life has anyone ever dared to address me like that. The more's the pity, of course. If only they had, I should be more tolerant now."

"I do not find you intolerant, madam."

"I'm much obliged," said the Duchess; "but don't let's get on to my faults, or we shall be here all night. One picks up quite a number in seventy years. And now unfold those arms and sit down in that chair. You shall have your cake in due course. But first, as once before, I must take a hammer and chip the scales from your eyes. I like to think, Richard Exon, that when you came into this chamber you found your reception cold. I mean, I didn't burst into tears and throw my arms round your neck."

"You have been kinder, madam."

"Well, I'm glad you got it," said Old Harry. "Your reception was cold, because it was meant to be cold. I deplore and despise the sex to which I belong. I always have. We have few virtues and many contemptible traits. But who is Richard Exon to tread on our traditional corns?"

"Madam," said I, something startled, "I've no idea what you mean?"

"Of course you haven't," says she. "But that's because you're a fool. *Women are curious*, Richard – get hold of that. They must know – everything. And what is more to the point, they've got to know it at once. It's got to stink of the stable…" She held up my letter. "And you walked out of my life…and left me this." She covered her eyes. "And, damn it, *I helped you to do it*. I helped you to keep me waiting for six full days."

"Madam, I – "

"Listen to this. *I told him that he would be arrested, unless he made himself scarce*. That's all. That is your dispatch – your account of the fall of a stronghold which I had been racking my brain how best to assault. Fall? Crash. The man left Brief the same night... And now perhaps you'll tell me by what supernatural means you uprooted in half an hour, without any tools, a tree which has stood and flourished for twenty-two years. And that, if Parish may be believed, upon an empty stomach."

"Madam, I'm sorry. I – "

"Damn your sorrow," screamed Old Harry, waving her arms. "Declare to me how you did it, you wretched boy. Cool my brain in explanation. Assuage my thirst. That's all I sent for you for – to learn the truth."

I tried not to laugh, and failed. And the Duchess got up and shook me, and then pulled me on to a sofa and sat with my hand in hers.

"Word for word," she said quietly. "Don't leave a syllable out."

I told what there was to tell: and, when I had done, she thanked me very sweetly and then apologized for saying that I was a fool.

"I'm afraid that's true," I said. "I've managed to scramble home, but I've made a pile of mistakes."

"That's the way of a man," said Old Harry. "The finest brains in the world are always making mistakes – because they belong to men, and not to machines. *Humanum est errare.* But no fool could have done as you did. Be sure of that. And, what is still more certain, no sage could have done as you did. You see, it wasn't a question of *savoir faire.* You used your precious instinct as instinct ought to be used. You didn't strain your eyes to see the fences ahead: you jumped each one as it came – and, as it came, you found it was nothing at all. As you approached them, they shrank, because you were in your stride and you could not be stopped... And now I see how to bring you to the top of your bent. And that is, to make you angry. *Ferdinand made you angry.*"

"By God, he did," said I, thickly. "You know what he said in that note."

Exactly. When he signed that note, he signed his death-warrant. He made Richard Exon angry…" She drew in her breath. "I'd have given a year of my life to have been behind a screen."

"I was very lucky, madam. The fellow played into my hands."

"Rot," said Old Harry. "If you'd never done anything else, you could cock your hat for this for the rest of your life. No one could have done better: and no one I've ever met could have done one half so well. You made him plead guilty to treason, and then carried out the sentence which those who are guilty of treason used to receive. You disembowelled the traitor and burned his beastly entrails before his eyes. Parish was quite bewildered. He said that the man had lost stature – as well as weight. He said that, if he hadn't seen it, he never would have believed that a human being could shrink. And now let's dismiss the matter. 'Let the dead bury their dead.' "

I often feel that a more appropriate epitaph never was used; for poor Matthew Gering, though dead, had buried the treacherous brother that brought him down, and Ferdinand, by indorsing the statement his brother had made, had laid to his proper rest the ninth Count of Brief.

Then I asked of Elizabeth and Herrick, to learn that the latter was at Raven and the former at Brief. Since there was much to be done, Herrick went over to Brief for the whole of each day, assisting my lady as I could never have done, for he was a fine man of business and, as I have said, could speak German without a fault.

And then we came back to myself.

"You must understand this," said the Duchess. "Exactly ten days ago, before ever we left for Brief, Elizabeth told me plainly that she meant to become your wife. Well, I didn't argue with her, because I approved her choice. The difficulty confronting me was to make Richard Exon – not worthy to be her husband, but eligible to marry the Countess of Brief. Well, I think I can bring it off – but only by your consent.

"You bear a very good name. And I'm sure you are proud of it. Parish remembers Usage – which was your home. His sister was your mother's maid, and when your mother died she stayed on till the house was sold. It should not have been sold, of course: but your father was killed in action, and, as you know, things went wrong. Very well. Now I, too, bear a good name. My family name is Saying: and, though you and I know better, the *Almanach de Gotha* will tell you that it is royal. And if you will change your name – it's easy enough, by deed-poll – and will call yourself Saying-Exon from this time on, I think you may very well marry the Countess of Brief. Apart from anything else, it is, as the three of us know, most right and proper that she should bear my name: and in view of all that has happened, it is most right and proper that she should take it from you. But the principal thing is this – that I am very fond of you, Richard, and should derive infinite pleasure from the thought that you and your sons were to bear my name, for I know you will do it honour and I find it hard to believe that, with such a mother to bear them, your sons will prove unworthy to hand it down."

She hesitated there and put a hand to her eyes. Then she went slowly on.

"The workings of Fate are very wonderful. Saying is my own name. When I was married, I took my husband's title, but not his name. And because the name is royal, his sons by me would have borne it... But, you see, I have had no children... And when I come to die, the name will die, too...unless you – you care to humour...a sentimental old fool..."

What I said I cannot remember, because my heart was too full: but I know I was down on my knees and her hands were in mine, as I tried my best to thank her for doing for me what only a king can do.

Then she kissed me on either cheek and told me to ring for wine, "for we must have a drink," she said, "to celebrate this. You seem to like the idea, and, as good John Herrick would say, it suits me down to the socks. The thought of that name going out has given me sleepless nights. But now…all's very well, for if you and Elizabeth Virgil aren't fit to fly my flag, then my eye is dim and my natural force abated. And that I refuse to believe, for I never wore glasses yet and, though I take it easy, I'm still as strong as a horse."

When the wine was brought she pledged me and wished me luck, and I tried again to thank her and drank her health. Then she picked up a sheet of paper and put it into my hand.

"Your cake," she said simply. "You can have it now – and can eat it, as soon as you've changed your name."

A marriage has been arranged and will shortly take place between Richard Saying-Exon, late of Usage in Wiltshire and now of Tracery in Austria, and Elizabeth Virgil, Countess of Brief.

I lifted my head, to stare at the Duchess of Whelp.

" 'Now of Tracery', madam?"

"That's what it says," said Old Harry. "You can cut it out, if you like. But I understand you're short of a residence, and it would give me great pleasure, if you were to make this your home."

After lunch I left for Raven, where I was to stay for three nights, after which I was to return – with the Countess of Brief and Herrick, to settle future arrangements and, generally, "chew the cud". But, before I went, Old Harry made me promise that I would drive straight to Raven and would not visit Brief until the following day.

"You owe John Herrick something. He's been a good friend to you, and he mustn't feel left."

In view of all that had happened, I could not protest: but I could not help thinking that Herrick could hardly 'feel left' if I paid my lady a visit, before returning to Raven to spend the evening with him. Still, if Old Harry was wilful, I owed her caprice so much that if she had seen fit to direct that the Countess and I should not meet for another ten days, I must have honoured her precept without a word.

So I took my leave and entered the Rolls once more and, driving leisurely, came to Raven at six – to find the homestead fit for a Morland's brush.

As we stole between the two chestnuts and on to the apron beyond, I saw that Brenda was standing at the foot of the steps. She must have seen the car coming along the road of approach.

I brought the Rolls to her side and put out my hand.

"Well, Brenda," I said, "how are you? You see, I've come back."

She took my hand in both hers.

"I am so glad to see you," she said. "Your room is all ready, of course. Mr Herrick is not back yet. He goes to Brief every day and I doubt if he will be here for another half hour. I think you will sit in the meadows, until he comes."

"You're perfectly right," said I, and got out of the car. "But, first, I must have a drink. Will you go and draw me some beer, while I'm washing my hands?"

Brenda hesitated.

Then –

"You – you won't have a bath, will you? I mean, the water's not hot."

In some surprise –

"I'd like one before dinner," I said. "But why mustn't I have one now?"

"It would take too long," said Brenda. "The meadows are now at their best, but the sun is low."

With that, she was gone.

I turned to my faithful man.

"Glad to be back, Winter?"

He smiled all over his face.

"This is the place for me, sir. Them 'igh an' mighty 'ouses is all very well in their way, but the country seems frightened of them. The woods and the meadows seem shy. But here they'll come right up – an' eat out of your hand."

"You've said it," said I. "And take it easy tonight. Wash the Rolls tomorrow."

"I'd rather do her tonight, sir. It won't take me very long, an' when you come to think, she deserves the best."

And that was another true saying.

"Do as you like," said I, and walked into the house.

I do not know what made me do it, but when I had used the bathroom I strolled across the landing and entered the pleasant bedroom I knew was mine.

For a moment I stood looking round. Then I moved to the open windows, commanding the friendly meadows and the sheltering woods beyond.

The scene was as rare as lovely, for the sun was going down and the pleasant Georgic was flooded with amber light. All things were throwing shadows as clean and as black as print, slashing the turf with sable and making the vivid green more vivid still. On every side the tapestry of woodland was shot with gold, the stream was afire with splendour...*and sitting beside its water was Elizabeth, Countess of Brief.*

Her beautiful head was bare and her eyes were fixed upon the tree-tops as though she were expecting the heaven above to open and make her rich: but for me the heaven had opened...and I seemed to be regarding some idyll that did not belong to earth, but had been sung by Shakespeare to please the gods.

So I looked upon my fortune.

Then I went down to the meadows, to see the light in her eyes.

Nearly an hour went by before Herrick arrived – for which I was very thankful, because his car was to take Elizabeth back.

As we heard the drone of his engine –

"Oh damn," said the Countess of Brief. "Now that I've got you back, I don't want to let you go. But you won't go mad again, will you? Remember that the Duchess of Whelp has set her heart on this match, and that, after all that she's done, you can't let her down."

With a sudden movement, I picked her up in my arms.

"Shall I tell you something?" I said.

"Yes, please."

A warm arm slid round my neck.

"Today I came back to my dream: and as long as my dream will have me, I shall never leave it again. I must go to London later, if only to change my name. But I will not go, unless you go with me. Take what companion you like. Take half a dozen women – to shut Propriety's mouth. Kick your heels, while I'm doing my business. Only, be there... You see, you are my dream. A week ago I rendered you unto Caesar – and tore my heart. And now Caesar has given you back – has given me back my dream. Well, that's all right: but the wound in my heart will reopen if ever I leave you again. And that, I tell you frankly, I cannot face. When I left you, I knew very well I was leaving my life behind. But not until I was gone did I know what it meant to be dead – a dead man having his being amid a workaday world."

For two or three moments she held my head against hers. Then she let it go and turned to look into my eyes.

"My blessed," she breathed, "I'm so thankful I mean so much. You see, I've given you all. I've no more to give. Heart and soul and body – you hold them in your strong hands. They're not mine any more. They're...at your disposal, Richard. And if ever you ceased to care, the body would wither, for the heart and the soul would die."

I would have answered her, but the words would not come, for I could think of nothing but the look in her glorious eyes. I cannot tell what exquisite language they spoke, but I understood their saying better than any words. I had that day been ennobled by the Duchess of Whelp; but now I was exalted in spirit, and a spring seemed to break within me for joy that Elizabeth Virgil had come to love me so well.

Then she smiled, and I kissed her mouth and set her down on her feet.

"Shall I tell you something?" she said.

"Yes, please."

"When we got the telephone message to say that you had been stopped and were going to come back, I – I burst into tears."

"My sweet!"

"It was natural enough... But listen. Old Harry called me a fool – and then burst into tears herself. We turned to John for comfort – John who had been our mainstay and simply kept us going for thirty-one hours...and John was standing there with the tears running down his cheeks. So you see, my darling, I'm not – peculiar. There's something about Richard Exon that gets us all under the ribs."

Which was, of course, absurd, for else I should not have suffered in Red Lead Lane.

Four hours had gone by, and I was sitting, smoking, with Herrick, under the stars.

Raven was fast asleep: only our sitting-room casements were framing two squares of light: the Rolls was within her coach-house: Winter had gone to his rest.

"I suppose it's all true," said Herrick: "but I must confess there are moments when I wonder if I've been translated before my time. I mean, a month ago I was not only down and out. The immediate future was hideous. Pawnshop, doss-house and gutter were staring me in the face, and I didn't like the look in their eyes – you see, I'd met them before... And now I'm ruling a castle, with fifty servants hanging on my lips. Compared with me, Elizabeth doesn't count. I'm a sort of Lord Protector, appointed by the Duchess of Whelp. And when that's done, I'm due at Tracery. I have been desired by Old Harry to take her estate in hand. 'Put my house in order,' she said. 'You're just the man to do it, and it's time it was done. If my agent's right, that'll just about carry you home. He gives your uncle six months...' So you see, my gay crusader, you've made my fortune, too – to say nothing at all of the fact that I've never enjoyed myself as I have in the last three weeks.

"Three weeks and one day – no more. Yet their burden has been so brilliant that, though I've seen quite a lot, the rest of my life beside them seems strangely dull. And that's not really strange, for never before have I entered the Middle Ages and tasted their mighty fare. Talk about food for the gods...

"Our first view of Brief, grey against green in the sunshine, as we stood on the bridge that trembled before the Vials of Wrath: Percy Virgil, afraid to writhe, whilst I drew his description from life for the eager police: Elizabeth here at Raven – Rosalind, Viola, Beatrice, rolled into one, with the secret of all the ages snared in her glorious eyes: the dead king, sunk in his stall, staring before him as he had stared before him, day and night, for almost five hundred years: dinner for four at Tracery – gold and silver and scarlet and powdered hair, Elizabeth worshipful and the Duchess of Whelp's most excellent majesty: Percy Virgil confronted with Winter... 'the Count' of Brief at bay, and the awful uncertainty flaming in Bertram's eyes: and then, one evening at five, the stammer of a telephone-bell and Old Harry's voice rock-steady and very clear... 'Is that you, Henderson? Yes?... *Stopped and returning tomorrow.* I'm much obliged.'...

"And you can add to that list – some very monstrous moments... Elsa's laugh in the staircase-turret...the darkness of Palfrey's court...the shock of that icy water...the straws you caught at to save your tottering life...and then Lord Ferdinand Virgil, broken and craven and cringing to be permitted to bury himself alive – I shall never get over that as long as I live. You're a blasted lion in sheep's clothing, and that's the truth. You sit there, as meek as mild and apparently dumb with admiration for Old Harry's efforts and mine to kick at the gates, and the next day, before we're up, you walk bung into the fortress and kill the giant. Then you put on the sheep's skin again… When I think that you came into breakfast straight from the field – and merely begged my pardon for being late…"

As though overcome with emotion, he threw himself back in his chair and covered his eyes.

"I'm sorry," I said. "It seemed better – "

"Don't," screamed Herrick. "How dare you? When you apologize, I want to kick myself and burst into tears. If you must wear your sheep's skin, do: we all know it comes off. But for you to bleat is indecent… Oh, yes, I can see you laughing, but that's because you don't understand. We're cast in two different moulds. We come, I see, you conquer – I can't put it better than that. And I warn you, my simple serpent, I'm not going to let you go. You may take a Duchess' name and marry the Countess of Brief, but I knew you before they did and I'm not going to give them place. And when I change my name, as one day I shall – it'll mean that you'll have three houses, instead of two."

And there you have John Herrick, sterling, efficient, adroit, with a glorious sense of humour and the heart of a little child. His way with all was wonderful. Duchess, steward and scullion – he was at ease with the lot; and they with him. What is more, he inspired affection. It gave him pleasure to make his neighbours glad: and his neighbours recognized this and thanked God for such a man. Upon what I owe him myself, I will not insist, for I think these pages have shown that, but for his present help, I could have done nothing at all and Elizabeth must have been broken and Percy Virgil succeeded to her estate.

To three others I must pay tribute before I end this tale – for I shall leave it at Raven, which was for me journey's end.

Winter is still in my service, but soon will leave it to marry Brenda Revoke. I often think that his was a trying office, for all the time he stood upon the edge of the fray. No vengeance was his, and three times he missed the battle for which he longed. He knew too much or too little from first to last, and yet he never complained, but kept his eyes upon his duty and did it with all his heart. No servant was ever more faithful or gave a fuller measure than Winter did, and it gives me lasting pleasure to think that to some extent he found his fortune with me – for Brenda will make a fine wife and Raven is his idea of heaven on earth.

Of Elizabeth, what can I say? I think there is no one like her, but that is natural enough. Still, Herrick is a fair critic and the Duchess is hard to please. And both of them commend her. Of course, she has her faults: but I am thankful for these, for otherwise she would be too good to be true. Her beautiful features have lost their wistful look, and a gaiety, long confined, is now at large to leaven her dignity: but her ways are as gracious as ever, her gaze is as level, her shining head is as high, and, though I know her so well, I never can lose the impression that she in fact belongs to the age of chivalry, for she has in fee the haunting, fabulous beauty of ballad and story-book, and she never seems to notice that, wheresoever she goes, she always receives a duty which is not accorded to others because it is not inspired. 'Was this the face that launch'd a thousand ships?' I sometimes think that it was. Though God knows I am no Paris… Perhaps Menelaus was burly, and could not tell 'judgment' from 'instinct', and went with scales on his eyes. In any event he set great store by his wife…

And as, when a play is over, the most illustrious player stands last and alone upon the stage, the latest to figure here must be Harriet Vincentia Saying, Duchess of Whelp.

Till the first day I stood before her, lying abed, I never had comprehended what personality meant – that indefinable presence which needs no help of the body to make itself felt. And then I knew…because I was immediately subject to something far greater than me. Had she taken no action and never opened her mouth, that sense of subjection must nevertheless have endured, because her spirit ruled mine from the moment I entered her room. It was the same with us all. High and low went down before her, as grass goes down before the scythe, and I can think of no one who could today stand up and meet her on equal ground. Proud and strong and fearless, keen-witted, humorous, wise – above all, full of that 'drive' that made a Conqueror out of a tanner's stock, she moved upon a plane that others sometimes climb to – and find the air too rare for their physique. And so she came down…for us. The fine, old eagle came down… and showed us her royal heart. I use the word advisably. Royal is as royal does: and the Duchess of Whelp does royally, because, I believe, she knows no other way.

That I cannot compute what I owe her is natural enough. There are some debts before which arithmetic pales. For one thing only, I owe her Elizabeth's life: for, had she not seen and shown me the deadly peril in which, whilst Virgil lived, my darling must be, I should never have gone to keep watch on the turret-stair. Then, again, it was she that had me into the castle and gave me the chance of doing whatever I did.

Unearthly shrewd – and swift to act upon her shrewdness, handling men and women as a horsemaster handles a horse, filling the weaker vessel with the virtue that ran in her veins, kind and understanding and generous, using us pygmies as equals, yet asking far less of us than she did of herself – from the hour that we called upon her she was the driving force behind all we did.

Though now there is no more to be done, our allegiance persists…

'Tracery is her wash-pot; over Brief hath she cast out her shoe.'

The *mot*, which is Herrick's, is *juste*.

And we are as proud as content, because there is only one 'Old Harry the Great'.

DORNFORD YATES

AS BERRY AND I WERE SAYING

Reprinted four times in three months, this semi-autobiographical novel takes the form of a conversation between members of the Pleydell family; in particular Berry, recalling his childhood and Oxford days, and Boy, who describes his time at the Bar. Darker and less frivolous than some of Yates' earlier books, he described it as 'my own memoir put into the mouths of Berry and Boy', and at the time of publication it already had a nostalgic feel. A hit with the public and a 'scrapbook of the Edwardian age as it was seen by the upper-middle classes'.

BERRY AND CO.

This collection of short stories featuring 'Berry' Pleydell and his chaotic entourage established Dornford Yates' reputation as one of the best comic writers of his generation and made him hugely popular. The German caricatures in the book carried such a sting that when France was invaded in 1939 Yates, who was living near the Pyrenees, was put on the wanted list and had to flee.

DORNFORD YATES

BLIND CORNER

This is Yates' first thriller: a tautly plotted page-turner featuring the crime-busting adventures of suave Richard Chandos. Chandos is thrown out of Oxford for 'beating up some Communists', and on return from vacation in Biarritz he witnesses a murder. Teaming up at his London club with friend Jonathan Mansel, a stratagem is devised to catch the killer.

The novel has equally compelling sequels: *Blood Royal, An Eye For a Tooth, Fire Below* and *Perishable Goods*.

BLOOD ROYAL

At his chivalrous, rakish best in a story of mistaken identity, kidnapping and old-world romance, Richard Chandos takes us on a romp through Europe in the company of a host of unforgettable characters.

This fine thriller can be read alone or as part of a series with *Blind Corner, An Eye For a Tooth, Fire Below* and *Perishable Goods*.

Dornford Yates

An Eye For a Tooth

On the way home from Germany after having captured Axel the Red's treasure, dapper Jonathan Mansel happens upon a corpse in the road, that of an Englishman. There ensues a gripping tale of adventure and vengeance of a rather gentlemanly kind. On publication this novel was such a hit that it was reprinted six times in its first year, and assured Yates' huge popularity. A classic Richard Chandos thriller, which can be read alone or as part of a series including *Blind Corner, Blood Royal, Fire Below* and *Perishable Goods*.

Fire Below

Richard Chandos makes a welcome return in this classic adventure story. Suave and decadent, he leads his friends into forbidden territory to rescue a kidnapped (and very attractive) young widow. Yates gives us a highly dramatic, almost operatic, plot and unforgettably vivid characters.

A tale in the traditional mould, and a companion novel to *Blind Corner, Blood Royal, Perishable Goods* and *An Eye For a Tooth*.

OTHER TITLES BY DORNFORD YATES AVAILABLE DIRECT
FROM HOUSE OF STRATUS

Quantity		£	$(US)	$(CAN)	€
☐	ADÈLE AND CO.	6.99	12.95	19.95	13.50
☐	AND BERRY CAME TOO	6.99	12.95	19.95	13.50
☐	AS BERRY AND I WERE SAYING	6.99	12.95	19.95	13.50
☐	B-BERRY AND I LOOK BACK	6.99	12.95	19.95	13.50
☐	BERRY AND CO.	6.99	12.95	19.95	13.50
☐	THE BERRY SCENE	6.99	12.95	19.95	13.50
☐	BLIND CORNER	6.99	12.95	19.95	13.50
☐	BLOOD ROYAL	6.99	12.95	19.95	13.50
☐	THE BROTHER OF DAPHNE	6.99	12.95	19.95	13.50
☐	COST PRICE	6.99	12.95	19.95	13.50
☐	THE COURTS OF IDLENESS	6.99	12.95	19.95	13.50
☐	AN EYE FOR A TOOTH	6.99	12.95	19.95	13.50
☐	FIRE BELOW	6.99	12.95	19.95	13.50
☐	GALE WARNING	6.99	12.95	19.95	13.50
☐	THE HOUSE THAT BERRY BUILT	6.99	12.95	19.95	13.50
☐	JONAH AND CO.	6.99	12.95	19.95	13.50
☐	NE'ER DO WELL	6.99	12.95	19.95	13.50
☐	PERISHABLE GOODS	6.99	12.95	19.95	13.50
☐	RED IN THE MORNING	6.99	12.95	19.95	13.50
☐	SHE FELL AMONG THIEVES	6.99	12.95	19.95	13.50

ALL HOUSE OF STRATUS BOOKS ARE AVAILABLE FROM GOOD BOOKSHOPS
OR DIRECT FROM THE PUBLISHER:

Internet: www.houseofstratus.com including synopses and features.

Email: sales@houseofstratus.com
info@houseofstratus.com
(please quote author, title and credit card details.)

Tel: Order Line
0800 169 1780 (UK)
International
+44 (0) 1845 527700 (UK)

Fax: +44 (0) 1845 527711 (UK)
(please quote author, title and credit card details.)

Send to: House of Stratus Sales Department
Thirsk Industrial Park
York Road, Thirsk
North Yorkshire, YO7 3BX
UK

PAYMENT

Please tick currency you wish to use:

☐ £ (Sterling) ☐ $ (US) ☐ $ (CAN) ☐ € (Euros)

Allow for shipping costs charged per order plus an amount per book as set out in the tables below:

CURRENCY/DESTINATION

	£(Sterling)	$(US)	$(CAN)	€ (Euros)
Cost per order				
UK	1.50	2.25	3.50	2.50
Europe	3.00	4.50	6.75	5.00
North America	3.00	3.50	5.25	5.00
Rest of World	3.00	4.50	6.75	5.00
Additional cost per book				
UK	0.50	0.75	1.15	0.85
Europe	1.00	1.50	2.25	1.70
North America	1.00	1.00	1.50	1.70
Rest of World	1.50	2.25	3.50	3.00

PLEASE SEND CHEQUE OR INTERNATIONAL MONEY ORDER
payable to: HOUSE OF STRATUS LTD or card payment as indicated

STERLING EXAMPLE

Cost of book(s):...................... Example: 3 x books at £6.99 each: £20.97
Cost of order:....................... Example: £1.50 (Delivery to UK address)
Additional cost per book:.............. Example: 3 x £0.50: £1.50
Order total including shipping:.......... Example: £23.97

VISA, MASTERCARD, SWITCH, AMEX:

☐☐☐☐☐☐☐☐☐☐☐☐☐☐☐☐☐☐☐☐

Issue number (Switch only):

☐☐☐

Start Date: **Expiry Date:**

☐☐/☐☐   ☐☐/☐☐

Signature: _____

NAME: _____

ADDRESS: _____

COUNTRY: _____

ZIP/POSTCODE: _____

Please allow 28 days for delivery. Despatch normally within 48 hours.

Prices subject to change without notice.
Please tick box if you do not wish to receive any additional information. ☐

House of Stratus publishes many other titles in this genre; please check our website (**www.houseofstratus.com**) for more details.